A Perilous Plot

Berkley Prime Crime titles by Lorna Barrett

MURDER IS BINDING
BOOKMARKED FOR DEATH
BOOKPLATE SPECIAL
CHAPTER & HEARSE
SENTENCED TO DEATH
MURDER ON THE HALF SHELF
NOT THE KILLING TYPE
BOOK CLUBBED
A FATAL CHAPTER
TITLE WAVE
A JUST CLAUSE
POISONED PAGES
A KILLER EDITION
HANDBOOK FOR HOMICIDE
A DEADLY DELETION
CLAUSE OF DEATH
A QUESTIONABLE CHARACTER
A CONTROVERSIAL COVER
A PERILOUS PLOT

Anthologies

MURDER IN THREE VOLUMES

A PERILOUS PLOT

Lorna Barrett

BERKLEY PRIME CRIME
New York

BERKLEY PRIME CRIME
Published by Berkley
An imprint of Penguin Random House LLC
1745 Broadway, New York, NY 10019
penguinrandomhouse.com

Copyright © 2025 by Penguin Random House LLC
Penguin Random House values and supports copyright. Copyright fuels creativity, encourages diverse voices, promotes free speech, and creates a vibrant culture. Thank you for buying an authorized edition of this book and for complying with copyright laws by not reproducing, scanning, or distributing any part of it in any form without permission. You are supporting writers and allowing Penguin Random House to continue to publish books for every reader. Please note that no part of this book may be used or reproduced in any manner for the purpose of training artificial intelligence technologies or systems.

BERKLEY and the BERKLEY & B colophon are registered trademarks and BERKLEY PRIME CRIME is a trademark of Penguin Random House LLC.

Book design by Laura K. Corless

Library of Congress Cataloging-in-Publication Data
Names: Barrett, Lorna, author.
Title: A perilous plot / Lorna Barrett.
Description: New York: Berkley Prime Crime, 2025. | Series: A Booktown mystery
Identifiers: LCCN 2025005729 (print) | LCCN 2025005730 (ebook) |
ISBN 9780593819210 (hardcover) | ISBN 9780593819234 (ebook)
Subjects: LCGFT: Detective and mystery fiction. | Novels.
Classification: LCC PS3602.A83955 P47 2025 (print) |
LCC PS3602.A83955 (ebook) | DDC 813/.6—dc23/eng/20250210
LC record available at https://lccn.loc.gov/2025005729
LC ebook record available at https://lccn.loc.gov/2025005730

Printed in the United States of America
1st Printing

PUBLISHER'S NOTE: The recipes contained in this book are to be followed exactly as written. The publisher is not responsible for your specific health or allergy needs that may require medical supervision. The publisher is not responsible for any adverse reactions to the recipes contained in this book.

The authorized representative in the EU for product safety and compliance is Penguin Random House Ireland, Morrison Chambers, 32 Nassau Street, Dublin D02 YH68, Ireland, https://eu-contact.penguin.ie.

Acknowledgments

It takes a village of support to write a book, and I'm lucky to have friends who are there for me along the way. My thanks go to members of the Lorraine Train: Amy Connolley, Debbie Lyon, Rita Pierrottie, and Kim Templeton, as well as my author friends Shirley Hailstock and Mary Kennedy for comments, catching typos, and sharing their collective knowledge. I'm also lucky to have my agent, Jessica Faust, who's always in my corner. Thanks, guys!

And if you haven't already checked out Lorraine's and Lorna's Cozy Perpetual Tea Party page, you can find the group on Facebook. (See you there!)

Cast of Characters

Tricia Miles, owner of Haven't Got a Clue vintage mystery bookstore

Angelica Miles, Tricia's older sister, owner of the Cookery, the Booked for Lunch café, and the Booked for Beauty day spa, and half owner of the Sheer Comfort Inn. Her alter ego is Nigela Ricita, the mysterious developer who has been pumping money and jobs into the village of Stoneham.

Pixie Poe, Tricia's assistant manager at Haven't Got a Clue

Mr. Everett, Tricia's employee at Haven't Got a Clue

David Price, Stoneham's new children's librarian and Tricia's special friend

Antonio Barbero, the public face of Nigela Ricita Associates, Angelica's son

Ginny Wilson-Barbero, Tricia's former assistant, wife of Antonio Barbero

Grace Harris-Everett, Mr. Everett's wife, manages their charity, the Everett Foundation

Ian McDonald, chief of police, Stoneham Police Department

Becca Dickson-Chandler, former tennis star, Tricia's sort-of friend

Cast of Characters

Cleo Gardener, innkeeper at Stonecreek Manor

Sheila Miles, Tricia and Angelica's mother

John Miles, Tricia and Angelica's father

Bunny Murdock, honorary aunt to Tricia and Angelica, their mother's best friend

A Perilous Plot

ONE

"**I hate** this place."

Tricia Miles glanced at her older-by-five-years sister, Angelica, who sat beside her in the Baker Funeral Home's comfortable family room. Luckily, Mr. Baker—the home's owner and head mortician—had left them, taking with him the urn containing the earthly remains of their father, John.

The sisters decided to commemorate the anniversary of their father's birth by celebrating his life with mourning jewelry. It wasn't Tricia's idea, but she didn't find it morbid. Well, at least, not *too* morbid. Angelica had chosen a hummingbird charm, while Tricia had selected a dragonfly—both creatures that flew free.

Six months had passed quicker than Tricia could have imagined. Back in October—and out of the blue—their mother had shown up with the urn. They still weren't clear what malady had taken their father's life. Sheila Miles had been pretty vague about the details. And then she'd checked out of Stoneham's Brookview Inn early the next morning, leaving the quaint New Hampshire village without a word.

Tricia's relationship with her mother had always been rocky. Three years before, it seemed that Sheila had a change of heart. She even spoke about the four of them attending family therapy, but that never happened. Months went by. Angelica tried to keep in touch, but Sheila and John went back to traveling to their various homes—and in different countries—and their usual communications blackouts. Also, as in the past, they resumed their previous roles. Sheila wearing the pants, John being browbeaten, Angelica the favored child, and Tricia persona non grata.

She was used to that.

Upon Sheila's disappearance, Angelica hadn't had any luck tracking her down, either. With all the business deals and projects she juggled, it wasn't at the top of her list of things to do. Dealing with their parents was just one task too many.

Finding their mother wasn't on *any* of Tricia's lists. For most of Tricia's life, she and her mother had been at odds—not Tricia's fault. Tricia's twin brother was a SIDS baby. Sheila had never forgiven Tricia for the sin of surviving infancy when Patrick hadn't. Three years before, they'd come to a sort of understanding, but it hadn't lasted long. They hadn't spoken in over a year before Sheila's abrupt arrival and equally fast departure. They'd barely spoken the evening Sheila dropped in on one of the weekly dinners with Tricia's chosen family. Those people included Angelica's son, Antonio Barbero; his wife (and Tricia's former employee), Ginny; and their two children, Sofia and baby Will; as well as Tricia's current employee, Mr. Everett, an older gentleman; and his wife, Grace. Last but not least, Tricia's current beau, David Price. She'd introduced the young man—twenty years younger than Tricia—as her friend. David could have taken offense at the apparent slight, but she'd previously filled him in on the complicated relationship she and Sheila shared. No doubt he wasn't keen to be a victim of Sheila's acid tongue. David was about to graduate with a master's degree in library science and currently worked at the Stoneham Library as its children's librarian, a job he loved. He also had a love for antiques and fine china, and he and Angelica had bonded over that.

"How are you going to wear your charm?" Angelica asked.

Tricia shrugged. "I bought a chain, but then I thought I might add it to the bracelet I've had since junior high."

"I bought a silver chain. I'm going to wear it twenty-four/seven."

Good for you, Tricia thought. She intended to add the charm to her bracelet and place it in the back of her jewelry box. She might wear it once or twice a year.

Maybe.

The sound of someone clearing his throat caused the sisters to look up. Mr. Baker stood at the doorway, looking even more somber than usual.

Tricia stood, but Mr. Baker waved to her to retake her seat and entered the room, placing the urn on the coffee table before taking a seat on the couch opposite the sisters.

Angelica gave her sister a side-eye. No other form of communication was necessary to convey what she was thinking: something about the urn wasn't on the up-and-up.

Sheila Miles had always kept her husband on a short leash, and it became apparent why three years before when the sisters learned (through bitter experience) that their beloved father was an experienced con artist. They'd grown up in privilege, but it was their mother's inherited money that paid the bills, not what their father earned. In fact, Tricia never really knew what kind of job her father worked—or if he worked at all.

"Is something wrong?" Tricia asked innocently, dreading the answer.

"Well, yes." Mr. Baker seemed reluctant to explain.

"And?" Angelica queried.

Mr. Baker chewed his lip, apparently choosing his words carefully before speaking.

"Some kind of fraud appears to have been perpetrated."

"Oh, God, now what?" Angelica grumbled.

"It pains me to be the purveyor of unwelcome news, but the urn did not contain human remains," the old gent said solemnly.

"What kind of remains does it hold?" Angelica asked sourly, glaring at the offending piece of porcelain.

"Not remains but . . . kitty litter."

"Kitty litter?" Tricia asked, shocked.

"Uh, yes, of the clay variety."

"I have a cat. I know what kitty litter is," Tricia said. And then she remembered hearing that unscrupulous funeral directors had sometimes passed off cat litter as cremains while leaving the bodies left in their care to decompose in sheds and other inappropriate places.

"We don't know who . . . who did the work," Angelica said in a tone Tricia knew well. *Do. Not. Cross.*

"Yes, containers usually have some kind of documentation to certify the cremation. Do you have such paperwork?"

"No," Angelica said, her voice almost a growl. "Our mother gave us the urn—telling us our father had passed. She didn't share much more about the circumstances of his passing."

"That's quite unfortunate," Mr. Baker said gravely. "However, that isn't the only anomaly."

Tricia raised an eyebrow. Angelica's expression seemed to convey two messages: *Now what?*—and—*Of course!*

"There was something else in the urn," Mr. Baker said.

The sisters waited expectantly as Mr. Baker reached into his suit coat pocket and withdrew a dusty plastic object. As though reluctant to place it in their hands, he set it on the table, beside the urn.

Again, the sisters exchanged glances. It was apparent that Angelica

A Perilous Plot

had no intention of touching the item, even though it hadn't been covered with cremains. It was up to Tricia to do so.

And she did.

The item was sealed in several layers of plastic, as well as a layer of Bubble Wrap. Tricia could have extricated it a lot faster if she'd had more than just the nail file she'd retrieved from her purse.

With every second that passed, Angelica seemed to get more and more frustrated. Finally, Tricia extracted the item.

"A watch?" Angelica grumbled.

"Not just any watch," Tricia said. "It's a Rolex."

Angelica shook her head. "It's probably fake—or stolen," she grated.

Mr. Baker raised an eyebrow but didn't comment.

"Well," Tricia said, standing, "I guess we won't be needing your services today, Mr. Baker. What do we owe you?"

"No charge. I'm only sorry I couldn't fulfill your wish to add cremains to the charms." He reached into his other pocket and withdrew a folded envelope, presumably containing the sterling silver trinkets. "Please let me know if I can be of service in the future."

"We'll do that," Angelica said, and stood. "I just hope it won't be too soon."

"As do I," Baker said gravely. Tricia idly wondered if his voice had atrophied from speaking softly for so many years.

The sisters left the home and walked in silence to Angelica's car. Getting in, they sat staring at the empty parking lot for long seconds before Angelica spoke.

"So, do you think Daddy's actually dead? Had he fooled mother into *thinking* he was dead? Or this time, was it Mother who pulled a scam on us?"

Tricia sighed. "Well, if Daddy *did* want to fake his own death, he hasn't resurfaced to ask us—you—for money. Yet," she muttered.

"Why do I feel like we have to wait for the other shoe to drop?" Angelica griped.

"It's been this way ever since Mother and Daddy left Rio and came back to the US."

"Maybe they should have stayed in Brazil." Angelica placed her hands on the steering wheel, gripping it tightly. "What do we do next?"

"One of them is bound to surface—eventually. I might take on the task of looking for Mother," Tricia said. "But first, I'll see if I can track down more information—like try to locate a death certificate."

"That could be a rabbit hole you'll never escape from. Our parents have at least four homes scattered around the globe. In what jurisdiction would you look?" Angelica asked.

Tricia shook her head.

"Or . . . we could do what we should have done when Mother disappeared from Stoneham back in the fall," Angelica suggested.

Tricia's heart sank. "Oh, no—please don't suggest we—"

"—call Aunt Bunny?" Angelica finished. "Why not?"

"Because I can't stand the woman. I never could," Tricia asserted.

"She always liked you. She's just a little off-kilter. I'm sure she's outgrown that by now," Angelica said, her tone flippant at best.

Tricia gave her sister the evil eye. "If you invite her here, she's *your* problem. I refuse to deal with her."

"She's not *that* bad," Angelica insisted.

"Oh, yes, she is. She causes almost as much trouble as Daddy. I don't understand why Mother ever put up with her."

Of course, Aunt Bunny wasn't their aunt by blood, but Sheila's lifelong friend. Because of her name, Tricia had always thought of the woman as a *dumb* bunny—and a bit of a flake.

Angelica gripped the wheel once again. "Isn't it strange that, instead of thinking a mistake had been made at a funeral home, we immediately assume something underhanded is going on with our parents?"

"Nope," Tricia said succinctly. She withdrew the heavy, man's watch from her purse. "If I'm not mistaken, each Rolex has a serial number. Call me suspicious, but I'll bet it isn't registered to Daddy."

"He *could* have bought it used but, as I said, it's more likely a phony," Angelica declared.

Tricia lowered her gaze. "Mother would never stand for Daddy wearing a phony watch. I'll bet it's the real thing, and I intend to find out. Today."

Angelica shrugged. "Go for it. And if it *is* hot?"

"Then I'll be paying Chief McDonald a visit." And PDQ. "One way or another, there's some kind of fraud going on."

And Tricia was determined to get to the bottom of it.

TWO

 The associate at the Milford Diamond Exchange wanted to be helpful but wasn't all that much. He did at least confirm that the Rolex was the genuine article, was worth at least ten grand, and did Tricia want to sell it?

No, she did not.

She asked about the serial number. Yes, it could be looked up online, but it wasn't a service they offered to customers.

Her next stop was the Stoneham Police Department, where she hoped to speak to Chief McDonald.

As always, Polly Burgess sat behind the receptionist's desk. Dour, white-haired, and what some called fluffy (Tricia wasn't about to label the woman as overweight), but always well-groomed. They'd started out on the wrong foot when Polly came to work for the former chief of police, and it was McDonald's threat of unemployment that had Polly interacting with the public in a more pleasant manner. Polly had, therefore, adopted a saccharine-sweet demeanor that Tricia found increasingly annoying. But they hadn't had to interact for nearly six months, which was probably a welcome relief for both women.

"The chief is in," Polly said brightly. "Let me just call and ask if he has time to see you."

"Thank you," Tricia said, and listened as Polly lifted the phone and announced her presence.

"You can go right in," Polly said, and smiled, but there was a shadow of something in her gaze. Tricia thought she'd observed the same look back in the fall. A sadness . . . or something else. She didn't feel comfortable asking.

Tricia knocked and waited for McDonald to call, "Come in," before she turned the door's handle and entered.

McDonald stood. "What can I do for you today, Tricia? Don't say you've found another body."

Tricia was used to such quips. Since her arrival in Stoneham, New Hampshire—also known as Booktown because of all the used bookstores that had saved the once-failing village—she'd become known as the village jinx due to the excessive number of corpses she stumbled upon.

"It's personal," Tricia said, taking one of the seats before his desk.

Ian's usual expression was perturbed—at least it was whenever Tricia came to see him at his office. That it wasn't going to involve a death seemed to please the chief.

"Well," Tricia amended, "I don't *think* anyone's dead. In fact, someone I thought *was* dead might well be alive."

McDonald's brow furrowed. "Go on."

Tricia explained about her mother's sudden appearance with the urn and a sketchy tale of her father's death and then what Baker had found inside the urn. And then she pulled out the watch, handing it to him. "I visited a jewelry shop in Milford, but they wouldn't tell me who the watch originally belonged to."

"You don't think it was your father's?"

Tricia thought about how she'd answer the question. No, because her father was a known con man. Had McDonald's predecessor chronicled the misadventures her father had perpetrated when he'd last visited the village? If not, should she tell him about those illicit deeds?

Tricia decided on the truth. "As much as I love my father, I'm also ashamed that he's been proven to be less than honest in his word and dealings."

McDonald pushed back in his office chair. "That's a rather bold statement."

"Sadly, it's the truth. No one wants to admit that their gene pool has been tainted by crimes—and for the most part, petty ones."

Tricia's cheeks felt hot with embarrassment as McDonald scrutinized her face.

"I'm sorry to hear that. I'll have Polly search our site's archives to find out whatever my predecessor chronicled about your father."

"Please don't," Tricia said. It wasn't a plea, just a request.

"And why's that?" McDonald asked.

Tricia let out a weary sigh. "Polly already hates me. I don't want to give her another reason to do so."

"She doesn't hate you," McDonald said.

Tricia gave him the fish eye, and the chief looked away. "Just what is Polly's problem?" she asked.

McDonald shook his head. "That's her decision to share with the world at large. Or not."

So, the woman *did* have a problem. Tricia had never liked Polly, but she always had compassion for souls in difficult situations—even if they weren't necessarily the kindest people on the planet.

"I respect your reticence," Tricia said. But then her thoughts returned to her own troubles. She offered the chief the watch. "In your official capacity, could you find out who the rightful owner is?"

A Perilous Plot

"And you don't think it's your father?"

Tricia thought long and hard before she answered. "My father was known to gamble. For all I know, he may have won it in a poker game. But perhaps that might be a clue as to what happened to him and point out where Angelica and I might track down our mother. She's got the answers to the questions we never got to ask last fall."

McDonald nodded. "I'll see what I can come up with."

"And if it belongs to my father?" Tricia asked.

"I'll be sure to return it. Is there anything else you want to tell me?"

Tricia shook her head. "I just wish—" But then she said no more. What was it she wished? That her parents had loved her more? That there were no secrets among them? That, despite the love she felt for the people who raised her, if she never saw either of them again, she would be okay with that. And what would McDonald think about that declaration? How would he judge her? Should she even care?

Tricia stood, ready to leave, when McDonald spoke again.

"I've taken to heart what you said last fall," he declared.

Tricia's mind whirled. What had she said? To cover her memory lapse, she said, "And what's your decision?"

"That since I'm not allowed to write about specific investigations I ran while working security for the cruise line, I might try my hand at writing a fictionalized account of what I encountered."

Good grief! Why had she ever said that? And she could predict where this conversation was going to go. "And?" Tricia dutifully asked. "What genre?"

"Mystery, of course. Just up your alley."

So, McDonald, a recent resident of the US, had already learned at least one of the country's clichés.

"I've already got a couple of chapters down. I wondered if you'd take a look and give me your unbiased opinion."

"A couple of chapters?" Tricia asked.

"Well, no, actually."

Good grief! Just an outline?

"I've actually finished the whole book."

That was a lot more than most wannabe authors accomplished, but if he had no talent, was she supposed to tell him so?

Tricia braved a smile. "I'd love to read it." *Liar!*

"Great. I'll drop off a copy in the next day or so."

"I'll look forward to reading it."

Another lie.

Tricia forced a smile. "I've been away from my store for too long today. I need to get back to work."

McDonald nodded. "Either way, if I find out anything about the watch, I'll be in touch."

They looked at each other for long moments. During that time, Tricia wondered what would have developed between them had they not met other people—lovers. Tricia was with David, and the villagers assumed that McDonald had coupled with Tricia's sort-of frenemy, world-famous former tennis star Becca Dickson-Chandler, who had a reputation for being difficult. Tricia was happy with her choice. Was McDonald happy with his?

It wasn't Tricia's business, and she wasn't about to ask either McDonald or Becca about it.

Saturdays were always the best sales day of the week for most of the Booktown merchants. Tricia's assistant manager, Pixie Poe, worked weekdays, and her other employee, Mr. Everett, bridged the weekend gap. As soon as Tricia darkened her shop's door, Mr. Everett—ever astute—sensed her melancholy.

"Is something wrong, Ms. Miles?"

A Perilous Plot

Tricia had never made Mr. Everett privy to the complicated relationship she'd had with her parents. Still, rumors had circulated the last time the elder Miles couple had visited the village—especially when it came to John Miles's antics.

Tricia was glad no patrons roamed among the shelves at her store, Haven't Got a Clue, before she spoke.

"There's a possibility that reports of my father's death were premature."

Mr. Everett looked confused. "But your mother said . . ." Mr. Everett had been present the evening Sheila Miles had arrived to report Tricia and Angelica's father's death.

"Yes," Tricia agreed, and shrugged out of her jacket. "I . . . I really can't go into it at this time. But this morning, I learned something that casts doubt on what my mother told us last fall. I've asked Chief McDonald to make some inquiries on our behalf."

Mr. Everett's brow furrowed, and he seemed at a loss for words. "Well, then perhaps you'll soon have some happy news."

Happy? Not likely. If John Miles lived, his wife had perpetrated an unforgivable lie meant to torment the couple's daughters unnecessarily.

Ever thoughtful, Mr. Everett said, "If you'd like some time to absorb this information, I assure you, I can take care of the shop."

Tricia shook her head. "No, this is just another in a long—long—line of convoluted misadventures Angelica and I have been through with our parents."

Mr. Everett nodded sympathetically. "I'm so sorry you've had to experience that. If there's anything Grace and I can do—"

Tricia held up a hand to stave off the offer. "Believe me, you and Grace being our friends—and honorary grandparents to Ginny and Antonio's children—has been such a blessing. I can't tell you how much—" But that's where the lump in Tricia's throat became too large to continue speaking. She'd known Mr. Everett for only nine years, but that he had been kinder and, in his own way, more loving than her own father just about broke her heart.

Luckily, a customer entered the store. These days, they were as rare as hen's teeth. In another six or seven weeks, customers would file through in more significant numbers. At this time on the calendar, anyone who crossed the threshold was treated like a king or queen in hopes they'd help support the store's bottom line. Tricia was not disappointed, as the customer, a dapper man in a three-piece suit, was a collector. He was more interested in the vintage specimens in the big glass display case than the more-often-than-not reprints of mystery classics on the store's shelves. The three of them had a lively conversation, with the gentleman buying two books—probably the most lucrative sale the store had had in over a month.

After the man left, Mr. Everett surprised Tricia by giving her a high five, which made her laugh. It felt good to laugh after the dour beginning of the day. And upon that realization, she tried not to let it show that her mood had immediately sunk back into depression. She wouldn't, for the world, want to disappoint Mr. Everett.

Tricia forced a smile. "We need to replenish the stock in our display case. Would you like to style it?"

"I'd be happy to. We've got those vintage copies of Nancy Drew hardcovers with the lovely color dust covers. Shall we use them?"

"Perfect," Tricia told him.

"I'll pop on down to the storeroom and get a few," Mr. Everett said, and headed for the stairs that led to the basement.

Tricia watched him go. Mr. Everett had never been blessed with children, but Tricia knew he would have been a terrific dad. Thinking about her father, she felt that sometimes nature chose the wrong people to become parents.

THREE

 Tricia was on her own when it came time for her midday meal as Angelica and David were spending the afternoon antiquing—and hopefully bonding—so she didn't mind. She retreated to her apartment above Haven't Got a Clue to consume a lunch of leftovers before returning to her shop to spend the rest of the quiet afternoon with Mr. Everett in the reader's nook to catch up on their reading in peace.

When closing time approached, they put down their books, performed the end-of-day tasks, and set up for the next day.

"Are you feeling better?" Mr. Everett inquired as he shrugged into his light jacket.

"I always feel better after spending time with you," Tricia assured him.

Mr. Everett smiled. "As do I. Perhaps tomorrow we'll see more customers."

Tricia held up her hand and crossed her fingers. "We can only hope so." She waved good-bye to him before giving her cat a snack and heading over to her sister's apartment over the Cookery.

As usual, Sarge, Angelica's bichon frise, was ecstatic to see Tricia, and she tossed him a couple of dog biscuits to quiet his exuberance. She shrugged out of her jacket and stood before Angelica's kitchen island.

"Hi."

"Hi, yourself," Angelica said as she removed the chilled pitcher of martinis and two frosted glasses from the fridge.

"Anything new since this morning?" Tricia asked.

"Well, not exactly."

Tricia raised an eyebrow.

"With everything else that's going on, I may have forgotten to mention that I—or rather Nigela Ricita Associates—take possession of the Bookshelf Diner on Monday."

"Wow," Tricia uttered blankly. "That happened a lot sooner than I thought."

"Yeah, me, too," Angelica admitted, looking pensive.

"And what are you going to do with it?"

"That's the thing; I'm not sure."

"What?" Tricia asked, confused.

Angelica shrugged. "I could just install another cook, head of house, and continue as is."

"And why would you do that?"

"Because it's a brand," Angelica answered simply.

"Which went downhill in the diner's last year or so."

"But it *could* be brought back to life. At this point, I'm inclined to cut the menu, refresh the dining room, and leave it at that."

"Cut the menu?"

"Does it really need to have over a hundred choices?" she asked pensively.

A Perilous Plot

"Probably not." Angelica stared at the counter. "Is everything okay?" Tricia asked.

Angelica heaved a sigh. "No. What we learned this morning has knocked my world off-kilter."

If Tricia was honest, she was just as upset but not surprised, which tempered her feelings. Angelica had always had a better, closer relationship with their parents. She had to feel devastated.

"Would you like to talk about it?" Tricia asked, reaching out to touch her sister's arm.

Angelica shrugged. "What good would it do? I mean, we have no idea what was going through Mother's head when she showed up last fall and lied to us. Was she trying to establish some kind of—" But then she stopped.

"My first thought was *alibi*, and I have no idea why," Tricia admitted.

"Yeah," Angelica agreed. "What could her motive have been?" She shook her head. "Something is really wrong," Angelica said. "If I weren't so generous, I'd say nefarious. I don't for a minute believe there was a mix-up at the funeral home, so why would she want us to believe Daddy was dead?"

Tricia hesitated before commenting. "What's the con? Insurance fraud is the only thing I can think of. Had their fortunes dwindled so low that they decided to fake Daddy's death to collect?" But then she shook her head. "At the very least, they'd have to have a legitimate death certificate."

"Were you able to find one?"

Oops. Tricia hadn't made time to look for one. "Uh, not as yet," Tricia said. She'd have to put that search at the top of her to-do list.

Angelica took another sip of her martini before speaking once again. "Mother knew I paid off all the people Daddy bamboozled the last time he spent time here in Stoneham. They know I've got bucks, although thank goodness they have no clue about my Nigela Ricita holdings."

"Are you sure?"

Suddenly, Angelica looked anything *but* sure. Still, she continued. "I think Daddy would have hit me up for *something*—money, a place to escape Mother. Whatever. Anyway, if they were in financial straits, why wouldn't they come to *me* to bail them out?" Angelica asked, her tone a mix of puzzlement and chagrin.

Tricia shrugged. "Embarrassment?"

Angelica leveled a sour look at her sister. "Daddy wasn't the least bit ashamed when I bailed him out three years ago."

No. Tricia bet not much would mortify the man, and a small part of her felt guilty about it. But why? As a child, her father had made her feel special—probably because her mother had so blatantly ignored her in favor of Angelica. But once Tricia had left the nest and married Christopher Benson, she'd had minimal contact with her parents. And, honestly, she was fine with that. Just like she wasn't as upset as Angelica over this whole debacle. That said, she needed to be there for her sister. Angelica had been unconditionally loved by her parents—and loved them implicitly. Tricia didn't have that same history. She couldn't fathom the depth of the betrayal her sister must feel.

Tricia decided to turn the conversation to a lighter subject. "Did you and David have a good time antiquing this afternoon?" she asked.

Angelica shook her head. "I canceled. After this morning, I just wasn't in the mood to have fun."

"Maybe that was precisely the time you *should* have gone out," Tricia pointed out.

Angelica nodded. "Maybe, but it's too late now."

"Are we still on for our family dinner tomorrow?"

"I suppose so," Angelica said halfheartedly.

"You can cancel that, too," Tricia suggested.

A Perilous Plot

Angelica shook her head. "And miss the chance to be with my grandbabies? Not a chance. I haven't seen them in a week. It's just been so crazy, what with Stonecreek Manor about to open and taking possession of the Bookshelf Diner. I haven't even seen Antonio since last Sunday, although we've spoken on the phone at least once every day this week." Antonio was Angelica's son, although she hadn't publicly acknowledged that. Everyone saw him as the public face of his and Angelica's company, Nigela Ricita Associates. The dinner Tricia referred to was where she, Angelica, Antonio's family, and Mr. Everett and his wife, Grace, got together every Sunday evening. Often, it was the highlight of the sisters' week—and more so for Tricia since David had been welcomed into the group.

"I'm feeling so down, I might just spend all of tomorrow in the kitchen cooking. If there's one thing that brings me joy, it's preparing food for people I love." She sighed. "Cooking reminds me of Grandma Miles. She would never have pulled the world's worst prank on us." Her lower lip quivered, and she looked about to cry.

"What would you make?" Tricia asked as a distraction.

"What?" Angelica asked, surfacing from her misery.

"What would you make that would be special?"

Angelica shrugged. "Comfort food. Maybe lasagna. It wouldn't be anything like Antonio enjoyed as a boy back in Italy, but the rest of the group would probably love it. Add to that, glasses of vino, a great big salad, and garlic bread, and it would not only taste great but soothe our souls."

Tricia didn't think the rest of the group needed such soothing, but they weren't likely to turn down the dish. And no doubt Angelica would pull out all the stops to ensure it was the best pasta dish they'd ever eaten.

"It sounds heavenly," Tricia said. "Which reminds me, what are we having tonight?"

Angelica's expression blanked before darkening. "Uh . . . can you believe it? I forgot to plan anything. My day was just so discombobulated that I never gave a thought to dinner."

The after-hours take-out options weren't great. It meant a pizza from a shop on the outskirts of the village—a business that never joined the Stoneham Chamber of Commerce, and the wait on a Saturday night could be hours. Their at-home choice meant cleaning out the fridge in hopes of finding something palatable.

"We could go to the Dog-Eared Page," Tricia suggested. "They make a mean fish and chips."

"Yes," Angelica agreed halfheartedly. "And their Hennessy sub is pretty good, too."

"And the fish tacos," Tricia suggested.

"And—" Angelica stopped, a slight smile gracing her lips. "I've suddenly got the urge to be in a place where there're people and music and—"

"Life?" Tricia asked.

Angelica nodded. "It wouldn't hurt to deviate from our usual evening, would it?"

"Not a bit."

"Do you suppose David's had dinner?"

"I'm betting not," Tricia said.

"I feel so bad canceling out on him this morning. Perhaps we should invite him to join us."

"I wouldn't mind," Tricia said. It seemed an age—which was almost twenty-four hours—since she'd spent time with her *amante*.

"Why don't you text him?"

Such an invitation would have been unheard of six months before. "I'll do that," Tricia said neutrally.

"Great. Let me change. I don't want to be seen in public in my

A Perilous Plot

ratty old clothes." Angelica wore a set of silk lounging pajamas—not appropriate for an evening at an Irish pub, but hardly ratty.

"You do that," Tricia said, watching as her sister drained her glass.

Once Angelica had left the room, Tricia pulled out her phone and quickly began a text.

What are you doing this evening?

David quickly answered. *What did you have in mind?*

Join Angelica and me at the Dog-Eared Page for dinner.

In no time, David answered: *How soon?*

As soon as you can get there.

Putting my shoes on now. He added a track shoe and a heart emoji, signaling to Tricia that the conversation was over.

Angelica returned faster than Tricia anticipated, looking smart in a black pantsuit with a crisp white blouse. Around her neck was a silver chain with the charm that was supposed to be filled with cremains earlier that day.

"Why are you wearing *that*?" Tricia asked.

Angelica looked down at her clothing and black flats. "I can't very well go naked."

Tricia rolled her eyes. "The necklace!"

"Oh!" Angelica's eyes narrowed. "I paid good money for that charm and chain, and I'll be damned if I discard it because of whatever stunt Mother and Daddy are playing on us."

It wouldn't have been Tricia's choice. She'd tossed her charm into one of her seldom-opened jewelry boxes, intending to forget that she'd ever bought it.

"Are you ready?" Tricia asked.

"You bet. Why don't we head over to the pub now?"

"David won't be far behind us."

Angelica took Sarge out for a quick pee, and then the sisters donned their jackets and headed out the door.

At least they'd have a nice, quiet dinner of comfort food and perhaps some camaraderie.

It was the best Tricia could hope for.

Saturday evenings at the Dog-Eared Page were always hopping. The manager, Shawn, often booked a musician to entertain the crowd, who ordered drinks and meals, played darts, and sometimes sang karaoke. The place didn't really come into its own until after nine, so there were still a few open tables when Angelica and Tricia entered.

Bev, the server who'd previously worked for Angelica at Booked for Lunch, greeted them enthusiastically. "Well, if it isn't the fabulous Miles sisters. Where have you been? We haven't seen you in ages."

"Oh, you know—just living life in the fast lane," Angelica said, but her tone held no enthusiasm.

"Just the two of you, then?" Bev asked with a raised eyebrow.

"We've got someone joining us. He should be along soon."

Bev crooked her lips. "Sure," she said, grabbed some menus, and steered the women to a booth. Once seated, Bev asked, "The usual?"

Tricia wasn't sure she wanted another martini. "I'll have a gin and tonic."

"And for you?" Bev asked Angelica.

"A gin martini, and not too heavy on the vermouth."

"Coming right up," Bev said, and turned toward the bar.

Tricia frowned. "We probably should have waited for David to arrive."

Angelica merely shrugged.

They didn't have long to wait before Tricia's beau arrived, with pink cheeks after a brisk walk from the municipal parking lot. He greeted Tricia with a kiss and settled down beside her before speaking to Angelica. "I assume you're feeling better now," he said hopefully.

Angelica heaved a heavy sigh. "Physically, yes. Emotionally . . . not so much."

David gave Tricia a side glance.

"We had some news today that was—" How on earth was she supposed to describe it? Unfortunate? Potentially good—but in a bad way? Devastating?

"Horrible," Angelica supplied.

David's eyes widened. "In what way?"

Tricia gave him a brief explanation, lowering her voice lest other patrons might listen in on their tale of woe.

"Wow," David said, and it wasn't with awe. It was more like confusion. He'd grown up with normal—sane—parents.

"Yeah," Angelica added, her gaze wandering to the bar and their lack of alcoholic soothers.

"That had to be quite a shock," David said.

"You're not kidding," Angelica said, sotto voce.

Bev finally arrived with the two drinks and took David's order for a Bashful Moose ale from the local craft brewery that also had a tasting room right across the street.

"Are you ready to order?" Bev asked, sounding hopeful.

"I am," Angelica said. "I'll have the Irish stew."

"Fish and chips for me," Tricia said.

"I'll go for that, too," David said.

"Great. I'll put the order in and be back with your beer in a flash," Bev promised.

They watched her head toward the bar before turning their gazes back to one another once again.

"So, what are you going to do?" David asked.

"About what?"

"About your family situation?" David asked.

Angelica nodded in her sister's direction. "Tricia's going to look for a death certificate. And if she finds one, I'll join the Foreign Legion."

"There's no such thing." David looked uncertain. "Is there?"

"No, there isn't," Tricia assured him.

"Well, there should be," Angelica grumbled, and took a big sip of her drink.

Tricia snaked her hand onto David's lap, fumbling to hold his hand. His fingers were warm as they gently clasped hers.

"Hey, Tricia!"

Tricia started, reclaiming her hand, and looked up to see a familiar gent—a dapper octogenarian with a full mustache and an Irish twinkle in his eye—approaching their table. Mike Thomas had been on the darts team with Tricia a few years before.

"I haven't seen you in here for a while. Care for a game of arrows?" he asked hopefully.

"That's sweet of you to ask, Mike, but we've had a long day and are just here to grab a quick dinner and go."

"That's too bad. But I'll hold you to a rain check."

"You bet," Tricia said, smiling.

Mike nodded. "So, how's John doing?" he asked, sincerely.

Tricia and Angelica exchanged rather panicked glances. "Uh, we haven't seen him in a while," Angelica said evasively.

"Really?" Mike asked. "We played darts the last time he was in the village."

A Perilous Plot

"And when was that?" David asked.

Mike looked thoughtful. "Let's see. Oh, about six weeks ago."

"Six weeks!" Tricia and Angelica cried in unison. Angelica's eyes had suddenly dilated. Tricia wondered if her own had undergone the same transformation. "Are you sure?"

Mike nodded. "I couldn't give you the exact date, but it was a Saturday night. Remember that last big storm at the end of February?"

"What was he doing here in the village?" Angelica asked, sounding as confused as Tricia.

"I assumed he was visiting you two. We talked mostly about sports," Mike reported.

That sounded like John Miles. He knew a lot about sports because he apparently gambled on them—a lot.

"We'll have to set a date and time for that game," Tricia said, hoping Mike would get the hint and retreat.

"Yeah, sure. When you see your dad, tell him I said hi."

"We'll do that," Angelica promised, her voice as tight as an overwound clock.

Tricia waited until Mike walked away before speaking. "What do you make of that?"

Angelica's eyes blazed. "What on earth was Daddy doing here in Stoneham—knowing he was *supposed* to be dead?" she hissed.

"Maybe he wanted to get caught?" David proposed.

The sisters turned their gazes on him. "You mean like to establish an alibi?" Tricia asked.

David shrugged. "Kind of."

Angelica scowled. "Sounds about right," she grumbled. Usually, Angelica defended their father's foibles. This time, it didn't seem like she was staunchly in his corner.

"Maybe he *wanted* to be seen by people who knew him, someone who could vouch he was *still* alive on that date," David suggested.

If that was so, then why hadn't he shown up in the town where he and Sheila had lived a great deal of the time they'd been married? The idea that one or both of their parents were perpetrating a scam seemed more and more likely. How many Stoneham citizens had interacted with John Miles some six weeks before—and why had none of them mentioned his presence in the village before now?

The pub's door opened, sending a blast of chilly air into the room. Walking hand in hand were Police Chief Ian McDonald and Tricia's sort-of friend/kind-of frenemy, Becca Dickson-Chandler, ex-tennis sensation, ex-wife of Tricia's former lover, and the latest Stoneham bigwig, with a soon-to-be-opened tennis club she hoped to turn into a franchise.

Becca made a beeline in Tricia's direction, pulling Ian along the way. "Hello, ladies and gentleman. And how are you this fine evening?"

Becca's moods usually ranged from blithe indifference to downright anger. Hence, no one ever knew what to expect from the woman.

"We're"—Tricia paused before finishing the sentence—"good."

"Marvelous. And?" Becca looked expectantly at the three as though to solicit a response of what she was up to.

"How are you?" Tricia dutifully asked.

Becca shoved her left hand in front of Tricia's face, flashing a solitaire diamond ring on her fourth finger. "We're engaged!" she squealed, like a teenager who'd just made the cheerleading squad.

"Congratulations, Ian," David said cheerfully. "And best wishes, Becca," he added.

"Yes, best wishes," Tricia managed in a somewhat strangled tone. Hearing about Becca's impending nuptials was the last thing she expected to hear that day. No, the second-to-last thing. Two shocks in one day were far too much for one to absorb.

"When's the happy day?" Angelica asked. She wasn't at all perturbed by the news.

A Perilous Plot

"It only happened today—just hours ago," Becca clarified. "We'll have to figure that out, won't we, darling?"

Darling? For some reason, that term of endearment had always grated on Tricia's nerves. It was so . . . saccharine. So clichéd. Tricia and David had no pet names for each other. Come to think of it, none of Tricia's lovers (and husband) had given her a nickname. Was she better or worse for it?

"I suppose you'll get married in Boston," Angelica said.

"We thought we'd tie the knot right here in Stoneham," Ian said. "After all, it's where we'll live."

"For the time being," Becca agreed.

Ian frowned but didn't comment.

"It depends on how well my tennis club franchises pan out," Becca clarified. "We're sitting on a potential gold mine!"

And would Ian have to sign a prenuptial agreement before the wedding day . . . just in case the marriage didn't work out? At that moment, Tricia gave their odds of reaching the altar at fifty-fifty, although she wasn't about to say so.

"Keep us informed about your plans," Tricia said.

"Of course. And, of course, I want *you* to be my maid of honor," Becca gushed.

Tricia started. "Me?"

"Of course. You're my bestie."

Tricia's eyes widened so far that they nearly popped out. Becca's BFF? That was news to Tricia, who somehow managed to smile, albeit forced. "We'll . . . we'll have to talk about it."

"It'll be an extravaganza, that's for sure," Becca quipped.

Tricia again glanced in Ian's direction. This was news to him.

"Let's do lunch next week," Becca said. "We have *loads* to plan."

"Sure thing," Tricia said, feeling like the wind had been knocked out of her. She looked in Ian's direction. "About the watch," she began.

"We'll talk about it tomorrow," McDonald promised.

Tricia nodded, and thankfully, Bev arrived with a big tray of plates for the table. "Here we go," she said, sidestepping the standing couple and plopping the entrées before the trio. "Eat hearty!"

"We'd better let these lovely people enjoy their dinners," Ian said genially.

Becca turned her adoring gaze at her newly minted fiancé. "As you say, sailor boy."

Tricia cringed. *Good grief.*

"We'll talk soon," Becca said—or was it a threat?

Angelica and David barely noticed the retreating couple, picking up their forks and digging into their meals. Tricia wasn't as quick to start eating. It was David who noticed.

"Well, that was some kind of announcement," he commented.

"Yes, it was," Tricia said, finally picking up her fork and poking at a French fry.

"Who knew you were Becca's best friend?" Angelica remarked.

"It certainly wasn't me," Tricia muttered.

"Isn't that a little odd?" David asked.

"Since I first met her, I got the feeling Becca doesn't have many people she can count on."

"Why's that?" David asked.

"I assume because most of the people she meets plot to exploit her," Angelica said mildly.

"And why's that?" Tricia asked.

Angelica shrugged, snagging a hunk of meat from her stew, and ate a bite. "Because I've often found myself in the same situation."

"People exploit you?" David asked, puzzled.

"No, but they'd sure like to. How many people in the village do you think I consider friends?"

Tricia thought about it. "Ten? Fifteen?"

A Perilous Plot

"Apart from family? Four."

"Really?" Tricia asked, frowning.

"Yes. Mr. Everett, Grace, Pixie, and David."

It was Tricia's turn to look puzzled. "No one else? Not even June?" June managed the Cookery for Angelica.

Angelica shook her head, finding her stew incredibly interesting. "She's my employee. Let's face it: As you get older, it's a lot harder to forge new relationships. And if you have money, you have to question *why* people want to cultivate your friendship."

"That's a sad commentary on man- and womankind," Tricia said.

Angelica squinted at her younger sibling. "And how many people here in Stoneham do you consider to be a friend?"

Tricia considered the question. Her list was pretty much the same as Angelica's. Tricia had many acquaintances in the village, but not many she'd confide in. And the friendships she had from high school, college, and the business world had fallen by the wayside—especially since she'd moved to New Hampshire. The list of friends she'd once exchanged Christmas cards with had dwindled to next to nothing. She'd had a huge wedding with five attendants, but she hadn't heard from any of them in over a decade.

"You make us sound like hermits," Tricia muttered.

"Well, aren't we?" Angelica asked. "How about you, David? How many people do you consider as close friends?"

"Loads," he said, stabbing a French fry as though in defiance.

"Count them on fingers and toes," Angelica challenged.

David set down his fork, looked heavenward, and counted on his fingers. "Okay, maybe eight. And, like you, almost half of them are you, the Everetts, and Pixie. Julie at the library has become a great buddy, too." Julie was an elderly volunteer who came in most days of the week to read to toddlers in the children's section of the library where David worked.

"I thought so." Angelica polished off the last of her martini and heaved a sigh before changing the topic. "With everything that's happened, I forgot to mention that Cleo Gardener is moving in tomorrow." Ms. Gardener had been hired as the innkeeper for the village's newest hostelry, formerly known as the old Morrison Mansion, recently renamed Stonecreek Manor, which was the newest addition to the Nigela Ricita Associates portfolio.

"Is Ginny going to meet her?" Tricia asked. Ginny was the face of NR Associates on the project, in addition to her regular duties as head of their public relations/marketing division.

"Yes. I'll be with her, too, of course, acting as . . . well, her friend, I guess. Would you like to join us? Cleo's supposed to arrive at ten—that gives you two hours before your store opens."

"Yes, I would. I haven't seen all the finished rooms."

"I'd like to be there, too, to show Tricia my contributions to the project," David said.

Angelica sighed. "That'll be quite the welcoming committee, but I don't see why not."

"We won't get underfoot," Tricia promised. Her gaze wandered to the booth where Becca and Ian had settled. Becca leaned across the table, smiling, looking relaxed. Tricia had seldom (ever?) seen her look so happy, and she wondered how long that sense of euphoria would last.

The trio finished their dinners and Angelica pulled out her credit card to pay.

"Thanks for the meal," David said.

"I'll second that," Tricia agreed.

Angelica shook her head sadly, her lips falling into a pout. "How pathetic is it that the last forty-five minutes were the highlight of my day?"

"Tomorrow *has* to be better," Tricia assured her.

A Perilous Plot

The ghost of a smile crooked Angelica's lips. "Sundays, when I see my little family and friends, always is."

Family. Tricia and Angelica's family had begun with their parents. People who had become mere strangers as opposed to people who weren't tied to them by their DNA.

It would take some expert sleuthing for Tricia to figure out just what was going on with her parents, and, more important, why they'd decided to deceive their children.

Tricia wasn't sure she'd ever be able to forgive them for that.

FOUR

Upon waking the following morning, Tricia's fervent hope was for a quiet day devoid of drama. David was up before her and laid a beautiful tablescape on her kitchen island. He collected bone china and porcelain and often gifted Tricia with eclectic pieces. When she dined at his place, each place setting was adorned with a freshly ironed linen napkin, often folded into an intricate shape, and fresh flowers. David wasn't one to save his best china for only special occasions.

He greeted her with a kiss and pulled back one of the stools on the kitchen island to seat her. He'd made eggs Benedict, fresh-squeezed orange juice, and ground Kona beans for their morning coffee.

"You went to a lot of trouble," Tricia commented with pleasure.

"No trouble at all for you, dear lady. But we can't dillydally. I'm eager to meet Cleo Gardener."

Dillydally? David might be only in his midtwenties, but he was an old soul who embraced old dishes, old people, and old expressions.

"The least I can do is help you with the dishes," Tricia said.

A Perilous Plot

"You'll do no such thing. After breakfast, you shower and dress while I clear up everything. If you like, we could walk to Stonecreek Manor. Pixie's going to pick me up there to go to the estate sales. She can give you a lift back to your shop, unless you want to hoof it."

Tricia smiled and extended her hand to caress his cheek. "Okay."

They ate their breakfasts, ruminating over the previous day's events, something Tricia could have done without. And yet, those dour events weren't about to spoil her day.

By the time Tricia returned from getting ready for the day, the kitchen was tidy, her cat had been fed, and David had his jacket and cap on and was ready to go.

They took Tricia's usual walking route through the village until reaching the former Morrison Mansion. Along the route, cheerful forsythia bushes had popped into bloom. Tricia thought about the estate's gardens. She wasn't a gardener, but she'd taken an interest in them. They needed a lot of work to restore them to their former glory, but that would take years, not months, to happen. She'd like to help with that.

As they walked up the path toward the mansion's front door, a black SUV pulled up in front of the building.

"That must be Cleo," David said. "Should we introduce ourselves?"

Tricia pondered the question for just a moment. "Probably not. I mean, how *would* we introduce ourselves?"

"Friends of Nigela?" David suggested. He knew about Angelica's alter ego—and Angelica knew that he knew . . . not that they'd spoken about it. "Otherwise, it could be awkward."

Yes, it might.

"Okay," Tricia said, took a steadying breath, and strode ahead as the truck's driver's side door swung open and a woman of about forty, with short-cropped red hair, dressed in sweats, jumped down to the asphalt drive.

Tricia charged forward. "Hi. You must be Cleo."

The woman squinted in Tricia's direction. "And you are?"

"Tricia Miles. And this is my friend, David Price. We're friends of Nigela Ricita."

Cleo looked at them, her expression cool. "How nice."

Tricia and David exchanged furtive looks. Neither seemed sure if the woman before them would turn out to be a friend or foe.

"We're here to see how the rooms have evolved," David said. "I was invited for my input."

Cleo didn't seem pleased by that new information. "How nice," she said again, but an air of disapproval seemed to hover above her words. Angelica had an uncanny knack for hiring the best people. Had she made a mistake by hiring Cleo Gardener?

Tricia indicated the cars in the drive. "Shall we go inside?" Tricia suggested.

"Yes," Cleo replied.

Tricia forged ahead, found the manor's big oak door unlocked, and charged inside. "Ginny? Angelica?" she called.

Ginny's muffled voice replied, "In the kitchen."

Led by Tricia, the three callers marched through the home until they came to the large room that was the mansion's main food-production hub. The gleaming white subway tiles that clad the walls showed no sign of the fire that had been set to cover up a more heinous crime some six months before. Vintage oak paneling hid the industrial-sized refrigerator, and an eight-burner Vulcan combination stove/oven dominated the west wall.

"What a magnificent kitchen," Cleo said without preamble.

Angelica practically beamed but said nothing.

"I'm glad you like it," Ginny said. "It's so nice to meet you in person, Cleo."

"And you, too." Cleo's gaze swiveled to take in Angelica. "And you are?"

"Angelica Miles. I've partnered with Nigela on another hospitality property here in the village. I'm here as an advisor."

"Miles," Cleo repeated thoughtfully, and glanced in Tricia's direction.

"We're sisters," Tricia explained.

"Where she goes, you go?" Cleo asked with a raised brow.

"Something like that," Tricia agreed.

Cleo nodded. "I see." But it was evident by her tone that she didn't. "I'd like a tour of the house, and then I'd like to get settled in my quarters so I can start work bright and early tomorrow morning."

"I'd be glad to show you around. We're enormously proud of the house," Ginny proclaimed, with Angelica nodding vigorously.

Ginny took the lead, first explaining the wonders of the kitchen and butler's pantry, then leading the group on a tour of the public areas on the ground floor before climbing the central staircase to the guest suites on the floor above.

Tricia and David tended to lag behind the other women, with David pointing out each of his contributions to the rooms after the others had departed.

"You've really put your stamp on the place," Tricia remarked.

"And I enjoyed every minute of it," David exclaimed. But then his expression grew wistful.

"What's wrong?" Tricia asked.

"This was a once-in-a-lifetime event and I'll probably never get the opportunity to consult on such a project again."

"Would you rather do that than work at the library?"

"I'd say I enjoy both equally," David answered honestly.

"I'm sure Angelica isn't finished with renovating properties in the area."

"Yeah, and that's another problem," David said with chagrin.

"Problem?" Tricia asked.

"Gentrification tends to ruin the spirit of a neighborhood."

"In what way?"

"Making it too expensive for locals to afford to live in an area. It brings in people who can outbid them for properties, and landlords raise the rents higher than the local workforce can afford."

"There aren't all that many estates in Stoneham," Tricia pointed out.

"That's true, but rehabilitating the Morrison Mansion will raise property values in the neighborhood and lock some people out. Prices here in New Hampshire are already some of the more expensive in the nation. What happens when the village's worker bees have to move because they can't afford to live here?"

It wasn't a thought Tricia wanted to entertain.

"Stonecreek Manor will employ several people to take care of cleaning, food prep, and garden maintenance," Tricia explained.

"And *Nigela*," he emphasized the noun, "is generous to her employees, but what if someone else comes in and rehabilitates a property and they *won't* pay a living wage? Have you noticed how many mansions languish in the area and are ripe for gentrification?"

No, Tricia admitted to herself, she hadn't.

"I thought you were all for restoring this beautiful old home," Tricia said, confusion causing her to frown.

"I am. But I'd be a lot happier if this place had been turned into a museum. It's the librarian in me. We're teachers, too."

"I get that, but how many museums do you think a village like Stoneham could support?"

"Well, if we were as inventive as the Brits, quite a few. But the Stoneham Historical Society has been struggling for years, and their gardens are nowhere near a total restoration. That'll take decades."

And it was a seasonal feature, as well.

"So, what do you propose?"

David shook his head. "Nothing."

That sounded like a cop-out. "Have you discussed this with Angelica?"

"No, why?"

Tricia sighed. "Because if you guys brainstormed, you might just come up with a solution."

David shrugged. "Maybe."

Approaching footsteps disrupted their conversation.

"So, what do you think?" Ginny asked Cleo as the trio of women reentered the room.

"The house is everything I hoped it would be," Cleo said, looking pleased. "I'm going to enjoy working here."

"I'm glad you feel that way," Ginny said, cheerfully. "And now, would you like to tour your living quarters?"

"Yes, I'd like to get settled today so that I can jump right into work in the morning." Cleo eyed David with what looked like disdain. "I was hoping I'd have help unloading my things into the carriage house."

All eyes turned to David, who was not smiling.

"We're *all* willing to help you get settled in," Ginny said, although she didn't sound as enthusiastic as she might have been.

So, while Ginny and Angelica gave Cleo the tour of her apartment, Tricia and David huffed and puffed up and down the stairs, transporting boxes of what might have been lead ingots they were so heavy, but were probably books. Tricia couldn't fault a person with an extensive library. In a village with so many bookstores, Cleo just might fit right in.

Then again, after all their effort, it seemed to slip Cleo's mind to thank them for their efforts.

David had trundled down the apartment stairs for the last time when Pixie's car pulled into the mansion's drive to pick him up for their usual Sunday estate sales.

"Hey, Tricia, want a ride back to the shop?" Pixie asked. That day, she was dressed in a denim jumpsuit with a blue-and-white bandanna covering her mop of maroon hair. Pixie liked to mix things up when it came to her hair and nails.

"No, thanks. I can use the extra steps." As though schlepping up and down the carriage house stairs hadn't counted toward her ten-thousand-plus step goal.

"Great," Pixie said as David hopped into the passenger side of her big car. "We'll see you later. Cross your fingers we find a lot of treasures."

Tricia held up her right hand, her middle finger crossing over the index. "You got it!" She blew David a kiss, and Pixie backed out of the drive. Tricia watched the car steer toward the main drag before looking back toward the carriage house, where Ginny and Angelica were still consulting with Cleo. There was nothing more for her to do than leave.

As she headed back toward her store, Tricia had a lot to think about: gentrification, Cleo's aloof demeanor, and what she might contribute toward the Sunday family dinner hosted by Ginny and her family and attended by the rest of their makeshift family later that day.

And, of course, the phantom presence of her father, who was apparently still alive and out there lurking . . . somewhere.

Of all the things on Tricia's mind, that last was the one that weighed the heaviest.

A smiling Mr. Everett arrived for work some fifteen minutes before his reporting time. Hot on his heels was Ian McDonald.

"Mr. Everett has just made a fresh pot of coffee. Would you like a cup?" Tricia offered.

McDonald shook his head. "I'm here on official business." He removed the Rolex from his jacket pocket but didn't offer it to Tricia.

A Perilous Plot

"I'll just go take a look at the inventory," Mr. Everett said, escaping to the basement office to give the others some privacy.

Tricia sighed. "Stolen?"

McDonald nodded.

Tricia wasn't surprised by the news. It seemed her father found more and more ways to disappoint her. "What happens next?"

"I've been in contact with my counterpart in North Haven, Connecticut. It seems it was put up as collateral in a poker game, but the owner won the hand. Soon after, the game broke up and while the gentleman was using the restroom, the watch disappeared. So had your father, who was not a regular in that circle of friends."

John Miles had an ingratiating personality and used it to excess. "And?" Tricia asked.

"Even used, the watch is worth about eighteen thousand dollars."

"Good grief!"

McDonald nodded. "There was a warrant out for your father."

"And then he conveniently died," Tricia said sourly.

"No death certificate was filed in North Haven. So, shall we say he disappeared?"

Tricia nodded, her heart heavy. "Last evening, I spoke to Mike Thomas at the pub just before you came in. He said he'd spoken to Daddy about six weeks before in the Dog-Eared Page."

McDonald raised an eyebrow. "Interesting."

Again, Tricia sighed. "I get the feeling Mother and Daddy are not too far away, plotting something."

McDonald scowled. "That's a pretty cynical point of view."

"Don't you think I have reason to be cynical?" she asked.

McDonald nodded reluctantly. "Will you keep an eye out for him?"

"Oh, you better believe I will," Tricia said firmly.

"Yes, but would you report your own father to law enforcement?"

Tricia hesitated.

"I see," McDonald said.

"You can't blame me for having qualms," Tricia remarked.

"No, I can't. But will you blame yourself?"

That was a question Tricia didn't want to answer. "What happens with the watch?"

"It'll be returned to its rightful owner."

"And what happens to the person who appropriated the item?"

"A Class A felony covers anything over fifteen hundred dollars in value. This watch far surpasses that."

"And what's the charge carry?" Tricia asked.

"The possibility of seven and a half to fifteen years in prison."

Tricia let out a low breath. If charged, John Miles might well die in prison. Did she want to be responsible for that?

McDonald pocketed the watch. "I'd better get going. We'll speak again soon."

Tricia nodded and watched him leave the shop. She moved to stand behind the big glass display case and settled on the stool behind it, her gaze falling to the carpeted floor, wondering if she ought to give in to tears. Her father, whom she'd dearly loved in the past, had pushed the limits of her affection and trust. She doubted their relationship could fully recover from that. She needed to speak to Angelica about what she'd learned, but it would have to wait—perhaps until the next day.

In the meantime, Tricia had a store to run. The door opened, the cheerful bell over it welcoming the first customers of the day. Tricia plastered on a smile and spoke.

"Welcome to Haven't Got a Clue."

FIVE

 After McDonald's visit, Mr. Everett seemed to sense Tricia's emotional upheaval. Of course, he would never ask for specifics, but he let her know by his words and actions that he was in her corner. It made the gray day feel that much brighter.

By closing time, Tricia was feeling almost her old self, but she promised herself she would look for an opportunity to speak to Angelica alone.

Tricia and Mr. Everett were the last to arrive at the Barberos' home, and David was in the kitchen helping Angelica pull the dinner together. His mood was buoyant, thanks to a good day of thrifting with Pixie.

"Don't tell me," Tricia teased, "you bought yet another set of dishes."

"No, but I did find a tureen and some bone dishes that match the set at Stonecreek Manor."

"Just in time for the big reveal," Angelica said, sounding pleased.

"I didn't know you were going to do a dinner for your shakedown visits."

"Just a few appetizers and a bit of a bar. Just wine and beer."

It was then a bell rang.

"That's the chicken nuggets," David said, grabbed a pot holder, removed a tray from the oven, and arranged the nuggets on a platter. "Shall I take these out to the others?" he asked.

"If you wouldn't mind," Angelica said, and smiled benevolently.

"My pleasure." David picked up the platter and headed for the living room, where the others had assembled.

"Speaking of the manor, what do you think of your new innkeeper?" Tricia asked flippantly.

Angelica's expression wasn't at all jovial. "I don't know."

Tricia frowned. "What do you mean?"

Angelica turned toward the stove, spoon in hand, to stir a pot of gravy. "That I think I should have vetted her in person instead of a Zoom call."

"Why?"

Angelica's answer was a combination of a shrug and a shudder. "I don't know. She *seems* okay by every usual measure—"

"But?" Tricia asked.

Again, Angelica seemed to shudder, turning her full attention to the gravy. "I don't know. I guess I just have to trust that Cleo is all she said she is."

"What part of her résumé *aren't* you believing?"

Again, Angelica shook her head. "She just gave me weird vibes."

"Well, if it's any consolation, my first impression wasn't especially favorable, either."

"Why's that?" Angelica asked.

Tricia turned her gaze toward the tile floor. "Like you said, it was just a vibe I got."

A Perilous Plot

"Well, I've got to give her a chance to prove my initial reaction to her as wrong. The sad thing is, I won't see how she interacts with real guests until the manor opens."

"Are you regretting having her start the job six weeks before the grand opening?" Tricia asked.

"No. I wanted a shakedown period. But if I have to let her go before my first guests arrive, I'll be skunked."

"Perhaps you ought to hire someone else—you know, as a backup. After all, Cleo can't work twenty-four hours seven days a week."

"That's a good idea. We'll also be hiring cleaners and kitchen staff to start a few days before opening."

"Should you wait that long?"

"Since Antonio put out feelers, we've had a ton of interest. Word of how well Nigela Ricita takes care of her employees has spread. We've got inquiries from people who live in Nashua, Portsmouth, and Concord."

Tricia nodded. "Impressive."

"And Jake"—the chef at the Brookview Inn—"and his team are going to interview applicants for the kitchen staff. We'll have a first-class operation."

"Will David and I be invited for the shakedown?" Tricia asked hopefully.

Angelica frowned. "To be honest, I'd prefer not."

"Why?" Tricia asked, feeling hurt.

"I was thinking of inviting members of the Brookview staff—those who are used to providing an exceptional inn experience might be my top critics and have the best suggestions for providing an extraordinary hotel experience. And I think they'd feel good about having their opinions respected."

Tricia couldn't argue with that logic. She sighed. "I'm disappointed, but I agree you should reward your Brookview employees. I'm sure they'll give not only honest reviews but endear themselves to the Nigela Ricita brand."

Angelica nodded. "But don't worry, you and David can make use of the manor's amenities at some point. Just not at peak times."

"Thanks for that," Tricia said, and held up her glass in salute. "And what about you? Will you try a night at the manor?"

Angelica looked smug. "Oh, I've already done it—multiple times—checking out all the rooms."

Tricia frowned. "What?"

"Well, you didn't think I'd just trust the word of strangers, did you?"

"But when?"

"On nights you spent with David. And, more often, after our happy hours and dinners. I'd pack a bag, and Sarge and I hit the road for the manor."

"And your assessment of the place?"

Angelica flashed a wide grin. "Fabulous!"

"Have you cooked there?"

"A few omelets, toast, coffee, and a coffee cake recipe or two—all delicious."

"And did you cover your tracks?"

Angelica nodded. "No one had a clue I was ever there."

Tricia doubted that but didn't dispute the claim.

"Speaking of food, what are we having tonight?"

"I decided against lasagna, so we're having pot roast, honey-glazed carrots—Sofia loves them—mashed potatoes, asparagus, Parker House rolls, and for dessert, angel food cake with lemon curd."

"Sounds delish. Can I help with something?"

"You sure can. Those potatoes aren't going to mash themselves."

After dinner, it was customary for Ginny to put the children to bed, with Mr. Everett and Grace giving them a good-night story and kiss. While they attended to that, Antonio and David were steeped in

A Perilous Plot

conversation while Tricia and Angelica rinsed the dishes, loaded the dishwasher, and washed and dried pots and pans.

Tricia eyed the men in the other room before lowering her voice and speaking.

"Ian came to visit me at the store this morning."

Angelica looked up from the soapy steel wool pad she'd been scrubbing the gravy pan with. "And?"

"Stealing a Rolex could put Daddy in the slammer for up to fifteen years."

Angelia let out a breath, shook her head, and turned her full attention back to the guck on the side of the pan. "I don't get it. What was the point of stealing the watch if he didn't intend to hock it?"

Tricia shrugged. "Maybe he wanted it to cool down before he did."

"Do you think Mother knew it was in the funeral urn?"

"Maybe. Maybe not. But she sure as heck knew Daddy wasn't dead when she waltzed in here and gave us that phony story about his supposed death."

Angelica rinsed the pan, decided it needed more attention, and attacked it with the steel pad once again. "Did she?"

"Are you suggesting Mother was delusional?"

Angelica shrugged.

Tricia looked thoughtful. "What if Daddy and an accomplice were pulling a con on Mother?"

"Who would he collude with?" Angelica asked.

"That's a good question."

"That still doesn't explain how the watch got hidden in the kitty litter," Angelica commented.

No, it didn't.

Angelica rinsed the pot and handed it to Tricia to dry. "I've got my own news to share."

"Oh?"

"There's been another sighting," Angelica said cryptically.

Tricia frowned. "Of what?"

"Daddy, of course."

Tricia's eyes widened, and her heart began to pound. "In Stoneham?"

Angelica shook her head. "Milford."

"By whom?"

"Fred Pillins." Pixie's husband.

"Did he come to you with that information?" Tricia asked.

Angelica shook her head. "No. He spoke to Tommy"—the short-order cook at Booked for Lunch—"during a drop-off." Fred worked as a deliveryman for a meatpacking firm that served the area.

Tricia's frown deepened. "Why didn't he mention it to you or me?" Tricia and Fred were more than mere acquaintances. That said, Fred probably hadn't known John Miles had been pronounced dead by Tricia and Angelica's mother months before. Had he mentioned that encounter to Pixie? If so, why hadn't she said anything?

Tricia thought about her response. "So, what's the context?"

"They had lunch together at the Milford diner."

"And?" Tricia prompted.

"That was it."

"When was this?"

"A couple of weeks ago."

"We need to talk to Fred. I'll mention it to Pixie tomorrow. Maybe she knows what's going down."

"I highly doubt it. I mean, she knows what we've gone through, right?"

Tricia averted her gaze. "Er . . . not really."

"What do you mean?" Angelica asked, perplexed.

Tricia's cheeks grew warm. "I didn't mention it to her, what with

A Perilous Plot

the way Mother disappeared and everything . . ." She let the sentence trail off.

"And you told Mr. Everett not to mention it to her?"

Tricia nodded. "That was the week Pixie called in sick with Covid. By the time she came back to work, I'd asked Mr. Everett not to say anything about it."

"But it wasn't ever a secret," Angelica asserted.

"No, but Pixie and I have never discussed it, either." Tricia tried to tamp down the anxiety that suddenly enveloped her heart. "Did Tommy mention what he and Fred discussed about our father?"

"Not really. Fred assumed Daddy had contacted us."

Just like Mike at the Dog-Eared Page. "And that's why Tommy didn't think to mention it to us?"

Angelica nodded.

Tricia frowned. And now she ought to track Fred down and interrogate him about that meeting.

"Do you suppose Daddy set Fred up? I mean, that he wanted to be seen, just like Mike running into him at the Dog-Eared Page?"

"I can't think why," Tricia said.

Angelica didn't look convinced. "You realize Pixie knows *everything* that goes on in the village."

Oops! That realization had escaped Tricia.

"Has Pixie acted differently toward you during the past two weeks?"

Tricia shook her head. "She's been her usual cheerful self." Tricia considered the situation. "Perhaps I ought to bring it up to her . . . just so she doesn't think I'm keeping secrets."

"Pixie's the one who keeps secrets," Angelica remarked.

Yes, Pixie had gossip radar and listened avidly but seldom, if ever, repeated it—a trait that had its good *and* bad points.

Angelica cleared her throat. "There's something else I should mention."

Tricia looked intrigued.

"Aunt Bunny arrives tomorrow afternoon."

Tricia's stomach took a tumble. "And where is she staying?" she asked, tight-lipped.

"With me, of course."

"Better you than me," Tricia muttered. "Gee, it's too bad I'll be busy tomorrow evening and won't—"

"You *will* show up for dinner as always, if only so that I don't have to repeat everything she tells me about Mother and Daddy."

Tricia sighed. "Oh, all right. But I *won't* enjoy myself. And you'd better break out the Hendrick's gin. I can't tolerate an evening with Bunny without something strong to deaden the pain."

"Oh, she's not *that* bad."

Tricia eyed her sister coldly. "How long is she staying?"

"A few days," Angelica said, her voice rising slightly.

"A few days?" Tricia questioned.

"Gee, I sure hope so," Angelica muttered.

Tricia had a feeling Angelica would need the Hendrick's more than she. As Ben Franklin said, "Guests, like fish, begin to smell after three days."

Tricia had a feeling Bunny would wear out her welcome long before then.

SIX

 As usual, after the family dinner, David stayed at Tricia's for the night, but he was up early the next morning, feeling cheerful as he went off to the job he loved at the library. Unfortunately, his joyful demeanor hadn't rubbed off on Tricia. She'd spent a good part of the night tossing and turning, dreading her talk with Pixie. The devil on her shoulder told her it hadn't been necessary to speak about her father's supposed death, while the angel begged to differ. She was on the angel's side but so tempted by the devil.

To distract herself, Tricia decided to whip up a batch of peanut butter cookies, choosing the recipe because she knew they were one of Pixie's favorites. While doing so, she reminded herself that her shop would be closed for at least two days that week—Wednesday and Thursday—while the carpet was replaced. Mr. Everett usually didn't work on Mondays, but that week he was scheduled to come in.

Tricia brought a domed plate with the cookies to Haven't Got a Clue and waited nervously as the hands on the clock inched toward ten o'clock and opening. Pixie arrived first. Her mood seemed as buoyant as David's had been.

"Did you have a good thrifting weekend?" Tricia asked.

"Did I ever! I picked up three new-to-me dresses and a gorgeous Roseville pottery planter for just two bucks." She shook her head sadly. "A few years ago, it would have sold for nearly a hundred bucks. I haven't checked the going rate lately, but I'll bet it's still worth over twenty bucks today."

"And will you grow flowers to put in it?"

Pixie laughed. "Not a chance. I have a brown thumb. But Fred brings me carnations—my favorites—on a regular basis so I can pretend."

Pixie mentioning her husband was the perfect opportunity for Tricia to bring up the subject of her parents and her father's supposed demise. But then Mr. Everett arrived, all smiles, and bearing a bag of bagels for them to share.

So much for Tricia's cookies, but then, the day's customers would enjoy them.

They sat in their usual places in the reader's nook, enjoying their coffee and bagels slathered with cream cheese. Pixie and Mr. Everett caught up with the highlights of their lives, while Tricia sat back and bit her lip, wondering how she could bring up the subject of her parents. She might have to wait until later in the day to do so and elicit Pixie's opinion on the subject—and hope she might spill what she knew and/or had heard about the couple.

The trio had drained their cups and finished their bagels when Pixie announced, "I left a box of books out on the back stoop." Pixie thrifted used books in good condition and sometimes came up with gems that would go for more on the shop's online storefront.

"Let me know what I owe you," Tricia said.

A Perilous Plot

Mr. Everett rose. "I'll bring them in and put them in the dumbwaiter to go down to the office and start the inventory."

"Thank you," Tricia said, as all three of them rose from their seats to start the workday.

While Mr. Everett left for the back of the shop, Pixie collected their mugs to wash and replaced them on the shelf below the beverage station. When she returned with the clean cups, Tricia figured there was no time like the present, but it took her long seconds to figure out how to present the subject.

"Angelica said Tommy at Booked for Lunch had a conversation with Fred about our father."

Pixie's expression flattened. "Oh, yeah?"

Tricia nodded. "Did you know my mother came to visit us last fall telling us he was dead?"

"So I heard," Pixie said, and again, her tone was subdued.

Tricia forced a laugh. "What do you make of that?"

Pixie shrugged. "What's the saying? That the rumors of his death were greatly exaggerated?"

Tricia bit her lip, considering how she should answer. "Yeah."

Pixie nodded. "Fred told me he ran into your father."

"And what did you think?"

"That something shady was going on," she answered bluntly. Pixie knew everything that went on in the village. She had to know about John Miles's exploits when he'd last visited Stoneham.

"I'm afraid you're right," Tricia remarked, lowering her gaze.

"What do you think's going on?" Pixie asked.

"I have no idea," Tricia answered honestly. She explained how she and Angelica had met with the local undertaker, the urn full of kitty litter, and the shock the sisters had felt at learning of the deception.

"What are you and Angelica going to do?" Pixie asked. She sounded remarkably calm. Perhaps she would have been more sympathetic if Tricia had confided in her some six months before.

"I don't know. Daddy seems to be lurking around the area, almost as though he *wants* to be caught, and yet he hasn't contacted either of us."

"How about your mother?"

Tricia shook her head. "We have no idea where she is."

"And the watch?" Pixie asked.

"It'll be returned to its rightful owner. But why would Daddy steal it and then not try to convert it to cash?"

"Your parents are—or at least *were*—rich mucky-mucks, right?"

Tricia nodded. "As an only child, my mother inherited the family fortune."

"Which was?"

"Was?" Tricia asked.

"Yeah, what did they deal in?"

Heat rose from Tricia's neck upward. "Uh . . . Hercules condoms."

Pixie's eyes grew so wide they looked dilated. "You've got to be kidding me!"

Tricia shook her head, embarrassed. "No. That was the foundation of my family's net worth."

Pixie's gaze narrowed. "Didn't I hear of a class-action suit against the company? They changed the product formula to save cash and the new condoms had like a fifty percent failure rate."

Tricia reluctantly nodded. "There was a lawsuit."

"And did the company go bankrupt?"

"Uh, the last I heard it was still solvent, but just barely."

Pixie shook her head. "In my former line of work, Hercules condoms were my protection of choice."

Tricia cringed. In another life, Pixie had been a lady of the night.

"So, because of the lawsuit, your parents are essentially broke."

"That sounds plausible," Tricia remarked.

A Perilous Plot

Pixie looked thoughtful. "I've read at least a thousand mysteries, and I can't come up with a reason why your mom and dad would try to pull a scam on you and Angelica."

"We can't, either," Tricia said.

The women looked at each other for long seconds.

"So, what are you going to do about this situation?" Pixie asked.

Tricia shrugged. "I have no idea. I can't understand why Daddy has let himself be seen in the area by people who were sure to mention it to Angelica and me—but that he didn't want to reveal himself to us in person."

It was Pixie's turn to shrug. "Maybe he's just a nutcase."

Tricia didn't think so. Not when there was some angle John Miles could exploit.

Tricia looked toward her assistant manager. "I guess we should have spoken about this sooner."

"Why?" Pixie asked. "It wouldn't have changed anything. You'd still be confused as to why your parents lied to you. And how does all this make you feel?"

"Like crap," Tricia muttered. "Who are these people I grew up with and thought I knew? What kind of scam are they trying to pull? Why would they want to involve Angelica and me in whatever petty little plot they've concocted?"

"I dunno," Pixie asserted. "What's that old saying, 'You always hurt the ones you love.' You, and especially Angelica, are pretty successful people. Success means money."

"But they haven't asked us for anything."

"Yet," Pixie said.

The one word cast a chill over Tricia's soul.

"I'm sorry you're going through this. If I can do anything to help, you know I'll jump to it," Pixie said.

"Yes, and thanks."

The shop door opened, allowing the day's first customers to enter.

"Back to work," Pixie chirped, and intercepted the visitors to greet them.

Tricia moved to stand behind the cash desk. Her conversation with Pixie had gone much better than she could have anticipated. Unfortunately, she didn't feel any better about the situation. She still had no idea what her parents were up to.

Becca arrived at the Brookview Inn before Tricia. This time, Tricia was determined not to get trapped into picking up the check. The hostess led her to the best table in the restaurant. Somehow, Becca always seemed to snag it.

"Ah, you're finally here," Becca said in greeting, her tone cool. She'd already ordered a cocktail—a margarita.

Tricia glanced at her watch. She was only a minute late. She took her seat, picked up the linen napkin on her plate, and shook it over her lap. "So, how are you?"

Becca didn't waste time on the pleasantries.

"I've been dress shopping. I've had my eye on a Vera Wang design, but she's gone awfully commercial. With enough bucks, just about *anyone* can wear one of her more pedestrian creations."

Tricia considered that statement. "You've got the clout. You could ask Ms. Wang to design something original, but as this is your second marriage . . ."

Becca scowled. "Are you saying I don't deserve a knockout gown?"

"I'm saying that second marriages are usually less flamboyant."

"This is *Ian's* first marriage. Doesn't he deserve the works?" Becca chirped.

"Why don't you ask him?" Tricia said innocently.

Becca actually pouted. "He wants *me* to be happy."

A Perilous Plot

"But will 'the works' make *him* happy?" Tricia asked.

Becca looked uncertain, like the idea of Ian's happiness hadn't occurred to her. She was to be the star of that marriage. And what would Ian's part be? Cheerleader or hanger-on?

Tricia signaled to a server and ordered a glass of the house white wine.

"Are you ready to order?" the server, whose name was Alice, asked.

"We haven't even looked at the menu," Becca said. "Check in with us in half an hour."

"Half an hour?" Tricia asked.

"We have a *lot* to talk about."

And I have a business to run, Tricia thought. "Make that fifteen minutes," she told Alice.

Becca did not look pleased, and Alice beat a hasty retreat.

Becca picked up her glass, took a healthy swig, and turned her gaze back to Tricia.

"As my maid of honor, you'll have specific roles to fill," Becca pronounced.

Tricia frowned. She hadn't yet *agreed* to fulfill that role.

"And of prime importance is the bachelorette party," Becca continued.

Tricia scowled. Weren't those parties for women under thirty, or had Tricia fallen into the dull age of fuddy-duddyness? "And who would you invite?"

"All my friends from the tennis world. Serena and Venus, naturally; Madison Keys, Simona Halep, Caroline Wozniacki, and, of course, Billie Jean."

Tricia struggled to stifle a smirk. She was pretty confident Ms. King was *not* Becca's lover.

"Are you sure these women are willing to spend the time and cash to come to Stoneham for the bachelorette party?"

"Oh, we wouldn't hold it here. It would have to be in a much bigger city. Vegas or LA, or—as a last resort—Boston," she said with derision.

"And who's going to arrange and *pay* for it all?" Tricia asked.

"Well, you, of course," Becca said offhandedly.

"Uh, I don't think so."

Becca's expression twisted from euphoric to menace in a heartbeat. "What do you mean?"

"That while I'm happy to stand up for you on your wedding day, I don't have the time"—or the inclination—"to devote to such an affair. While I'm flattered you want to include me in your big day, I really think you should enlist a friend who's played a much bigger part in your life."

"Are you trying to shame me?" Becca barked.

"Not at all. Knowing Ian, and since this isn't your first marriage, I just assumed you two were planning a more low-key event."

"Well, you thought wrong," Becca grumbled.

"What has Ian had to say about your big day?"

Becca looked confused. "What do you mean? This is *my* day."

"No," Tricia asserted. "Ian will be there by your side. He's a man of modest means."

Becca's expression darkened.

"I'm assuming you're asking him to sign a prenup."

"Of course. My lawyer and accountant insist on it."

"And how do you think that makes him feel?" Tricia asked.

Again, Becca looked confused. "It's a standard thing in my crowd. Gene"—her ex-husband, and Tricia's deceased lover—"did the same." Tricia had known "Gene" as Marshall.

"Gene had his own source of money. And as I recall, it wasn't a legal source," Tricia countered.

A Perilous Plot

Becca scowled. "We won't go into that." No, because Gene had testified against a racketeer and had gone into hiding for the rest of his life.

"Why are you being such a pill about planning what's supposed to be the happiest day of my life?" Becca demanded.

Because they were not really friends. Because Becca asking Tricia to take on an activity she wasn't comfortable with was a *major* imposition.

Tricia chose her next words carefully. "I think you and Ian should have a frank discussion about the wedding and what transpires ahead of it before we plan anything else."

"I told you," Becca said with authority, "this is *my* day."

"Unless you're marrying yourself, it's also Ian's day, and he should have an opportunity to express his thoughts on how the event unfolds."

"He doesn't care," Becca said flippantly.

"Are you sure?" Tricia demanded.

Becca finally looked unsure. "I think so."

"Well, until you know for sure, I don't think you should make any major decisions."

Becca scowled. "You are such a killjoy."

"No, I'm realistic—and pragmatic," Tricia amended.

It took long seconds before Becca replied. "All right, if *you* insist, I'll speak to Ian about our plans before we meet again to discuss the details."

And Tricia was determined to speak to Ian alone before she entered into another conversation with Becca about the wedding plans.

"You've assumed an awful lot. First of all, that I have consented to *be* your maid of honor."

"Well, why wouldn't you?"

"Because we're not that close. I like you. I think you're a smart, capable woman, but I wouldn't say we have the kind of relationship that warrants me being your maid of honor."

Becca bit her lip, her eyes filling, looking vulnerable—something Tricia hadn't witnessed in the two years the women had known each other. "Wouldn't you feel more comfortable with one of your tennis friends standing up for you? Say, Serena or Madison?"

Becca picked up her glass, taking a much smaller sip than she'd imbibed less than a minute before. She seemed to be struggling to come up with an answer.

Becca took another sip. "The truth is," she began, "my tennis buddies were more rivals than friends. It's a pretty cutthroat sport."

"But you're no longer competing against those women."

Becca nodded. "That's true. It's just . . ." But then she didn't elaborate.

Tricia took a wild guess. "It's just that you only have tennis in common with them—and for the most part, none of them play anymore."

Becca nodded.

"If you don't feel close to them, why would you want to have a destination bachelorette party?"

"Well, because . . ." But again, Becca had no answer.

Tricia had an inkling. Having had accolades for most of her adult life, Becca was hooked. She needed that dopamine hit of being the biggest cheese in the room. She missed the adoration that came with athletic fame. She missed being in the limelight. Did all former athletes feel the same? Was it a sharp, painful fall from the heights of celebrity to the hard landing of becoming just an ordinary citizen?

Alice returned with Tricia's wine.

"I'm familiar with the lunch menu, but could you tell us about today's specials?"

A Perilous Plot

Alice looked in Becca's direction, as though waiting to be chastised. "Uh . . . the quiche of the day is sausage and asparagus, and we're also offering a lamb shank on a bed of garlic mashed potatoes."

Tricia considered the specials. Angelica had demanded she appear to welcome their so-called aunt Bunny. She hadn't commanded that Tricia *stay* for dinner. "I'll take the lamb shank."

Becca frowned. "I'll have a house salad with raspberry vinaigrette—on the side," she added.

Becca wasn't heavy, but when thinking of fitting into a wedding dress, a diet was likely the first thing on a bride's mind.

"I'll get those going for you," Alice said, and left the women to their conversation.

Tricia and Becca sat in awkward silence for a couple of long minutes. Becca turned her gaze toward the brook outside the window. The still-icy water tumbled over mossy rocks, looking like something out of a nature documentary.

Finally, Becca polished off the last of her margarita. "So, you're saying you *refuse* to be my maid of honor?"

"I didn't say that. I meant it seemed like you were foisting the duty onto me."

Becca swallowed, and Tricia could see the woman was fighting tears—either of embarrassment or pique. "I'm sorry you feel that way."

"But as I mentioned, you should have a frank conversation with Ian before you make any more plans. Once you guys are on the same page, then I'd be glad to stand up and be a witness to your marriage."

Again, Becca's gaze turned toward the landscape outside the inn's window. She seemed to be struggling to find the words to reply. Finally, she simply said, "Thank you."

Tricia tried not to heave a heavy sigh. Still, she had no illusions that the impending nuptials would now travel on a steady course—as Ian would no doubt say in seafaring parlance. And, in another cliché,

Becca was still a loose cannon. Tricia wasn't sure the relationship could survive the engagement, let alone a marriage, which made her feel sorry for both partners. Tricia and Christopher had had much more in common than Becca and Ian. Their marriage had lasted ten years. Tricia wasn't sure the union between Becca and Ian would survive the honeymoon.

SEVEN

 The rest of the day progressed without incident, but Tricia couldn't shake off the feeling of impending doom. She was not looking forward to an evening—or even an hour—with Bunny Murdock.

Finally, she closed Haven't Got a Clue's doors and headed for the Cookery, letting herself in.

"Hello!" Tricia called as she ascended the stairs to Angelica's apartment. Unlike almost every other time she'd done so, there was no joyful barking from Angelica's bichon frise, Sarge. "Hello!" she tried again.

"Come on in," Angelica answered. Her voice sounded a tad off.

Tricia opened the door to the apartment. Still no Sarge.

Tricia entered and saw (not-so) good-old Aunt Bunny sitting in her usual seat at the kitchen island. Dressed in a shapeless caftan of brilliant orange-and-purple stripes, the older woman slipped off the stool and held her arms out to Tricia.

"Darling, Tricia. It's so good to see you."

The women embraced, and Bunny's hands patted Tricia's back and then slid down to pat her butt. Tricia pulled back, uncomfortable with the touch.

"My, you've put on a little weight since I last saw you," Bunny said.

Whatever good feeling Tricia felt toward the woman—and it wasn't much—totally evaporated.

"Not that you're fat," Bunny backpedaled, "it's just that you always looked like you could use a good meal and a pound of butter cookies to stick to your ribs."

Maybe so, but now Tricia felt like she was being fat-shamed for adding a mere eight pounds to her once-emaciated frame. She eyed the half-empty stemmed glass before Bunny. Apparently, she hadn't waited for Tricia's arrival to begin happy hour.

Angelica removed the crystal pitcher from the fridge, pulled out two more chilled glasses, and filled them before settling the olives on frill picks into the glasses. "Shall we retreat to the living room?" she asked brightly, her tone still higher than usual. Was she already tired of Bunny's company?

A tray with still-steaming pastry cups filled with Brie and raspberry preserves sat on the counter, apparently having just been retrieved from the oven. "Tricia, will you carry the tray of drinks, while I bring in the rest?"

"I'd be happy to," Tricia said.

Bunny lifted her bulk from the stool and preceded the sisters into the living room, settling into Tricia's usual chair.

Tricia paused to whisper to her sister, "Where's Sarge?"

Angelica looked embarrassed. "Up in my bedroom. He didn't take to Bunny. In fact, he lunged at her, trying to bite her."

Tricia blinked. Sarge loved everybody. He was the sweetest little canine Tricia had ever encountered and the only time he became aggressive was when he thought his mistress might be in danger.

A Perilous Plot

Apparently, the dog seemed to feel the same way Tricia did about Angelica's guest.

Tricia set the tray down while Angelica distributed the martinis.

"So, what have you been up to lo these many years?" Bunny asked Tricia.

"I run a mystery bookstore. It keeps me busy."

"So I gathered," Bunny said, not sounding at all interested. "Angelica tells me *she's* quite the entrepreneur with so many businesses. You must be a multimillionaire by now," she said, turning her gaze in Angelica's direction.

"I've been pretty lucky," Angelica replied.

"Not luck, my dear. Your mother tells me it's a trait handed down through the ages by the Tate family."

Tate was Tricia and Angelica's mother's maiden name.

Angelica shrugged. "Skill—and a good dose of luck."

Bunny turned her jaundiced gaze toward Tricia. "So, while Angelica has four businesses, you've only got the one?" Her tone had taken on a distinctly judgmental tone.

"It's all I need," Tricia said sweetly, but her hand tightened around the stemmed glass, and she fought against taking a massive gulp of her drink.

"Speaking of our mother, when was the last time you saw her?" Angelica asked, her tone neutral.

Bunny eyed the Brie pockets. "New Year's Eve," she replied.

"And where was that?" Tricia asked. Like her sister, she wanted the question to appear to be neutral.

"Oh, in North Haven."

"We haven't seen Mother since October," Angelica commented, and sipped her martini.

"And was Daddy with her?" Tricia asked.

Bunny's eyes narrowed. "No, as a matter of fact, he wasn't."

63

Angelica took a heftier slug of her drink before asking, "And when was the last time you saw him?"

"That's a good question," Bunny said, her expression turning thoughtful. "Last fall."

Tricia eyed her sister. At that moment, the siblings seemed to be communicating telepathically. "And how did he seem?"

Bunny shrugged, a slight smile creeping onto her lips. "Perfectly fine. *Exceptionally* fine." She said the words in a way that didn't sound exactly appropriate.

Again, the sisters' gazes met. Should they mention to Bunny what their mother had told them some six months before?

Angelica sat up straighter, and Tricia let her take the lead. "Mother came to visit us last October. She said Daddy was dead."

Bunny blinked. "Dead?"

"As a doornail," Tricia remarked.

"That's ridiculous," Bunny said, taking another small sip from her martini.

"Yes, it is. Especially since Daddy has been seen in the area at least twice since Mother's pronouncement."

Bunny's lips puckered. "Poor Sheila. Do you suppose she's in the throes of dementia?"

"You tell us," Tricia said.

Instead, Bunny picked up one of the pastry pockets and popped it into her mouth, taking great delight as she chewed. While she did so, she seemed to consider the question.

"No, I didn't get that vibe from dear Sheila."

"And why was that?" Angelica asked.

It was then that one side of Bunny's mouth crooked up. "We're all adults here, right?"

Tricia wondered where this conversation was going.

"Of course," Angelica said nonchalantly.

A Perilous Plot

Bunny fluttered her false eyelashes and simpered. "Because your father and I have been lovers for many years."

Angelica straightened higher in her seat. If Bunny thought that revelation would endear her to the sisters, she'd been tragically wrong.

Tricia was the next to speak. "And did our mother know this?"

Bunny's smile was smug. "Of course. I think she'd had enough of John's outrageous behavior years ago. But she kept him on, treating him like an escort. He's a divinely handsome man. Someone any woman would be proud to be seen clinging to his arm." Bunny sighed dramatically. She failed to see that her hostess was not enamored with that description—nor was Tricia.

An awkward silence descended upon the women—at least, awkward for Tricia and Angelica.

It was Angelica who broke the silence. "Didn't you think it odd that you hadn't seen Daddy in a while?"

Bunny shrugged. "They were always spending winters in some warmer clime. John's and my adventures almost always happened during the summer months."

"Adventures?" Tricia asked, wondering if Bunny had caught the edge in her tone.

"Oh, yes. We had weekends on Martha's Vineyard, Cape Cod, Boston, and sometimes New York." All locations within hours of the older Mileses' home in Connecticut.

"And how did Daddy explain his absences to our mother?" Angelica asked. She sounded cool, calm, and collected. On the other hand, Tricia felt ready to explode.

"Sheila would often go off on spa weekends to some health resort or another. That was when John and I would share our alone time."

How nice for you, Tricia thought sourly. If there was one thing she absolutely despised, it was a cheat. That her father displayed such tendencies shouldn't have come as a surprise, as he'd shown another lapse in fidelity well known to the sisters. But that it hadn't been a onetime incident did nothing to endear their father to them. And even if Tricia and her mother weren't on the best of terms, she could identify with the hurt she must have felt every time John Miles stepped out on her.

On impulse, Tricia downed the last of her drink and plunked the glass on the coffee table. "Well, it's been nice catching up with you, Aunt Bunny, but I really must go."

"Tricia," Angelica warned.

"Must you, dear? What's so pressing that you can't spend a little more time with your dear old aunt?"

First, she wasn't a blood relative. Second, she'd admitted to having a long-standing affair with Tricia's father, betraying their mother, who was Bunny's lifelong friend. And third, Tricia had never liked the woman—and it appeared with good cause. She'd been a good judge of character even at a young age.

"Are you sure you *can't* stay?" Angelica asked, her tone bordering on menace.

"Alas, no. But I do hope I'll see you at least one more time before you have to leave our fair village," Tricia told Bunny.

"Oh, I've got nothing on my plate for the near future. I can extend my visit for as long as I like," the older woman said sweetly.

Tricia risked a glance in her sister's direction. Angelica looked distinctly displeased.

Tricia headed toward the apartment's exit. "I'll talk to you tomorrow, Ange."

Angelica rose from her chair, and when she spoke, her voice was menacing. "You better believe you will."

Tricia faked a smile.

"Until we meet again," Tricia said in Bunny's direction.
"Don't do anything I wouldn't do," Bunny said with a nasty chuckle. Tricia didn't find the salutation amusing.

As soon as she returned to her apartment over Haven't Got a Clue, Tricia texted David.

Have you had dinner? I've got a frozen pizza.

Be there in fifteen with bells on, he replied.

Although Tricia had lived in Manhattan for over ten years, New York pizza wasn't her favorite. She preferred a chewier crust and lots of veggie toppings, like onions, mushrooms, peppers, and sometimes even broccoli, to enhance a plain frozen pepperoni pizza. David liked banana peppers, so she had those on hand, too.

Just after his arrival, Tricia shoved the pizza onto her oven rack and set the timer. She poured David a beer and a glass of wine for herself and they retreated to the living room, where Miss Marple made a big fuss over David. At one time, she'd done the same with Tricia's now-deceased ex, Christopher Benson. She hadn't taken a shine to all Tricia's male friends, but that the cat seemed to love David was a good sign.

"What a day," David said, leaning back on her sectional.
"Bad?"
"No, just long. But then, I wouldn't want to be anywhere else."
"Really?"
"Okay, maybe spending the next week or so helping to put the finishing touches on the rooms at Stonecreek Manor, but other than that—no. I love my job. I love the kids. It's all good. How did your day go?"

Tricia took a swig of her wine and shook her head. "You don't want to know."

"Yeah, I do," David said sincerely.

Tricia brought him up to speed on her conversation with Pixie before she shared with David what she'd gleaned during her lunch with Becca.

"Wow. I can't blame you for feeling uncomfortable with the situation. But I can also see things from Becca's perspective."

"What do you mean?" Tricia asked.

"Everybody wants their wedding day to be special."

"Yes, but a second wedding should be more subdued."

"Who says?" David asked.

"It's accepted decorum."

David shook his head, looking skeptical. "It looks like we're on different ends of the spectrum," he said.

"What do you mean?"

"Well, say we decide to marry someday."

Tricia's eyes widened. It wasn't *anything* she'd considered.

"I'd like a huge bash. I'd want all my friends and family to attend. I'd want all the pomp and circumstance. A big reception with a band, champagne, dancing, and a multitiered cake. The whole nine yards."

Tricia had had all that when she married Christopher Benson. They'd had ten years together after that special day, and then he'd left her. She'd had the bridesmaids. The big church wedding. The huge reception, which her parents had paid for and invited scores of their friends to. But in retrospect, she would have preferred a less grand observance with just a small circle of friends and family. Her parents had spent too much money on a party that had little to do with her and Christopher. It seemed more like a repayment her parents felt they owed for attending other people's celebrations. Tricia and Christopher had discussed it during their honeymoon, but he'd blown off

A Perilous Plot

her interpretation of the events . . . as he'd done on so many other occasions. With that kind of thinking, perhaps it should have been a relief instead of a devastating event when he left her. Again, in retrospect, Christopher leaving her had been one of the best things that could have ever happened. It caused her to reevaluate her life and what she really wanted. And what she'd wanted was to be a bookseller, something her parents would never have approved of. The fact that Angelica had taken on a bookstore was inconsequential because she'd branched out—and they had no idea how far Angelica had taken her business ventures.

Poor little, once-anorexic Tricia had one small business, while Angelica was an entrepreneurial genius.

Tricia shook away the thought and sipped her wine. "But that wasn't the end of my already too-eventful day." Before she could elaborate, the timer went off, and they retreated to the kitchen for pizza. While they ate, Tricia told David about happy hour with Angelica and Bunny.

"And she admitted having an affair with your father right to your faces?" David asked, aghast.

Tricia bit off the tip of her slice and nodded.

"What did Angelica say?"

"Like me, nothing. But I'm sure she was just as appalled."

"Do you think Bunny was telling the truth?"

"Absolutely."

"I'm sorry."

"For what?"

"That your father's a—" David hesitated.

"A cad?" Tricia supplied

David nodded. "An old-fashioned description, but probably applicable nonetheless."

"Absolutely," Tricia agreed.

"And how will you handle interacting with Bunny for the next few days?" David asked.

"By spending as little time as possible with her."

"Sounds reasonable," he agreed, and took another bite of his pizza. "I pity poor Angelica," David said, and took a swig of his beer.

"She invited Bunny here—knowing how she was. The woman is *not* my problem."

David frowned. "Come on, you can't let Angelica suffer alone when catering to the woman."

"Why not?" Tricia demanded.

"Because you love your sister, and it's not in you to be vengeful."

Vengeful? No. But sometimes, Tricia was more than ready to let people stew in their own juices—especially when they'd brought the problem on themselves.

The subject of Bunny had already gotten old.

"Why don't we do something fun tonight?" David suggested.

"Like what?"

"A board game."

"I don't have any."

"Then how about we snuggle and watch a rom-com?"

Tricia smiled. "Now you're talking my language."

"We could make some popcorn, have another drink, and then see where things take us."

Tricia's smile broadened. "I like the way you think. And then what?"

David shifted his gaze toward the stairs to Tricia's master bedroom suite. "We'll see what happens."

They would indeed!

EIGHT

 It wasn't until the next morning while making French toast for David's breakfast that Tricia remembered Angelica was supposed to close on purchasing the Bookshelf Diner the day before. There simply hadn't been an opening to discuss the situation with Bunny Murdock hanging on to their every word. Tricia was sure her sister wouldn't want to have the subject broached in front of their father's presumed lover. The less Bunny knew about their respective businesses, the better.

It was to be a long workday, as Tricia, Pixie, and Mr. Everett needed to clear the shelves and pack up the store's inventory before the day's end so the carpet installers could start work early the next morning.

The aroma of frying bacon permeated the kitchen by the time David showed up for breakfast, his hair still damp from a shower. "Are you making my favorite breakfast again?" he asked.

"But of course," Tricia said as David approached, stood behind her, and nuzzled her ear.

"With real, New Hampshire maple syrup?"

"Is there any better kind?" she answered, careful not to let her bathrobe's sleeve dip into the frying pan.

"Don't ask that of the people in Vermont." David kissed her neck. "Coffee," he breathed into her ear.

"You know where it is," Tricia said, grinning.

David stepped back, grabbed a mug from the cupboard, and poured the freshly made brew into it. After adding milk and sugar, he topped up Tricia's cup with a little milk.

"Thanks. What are your plans for the day?" Tricia asked.

"Processing new titles, two different story hours with toddlers—just the usual. And all while you pack up books."

"I should have done it back in February, but it's better to replace the rug now rather than wait. It should be good for another six or seven years."

He nodded. "What are your plans for the day—I mean, besides packing up books?"

Tricia sighed. "I need to talk to Chief McDonald about wedding plans."

David laughed as Tricia picked up a pair of tongs to remove the golden-brown pieces of French toast from the pan. "It sounds like *you're* the bride."

"Hardly," Tricia said dryly.

"What are you going to say to him?"

Tricia grimaced. "I'm not exactly sure. I don't think he has a clue about what Becca has in mind for their special day. He needs to make his ideas known."

"And what if you're just butting into their business?"

Tricia shrugged. "I didn't *ask* to be in their wedding. I would be perfectly happy as a guest giving them a check as a wedding gift and enjoying a rubber-chicken dinner and a nice, fat slice of cake instead

A Perilous Plot

of footing the bill for a bachelorette party in Vegas for a bunch of multimillionaires with whom I have nothing in common."

"You wouldn't ask for their autographs?"

"Don't be gauche," Tricia chided him. She pursed her lips, considering her next words before she spoke them. "I'm a very lazy person. I just don't want the kind of responsibility Becca expects me to shoulder."

"That's a bald-faced lie," David asserted. "You put all your effort into every task you undertake. Becca is asking more than she should of you, and I can't blame you for feeling put upon."

Exactly. And yet Tricia wasn't willing to agree to that assessment out loud.

She served herself two small pieces of French toast and a slice of bacon, poured a dribble of maple syrup over each, and dug in. She still wasn't sure how she'd approach such a delicate conversation with Ian, but it had to be done—because she was pretty sure Becca wasn't likely to broach the subject.

Now all Tricia had to do was come up with the courage to do so.

As soon as David left for work, Tricia—and her cat—trundled down to Haven't Got a Clue to start the great boxing of inventory. She hauled up the boxes she'd ordered online and began assembling them at least an hour before Pixie and Mr. Everett were to start their workday. If she was going to leave them for twenty to thirty minutes to chat with Ian McDonald, she at least wanted to get a jump on the task at hand.

Once her employees showed up for work, the trio didn't bother with their normal coffee klatch and immediately began work, not knowing how long it might take to pack up the shop's entire inventory. After about an hour, Tricia announced she had an errand to run. Neither Pixie nor Mr. Everett objected, and she promised she'd be back ASAP.

Tricia power walked toward the Stoneham Police Department and only after she was halfway there did she realize she should have called first to ensure that Chief McDonald was on the premises.

Upon reaching the station, Tricia was relieved to see the chief's SUV parked alongside the building.

As she entered the building and stepped up to the receptionist's desk, Tricia noticed that Polly sat hunched over her computer keyboard, wiping away tears.

Tricia crept closer. "Polly, are you okay?"

Polly swallowed hard, her hands balling into fists until the skin stretched taut. "I'm—" she choked. "I'm fine."

Tricia shook her head. "No, you're not. Is there anything I can do to help?"

Polly turned her gaze upon Tricia as though shocked by the offer. "I . . . I don't think so."

"Are you sure?"

Polly's lips trembled as her face crumpled into a deeper level of anguish. Then she shook her head. "No." She sat up straighter and shook her head, her features settling into a more normal expression. "I assume you want to speak to the chief."

"Yes, I would."

Polly cleared her throat before she touched the intercom key. "Tricia Miles here to see you, sir."

Seconds later, McDonald replied, "Send her in."

Polly waved a hand toward McDonald's office but said nothing.

"Thanks," Tricia said, and moved to stand before the chief's door. She knocked.

"Come in."

Tricia did.

McDonald waved a hand in the direction of one of the two chairs before his desk. Once Tricia was seated, he leaned forward and folded his hands. "What can I do for you today, Tricia?"

"First, tell me why Polly is so upset."

McDonald leaned back. "As I mentioned before, that's up to Polly to talk about her circumstances."

"Oh, don't give me that line of bull. The poor woman is obviously upset. Is your office doing anything to combat that?"

McDonald let out an exasperated breath. "It's not within our jurisdiction."

"That woman is in distress. She doesn't like me—never has—so she isn't likely to talk to me."

"Yes, well . . ." McDonald seemed to reconsider his previous stance. "It seems her son is suffering from some kind of kidney ailment."

"And?"

"He needs a transplant. Unfortunately, he lost his job due to his affliction, and his insurance went out the window as well."

"And?" Tricia demanded.

McDonald shrugged.

Tricia frowned. Did Polly know about the Everett Foundation? Mr. Everett had won the lottery several years before and set up a nonprofit organization to help those in need. Why hadn't Polly contacted them? Surely if Grace knew of Polly's son's plight, she would allocate funds to help him. Tricia decided she'd contact Grace first before she spoke to Polly. The receptionist might not welcome her family problems being discussed by outsiders.

McDonald changed the subject. "What brings you here today? Have you heard from your father?"

"No," Tricia said. "I'm here because I had lunch with Becca yesterday to talk about the wedding."

Ian raised an eyebrow. "And?"

"Has she consulted you on anything?"

Ian looked thoughtful. "Not really. I mean, isn't it the bride's prerogative to decide these things?"

"That depends. Is she expecting you to pay half the cost for everything that goes along with the celebration?"

Ian looked perturbed. "We haven't really discussed it."

Tricia nodded, trying to think of a tactful way to introduce a difficult subject. "I always considered you to be a man who enjoyed the simple things in life. A beautiful sunset, a nice bottle of wine . . ."

Ian nodded, smiling. "That sounds about right."

"And I figured you'd probably want a pretty straightforward wedding. Nothing too elaborate. A beautiful ceremony with heartfelt vows, a lovely dinner with friends and family, and a honeymoon in a quiet, secluded spot."

Ian smiled. "That sounds like heaven."

Tricia nodded and paused for a moment before speaking. "I'm not sure you and Becca are on the same page."

Ian frowned. "What do you mean?"

"Well, first of all, Becca wants me to plan, *and pay for*, a bachelorette party in Vegas and invite a lot of her celebrity friends from the tennis world."

Ian frowned. "That sounds expensive."

"It sure does." Tricia bit her lip, trying to come up with the appropriate language.

"No offense, but as I understand it, you're not living in poverty," Ian said.

"No, but I don't expect to pay tens of thousands of dollars to throw a party for a bunch of people I don't know, either."

"I thought you and Becca were best friends," Ian said, sounding shocked.

A Perilous Plot

"Well, if we are, it's news to me."

Ian's expression darkened. "I don't understand."

"The only connection Becca and I have is that she was married to Eugene Chambers, and I had a relationship with him after they divorced."

Ian's frown deepened, and he looked even more troubled.

"I've suggested to Becca that I may not be the best person to take on the role of maid of honor simply because . . . I don't really know her. I asked if she has friends she's closer to . . ." Tricia let the sentence hang.

"And?" Ian asked.

Tricia tried not to wince. "It doesn't sound like she *has* a best friend she can rely on."

Ian's expression grew darker still. "What are you saying? That Becca is incapable of being a true friend?"

"Not at all," Tricia said, backpedaling. "But I suspect that being in such a cutthroat sport, and under the kind of media scrutiny she's had to endure for decades, *and* the fact that she's probably been sold out by friends and foes alike, it would be hard for her to trust people. She has no reason *not* to trust me, as I'm pretty sure she knows I have no agenda when it comes to her past, present, or future."

"Well, I'm grateful for that because, yes, Becca has been exploited in the past by people she trusted—including those in her own family."

Tricia nodded. "The truth is . . . I'm not in her league and I really don't feel comfortable trying to navigate in the world she's accustomed to."

"Then why on earth did you agree to be her maid of honor?" Ian asked, sounding confused and more than a little annoyed.

"Actually, I *didn't* agree to it. Becca just assumed I'd take it on. I think no matter what I do, she's bound to be disappointed, and no bride wants that on her wedding day."

Ian's brow furrowed. "Then what do you suggest?"

An elopement immediately came to mind, but Tricia didn't voice that thought. "That you should talk about what *both* of you want on what's supposed to be the happiest day of your lives."

McDonald nodded, looking grim. "I'll do that."

Tricia stood to leave.

"There's just one thing," McDonald said, opening a drawer on the right side of his desk and removing a large kraft envelope. "Here," he said, proffering the package.

Tricia frowned. "Uh . . ."

"It's my manuscript. You said you'd look over it."

Tricia swallowed and forced a smile. "So I did." She accepted it. "I'll get back to you about it soon."

"Thank you."

McDonald offered nothing more, so Tricia turned, opened the office door, and left the room.

Tricia clutched the envelope to her chest and headed for the exit but paused before Polly's desk, wondering if she should say something about the Everett Foundation.

"Did you need something, Ms. Miles?" Polly asked.

"Uh . . ." Tricia chickened out. She'd find some other way to get the information about the Everett Foundation to Polly. "Nothing. Have a great day," Tricia said sincerely.

Polly's lower lip quivered. "It's doubtful."

Tricia didn't know how to reply to that sad statement. She also knew better than to discuss Polly's situation with Mr. Everett. He left all the decisions for grants from the Everett Foundation to his wife. Tricia would have to speak to her later.

A Perilous Plot

* * *

The packing crew made good progress before Pixie's and Mr. Everett's lunchtime rolled around. "Any idea when the Bookshelf Diner is going to reopen?" Pixie asked Tricia as she shrugged into her jacket.

"Sorry. If I hear anything, I'll let you know."

"I sure hope it opens before the tourist season starts. Either that, or I'll be eating PB and Js every day . . . again."

Tricia continued packing, reluctant to dismantle the stereo system until the last minute. As it was, they still had half the store to pack up. They weren't going to be able to fit all the stock into the basement stockroom, so the carpet installers were going to have to move some of the boxes as the old carpet went out and the new went in. She was so absorbed that it seemed the hour Pixie and Mr. Everett were gone went by in a flash.

Like the day before when she'd met Becca, Tricia was only one minute late for her standing lunch date with Angelica at Booked For Lunch. As it was off-season, the retro café was populated mostly by locals, and Angelica already sat at their reserved booth.

Tricia scooted into it. "Sorry I'm late."

Angelica was scrolling through her phone and barely noticed her arrival.

Molly, the waitress, swooped in with a carafe of steaming coffee, ready to fill their cups. "Today's special is enchilada casserole, and the soup-and-half-sandwich special is a BLT and tomato soup."

"We'll think about it," Angelica said, finally setting her phone aside. Molly nodded and moved on to the next table.

"I'm sorry I left you in the lurch last night," Tricia apologized as she wriggled out of her jacket.

Angelica waved a dismissive hand. "I *was* a little miffed, but I know Bunny isn't your favorite person."

Tricia noted that Angelica had omitted the title of *aunt* in her sister's description of the woman. "And after her totally thoughtless admission of being Daddy's mistress, it took all my resolve not to kick her to the curb."

Tricia felt the same way. "So, how are you going to deal with her being your houseguest for the foreseeable future?"

"I'm not."

Tricia's eyes widened in anticipation. "So, you *did* kick her out?"

"Don't be absurd," Angelica chided her. "Mother thought Bunny was her friend. Knowing how she betrayed her, I certainly don't want her under *my* roof—staying in Sofia's bed."

"So, what's your solution?"

"I'm sending her off to Stonecreek Manor," Angelica said, adding creamer to her coffee. "At first, she wasn't keen on the idea, but I can be pretty persuasive if I have to be."

"And what did you tell her?"

"That my dear friend Nigela was about to open the manor and was looking for people to participate in the shakedown."

"And she fell for it?"

"Hook, line, and sinker."

"And how did Cleo react to the news?"

Angelica leveled an unblinking stare at her sister. "What choice does she have? Nigela called her directly."

"That voice-altering gizmo you bought a few years back has served you well," Tricia remarked.

"It certainly has."

"So, when is Bunny leaving your home?"

"Right after we finish our lunch. She didn't get up until after ten. I offered her French toast and bacon, or eggs and sausage, or waffles

A Perilous Plot

and her choice of meat. She said yes, she wanted it all! Then she demanded that I sit with her as she consumed it."

"If you're hell-bent on getting rid of her, why would you offer her a perk like staying at the Stonecreek?"

"Oh, it won't *be* a perk," Angelica said with a touch of an edge to her voice.

Tricia offered half a smile. "And why's that?"

"Cleo has been instructed to do just the bare minimum for Bunny. She won't have access to the laundry facilities. The TV in her room won't be connected. And, unless there are others in for the shakedown, the Wi-Fi will be turned off."

"Why don't you just cut off the power to her room?" Tricia asked facetiously.

"Don't think I haven't considered it," Angelica said flatly.

Tricia nodded. "Mother and I have had our differences"—and boy, were they plenty!—"but I don't condone Daddy cheating on her, not when she's been paying the freight all these years."

Angelica shrugged. "And maybe that's part of the problem."

"What do you mean?"

"Apparently, Mother's financial situation caused her to tighten her belt to keep them afloat. To boost Daddy's ego, she always let people think he was the one with the bucks. I put the pressure on Bunny, who said Mother had to sell off some of their assets to keep afloat."

"Such as?"

"The house in Rio. The wonderful flat in London."

"Gone?" Tricia asked, her heart sinking. She'd always been fond of the London apartment, which was not far from the Houses of Parliament.

Angelica nodded.

Tricia sighed. "That's too bad."

"Yeah, if she'd only explained their circumstances and offered it to one of us, we could have given her top bucks for it and kept it in the family."

Tricia nodded. David had often spoken of a desire to visit the UK, and having a place to park for a couple of weeks would have been the perfect opportunity. Well, should they make such a trip, there were plenty of hotels and other rental options at their disposal. That didn't make the loss any easier to bear.

"And what room are you giving Bunny? The bridal suite?"

"Not on your life. She gets the only single we have. She's one person. She doesn't need the top-of-the-line room."

"And this is her punishment for her cheating with Daddy?"

"She'll get breakfast and a beautiful room," Angelica asserted.

"So, she's going to have to find lunch and dinner on her own?" Tricia asked.

Angelica nodded. "I'm treating her as I would any other guest. Besides, that's what everyone else who participates in the shakedown will receive."

Bunny had driven herself to Stoneham, so it wasn't like she'd be stranded. She could make her way to any of the local eateries to find sustenance for the other two meals of the day.

"And how much attention are you going to pay Bunny while she's staying in the village?" Tricia asked.

"As little as possible," Angelica said tartly.

"Ange, *you* invited her here."

"I did not—she invited herself. And I've learned all I want to about her relationship with our parents."

"But the fact that she hasn't seen Daddy in a while must mean—"

"What? Either that she's lying or that he didn't trust her not to blab about what he and Mother are up to?"

"Something like that," Tricia said. She felt odd being in a position

A Perilous Plot

to defend her mother—a woman who had treated her as less than lovable because of an accident of fate.

Molly arrived to take their orders. They both went for the enchilada casserole.

The sisters abandoned their previous conversation, and as Tricia hadn't had an opportunity to mention her lunch with Becca the previous day; she did so.

Molly arrived with bowls of tortilla chips and salsa. "Your entrées will be up in a few minutes."

Angelica nodded, and Molly retreated. "Do you think Becca will talk to Ian about her grand plans?"

"Eventually. But she can be a master of misrepresentation, so I'm betting he won't be privy to everything she's got in mind."

"So, are you going to tattle on her to Ian?"

Tricia frowned. "You make it sound so petty."

"Isn't it?" Angelica asked.

"No! Ian's my friend, and I've already spoken to him about it."

Angelica scrutinized her sister's face before shaking her head. "Sometimes I think you're too friendly with the man."

"What do you mean?"

"I saw your expression when Becca announced their engagement. You were shocked—*and* disappointed."

"I won't deny that," Tricia remarked.

"But were you disappointed because you thought one day *you'd* have a chance to be with Ian?"

"Don't be ridiculous," Tricia asserted.

"Is that what I'm being?" Angelica asked, her eyes wide.

"Yes! Besides, I'm gloriously happy with David."

Angelica nodded, but she didn't look convinced.

Luckily, Molly arrived with their lunch plates, which put an end to the conversation. After she left, Angelica picked up her fork to cut a piece of the casserole. "Do you mind if we have dinner at your place tonight?"

"Not at all, but why?"

"Because I told Bunny I had a last-minute business meeting come up. 'Last minute' being the operative description."

Tricia shook her head. "Okay, and I promise to come up with something yummy to eat."

"I'll take stale bread and water if it means I don't have to spend any part of the evening with Bunny."

Angelica had always liked the woman—much to Tricia's chagrin. Her change of heart was telling.

"With all that said," Angelica continued, "I suppose I'll have to pay her *some* attention while she's here."

"And how much time?"

"No more than thirty minutes a day."

Angelica really did want to encourage Bunny to leave. After all, besides a bed-and-breakfast, there wasn't much else to entice the woman to stay in Stoneham. Unless . . . she hoped to connect with John Miles.

Tricia didn't like to think about it.

After lunch, Tricia returned to her store, but she took ten extra minutes to hit the basement office's computer to peruse the Everett Foundation website. It plainly stated that those who wished help *had* to fill out the appropriate form and submit it online or via snail mail. Tricia downloaded the form, printed it, and put it in an envelope, printing out a sticky label addressed to Polly Burgess in care of the Stoneham Police Department. She sealed the envelope, put a stamp on it, and would put it out to be mailed the next day. After that, it was up to Polly to follow through.

But what if she didn't? She'd be a fool not to. And what if the

Everett Foundation turned down Polly's request for help? Should Tricia try to influence Grace to approve such an application?

There were other ways to solicit funds for someone in need of medical attention, which was a crime for a nation that billed itself as the most prosperous in the world. The sad fact was that people who had no insurance often died of their ailments because they didn't have the means to pay for expensive treatments. Tricia actually knew of a few women who had been failed by the country's for-profit health care system. In those days, she hadn't had the means to offer much more than sympathy. If the Everett Foundation couldn't help Polly's son, could she fund such an operation—and if not, could she convince Angelica to do so? The fact that Polly had a reputation for being difficult—if not hostile—was a huge mark against her. But it wasn't Polly who needed a transplant. As far as Tricia knew, no one had a beef against Polly's son.

Though Tricia, Pixie, and Mr. Everett diligently worked to pack up all the books, the task seemed just a little greater than their ability to do so.

Still, she found herself thinking about Bunny Murdock and the unwelcome information she'd shared. Tricia hoped her mother didn't know about the alleged affair. Sheila Miles had never been known to forgive and forget, and Tricia hated to think what the consequences might be if Sheila ever discovered Bunny's betrayal.

NINE

It was half an hour before closing when Tricia remembered she'd promised to feed her sister something yummy for dinner. But all she could remember residing in her freezer were some generic chicken filets, ciabatta rolls, and bags of various vegetables. Nothing that would constitute *yummy*. But then, Angelica said she'd be happy with bread and water. Tricia could supply that.

She cut her employees loose for the day and hurried up the steps to her apartment to try to come up with some kind of dinner to placate her sister. When it came to an appetizer, Tricia was just as skunked. She had a chunk of cheddar to cut into slices and a box of poppy seed crackers. It would have to do.

She'd assembled a makeshift dinner by the time Angelica arrived some twenty minutes later than expected, looking as stressed as Tricia had ever seen her. She broke out the pitcher of martinis she'd made, as well as the chilled glasses and olives, and poured the drinks.

"Rough day?"

Angelica rolled her eyes. "You don't know the half of it."

"Why don't we sit down in the living room and you can tell me all about it."

"Only if you want to feel as depressed as me," Angelica said as she snagged her glass and the plate of cheese and crackers and headed for her usual spot. Tricia put the pitcher back in the fridge, grabbed her own glass, and followed, settling down on the end of the sectional nearest to her sister.

"I never got a chance to ask you about the closing on the Bookshelf Diner."

Angelica selected a cracker. "I'm not the face of NR Associates. As usual, Antonio handled it. He's pushing me to make up my mind about how we move forward with the project. But honestly, I've had so much on my mind—first with the whole debacle with Daddy not being dead, and then Bunny's arrival . . ."

Angelica had had months to contemplate the diner's fate, so her excuses sounded lame at best.

"If it's any consolation, the customers are getting antsy."

"Like whom?"

"Pixie and Mr. Everett. Pixie's afraid there'll be no room for them at Booked for Lunch come tourist season and that she'll have to make her lunch every workday."

"Hmm . . . I guess I hadn't thought about that situation."

"Well, think about it." Tricia changed the subject. "How did relocating Bunny go?"

Angelica scowled. "It went. Just before I got here, she texted me with a list of complaints about the manor."

"Such as?"

"She said her room is drafty. I'll have the contractor see if the windows need caulking."

"What else?"

"She said the mattress was lumpy. That's impossible. Every one of them is brand-new and, except for me testing it out, she was the first to sleep on hers."

"Anything else?"

"That Cleo wasn't attentive enough."

"What was she expecting? A servant at her beck and call?"

"She said it's creepy being all alone in such a big house."

"Well, I can't blame her there. You aren't advertising a ghost, are you?"

"I've slept at the manor five times and never encountered one. And if someone was haunting the place, I'm sure Sarge would pick up on it. And, as I suspected, she wondered if she could stop over at my place for dinner and wasn't pleased when I had to tell her no."

"She always was tight with a buck," Tricia remarked.

"Yes, it was Mother who picked up the tab whenever they'd go out for lunch. Perhaps a day or so of buying her own meals will cause her to hurry home."

"I wouldn't be surprised if she asked you for gas money," Tricia quipped.

"Neither would I."

Angelica's phone pinged. She ignored it and sipped her drink before reaching for another cracker. A minute later, it pinged again. Finally, the phone rang and she glanced at the number. "It's Cleo. Now what's Bunny done?" she asked, annoyed. She picked up the phone and stabbed the little green icon and the speaker one, too. "Hello, Cleo. What's up?"

"I'm sorry to bother you, but I called NR Associates and only got voice mail."

"Yes, well, their offices are closed. What do you need?"

"I . . . I came over to the mansion to take out the sausage to thaw overnight for Ms. Ricita's guest's breakfast tomorrow and . . ." She stopped talking.

A Perilous Plot

Tricia and Angelica exchanged glances.

"And what?" Angelica demanded.

"I . . . I think Ms. Murdock's dead."

"What?" Angelica cried.

"I found her phone in the kitchen and figured she'd need it, so I went to look for her in all the common areas, and when she wasn't in any, I went to her room. The door was ajar . . . and I found her there, lying in a puddle of blood."

Tricia's jaw dropped. Cleo seemed remarkably calm reporting such a calamity.

"Lying where?" Angelica asked.

"Oh, on that beautiful Persian rug next to the bed."

"Oh, no!" Angelica cried in anguish, but Tricia wasn't sure if she lamented Bunny's passing or the ruin of an antique rug. "Did you call nine one one?" Angelica demanded.

"As she's dead, I didn't see what good the paramedics could do."

"Well, you need to call the police right away."

Cleo's words were slow in coming—probably from shock. "Okay, yeah . . . I'll do that!"

"I'll be there in minutes," Angelica promised. "Cut this call and contact them now!"

"Yes, I'll do that."

The call ended.

Tricia closed her eyes and sighed, feeling like a jerk as she wondered when she'd get to eat her dinner.

The police hadn't yet arrived when Tricia and Angelica showed up at Stonecreek Manor. Angelica punched in a code to unlock the vintage oak door and entered, calling for Cleo.

Tricia followed her sister through the main entry, but there was no sign of Cleo. "You find her. I'll stick by the front door to direct the police. Where's the room where Bunny was staying?"

"Second floor, last bedroom on the left at the top of the stairs."

"Go—and make sure Cleo hasn't messed up the crime scene."

"Crime scene?" Angelica asked, appalled. "Why would you immediately assume Bunny was killed? Couldn't she have just fallen, hit her head, and died?"

"Ange, she admitted to us that she was having an affair with our father. That's a motive for murder by a woman who's involved with something underhanded and may be lurking somewhere near—along with Daddy. It makes sense to—"

"No!" Angelica protested. "I won't believe Mother is a murderer."

"Then how about Daddy as a suspect? We don't know that Bunny wasn't blackmailing him."

"And we don't know that she was, either," Angelica said hotly.

"Just go," Tricia advised. "I'll direct the police on when they get here."

Angelica shook her head. "It's a bad omen," she muttered. "Two people died in this house within six months. I'm beginning to think the place is cursed." She turned away and headed up the stairs to the second floor.

Not ten seconds later, a police cruiser with lights flashing turned up outside the house. Tricia threw open the door to welcome the uniformed officers.

Officer Henderson spoke first. "What's this about a possible homicide?"

Why had Cleo reported Bunny's death as such? As Angelica hypothesized, she could have hit her head and died of blood loss.

"Where do we find the victim?" Officer Cindy Pearson asked.

"Up the stairs, and turn left, the last bedroom down the hall."

Nodding curtly, the officers jogged up the stairs with Tricia not more than a step behind them.

A Perilous Plot

The officers stopped at the open doorway, looking in. "Hey," Henderson called. "Get away from the body!"

Tricia peeked over the officer's shoulders to see Cleo and Angelica standing over Bunny's supine form. It wasn't a pretty sight. The woman was clad in a filmy nightgown of what looked like silk, soaked with scarlet around a jagged hole at the waist. After a quick look around the room, Tricia surmised that the weapon that had killed poor Bunny was nowhere in sight—probably the perpetrator had taken it with him . . . or her.

Officer Henderson knelt down beside the body, felt for a pulse, apparently finding none, and spoke into the radio attached to his uniform blouse, asking for the county medical examiner to be alerted.

So, Bunny really *was* dead. Tricia wasn't sure how she felt about that. She'd never been a fan of the woman, who seemed to be in sync with Tricia's mother when it came to finding fault with the Mileses' second daughter, but she'd never wished the woman dead.

Angelica stepped away from the body, her expression a mixture of grief and confusion. Cleo, however, seemed to have recovered from the shock Tricia had heard in her voice when she'd called upon finding Bunny's body.

The officers herded the women out of the room, and Pearson guided them down to the first floor's parlor. Angelica took a seat on the blue brocade love seat and Tricia sat on the matching chair, but Cleo crossed to the window, gazing over the brief patch of front lawn. The bulk of the estate lay behind the grand house.

Angelica pulled a tissue from her jacket pocket, wiping her nose. "Oh, goodness, I wish I hadn't done it," she muttered.

Pearson's head jerked up, and she checked the camera attached to her uniform. "Are you confessing to the crime?"

Angelica blinked. "Crime?"

"The murder of that woman upstairs?"

"What? Of course not."

"Angelica hasn't been near the manor this afternoon or evening," Tricia said, defending Angelica.

"You're her sister," Pearson practically spat. "You're not a credible witness."

"What?" Angelica cried.

"I'll ask again, are you confessing to the crime?"

"Of course not," Angelica said with conviction.

"Then what are you referring to?"

"Bunny *was* my houseguest, but I arranged for her to stay here at the manor—"

"Ange," Tricia warned. If the cops were going to report Angelica as a possible suspect, at that moment, keeping her mouth shut was her best defense.

Angelica stared at her sister for long seconds before she nodded in understanding.

"What have you got to say?" Pearson asked Cleo.

"It was me who found Ms. Murdock. She left her phone in the kitchen and I wanted to return it to her. I checked the common areas before I went to her room. The door was open and . . . I found her, just as you saw."

Pearson looked skeptical.

Tricia and the female officer had a rather rocky relationship. Pearson had nearly lost her job with the Stoneham Police Department two years earlier when it was revealed she had a relationship with a murder suspect and had kept it quiet. She'd been put on probation but had ultimately been kept on at the police department.

The women fell silent, listening to the officer's squawk box as Henderson called for reinforcements, including summoning Chief McDonald.

Tricia's mind raced to come up with various explanations for what might have happened. Although it wasn't late, Bunny was clad in a nightgown—and it wasn't flannel. Pink satin—or some facsimile—with a plunging neckline. Of course, lying as she was, covered in blood, the negligee looked anything but sexy. Had she donned it thinking she'd soon see her lover? John Miles seemed to be lurking nearby. Had he contacted Bunny before or after she'd arrived at the manor? And if so, was it for a tryst or to knock off his mistress, who might well implicate him in a crime? Bunny's phone might answer that question.

Tricia couldn't voice those thoughts, but as she glanced at her sister, she wondered if Angelica was coming to the same conclusions.

More flashing lights appeared outside the inn: a fire rescue truck, another patrol car, and Chief McDonald's SUV. Had his evening with Becca been disturbed and was he likely to take out his pique on Tricia?

No. That wasn't McDonald's style. The same couldn't be said for his predecessors.

The front door was propped open as more officers and the chief entered; the measure was sure to drive up the manor's heating costs.

"Don't say anything," Pearson warned Tricia, Angelica, and Cleo, and stepped just outside the parlor's door to have a word with the chief.

Back in high school, Tricia had learned American sign language as an elective course. This would have been the perfect time to communicate with Angelica. Unfortunately, the course had become available only *after* Angelica had graduated. Tricia wasn't quite sure she remembered enough to communicate that. What she *did* clearly remember was the manual alphabet, but that didn't help in this situation, either.

After a few long minutes of conversing with his officers, Chief McDonald entered the building and headed directly up the main staircase, no doubt to inspect the crime scene.

Meanwhile, Tricia, Angelica, and Cleo remained silent. The only sounds came from footsteps tromping around the upper floor and the growling of Tricia's stomach. Despite the gruesome scene upstairs, her appetite hadn't been completely suppressed. She'd never been a stress eater, but she could see how that might affect others.

Finally, thundering footsteps on the stairs announced McDonald's reappearance. He entered the parlor, his gaze landing on Angelica. "I understand you've confessed to the murder."

Angelica's cheeks burned a brilliant red. "I most certainly did not!"

"Did you not say it was your fault Ms. Murdock was dead?"

"No! What I said was taken out of context."

"And what *is* that context?"

"As I told Officer Pearson, I'm responsible for Bunny being here, but I had no hand in *killing* her." Angelica explained the situation, including that Bunny wasn't exactly the most hospitable guest— telling him of Bunny's confession to being John Miles's mistress, and that the supposedly dead man had been seen lurking around the area.

"So, you think your own father might have killed her?" McDonald asked, his voice more than a little judgmental.

Angelica sighed, and Tricia knew she was doing everything to keep her temper in check. "We've told you what we've learned about our parents and what's gone down these last few months. I'm not throwing our father under the bus when I say that he—or our mother—may have had a motive to silence Bunny."

Well, not really. For Tricia, it sounded exactly as though Angelica *was* offering up their parents as scapegoats to save herself. And yet, Tricia couldn't fault Angelica for it. If nothing else, their mother had been perpetrating a scam on them—and they had no reason to think well of her. And yet . . . Tricia still held some kind of loyalty to the woman who birthed her, no matter what her faults. And for that,

Tricia felt guilty. She *should* have abhorred the woman. That was the tragic course of abuse.

"Ian, Angelica has a rock-solid alibi. She was at the Cookery, and then she joined me for dinner, which was sadly interrupted by news of Bunny's death."

Tricia shot a glance in her sister's direction, but Angelica's expression wasn't one of implicit innocence. And it was then Tricia remembered her sister had shown up late for their usual happy hour.

"I understand you found the deceased's phone in the kitchen."

"Yes," Cleo answered. "One of the officers took charge of it."

"Will you be searching it for information on Bunny's last contacts?" Tricia asked, wondering if her father was among them.

McDonald nodded. "I assume all you ladies have cell phones."

The three women nodded.

"Would you all be willing to turn them over to the local police department?"

"Why?" Cleo asked.

"To see what the tracking software has to say."

"My phone is going to say that prior to Ms. Murdock's death, I was on the property, albeit *not* in the main house. My living quarters are in the carriage house across the drive. Am I to be considered a suspect because of proximity?" Cleo demanded.

"Not at all. It's just that we need to ascertain if—"

"If I'm telling the truth."

McDonald just stared at the woman.

Cleo took a few moments to consider her options. "All right. I'll give you my phone."

"Ms. Miles?" McDonald asked, turning to Angelica.

She was silent for a moment. "I don't know. I do a lot of business on my phone. I can't be without it for any length of time." Like most people on the planet, she'd come to depend on the device for much more than just making calls. Using it for its created purpose seemed to be the least of its functions.

"Is everything backed up on the cloud?" he asked.

"I don't know. I would need to consult with my—" She hesitated. Tricia was sure her sister wouldn't want to blurt that Antonio was her son and business partner. "My phone guy," she finished lamely.

"Tricia?" McDonald asked.

"I don't know. I have nothing to hide, and I'm sure Angelica and Cleo don't, either. But it seems like you're jumping to conclusions pretty quickly, especially since you know the backstory as to what's been going on around us."

"I'll take what you've previously told me into account," McDonald said.

"I would certainly hope so," Tricia said firmly. "Is this a decision that has to be made right this minute?"

"No, but if necessary, I can ask a judge to subpoena them to be turned over. I'm sure that won't be necessary if you intend to cooperate with the investigation into Ms. Murdock's death."

"Of course we want to cooperate," Tricia protested. "But like Angelica said, we do business on our phones. I'd like a little time to think about it—unless you can promise a fast turnaround time."

"I'm not sure how long it would take. But, as I said, a subpoena is always a possibility," he said, his words clipped.

At that moment, Tricia wasn't feeling especially fond of the man she'd thought of as a friend. And what impact was this investigation going to have when it came to being the maid of honor to the woman he hoped to marry?

As of now, standing up at their wedding seemed pretty iffy.

TEN

 It was nearly nine by the time Tricia and Angelica were allowed to leave Stonecreek Manor. "Are you coming back to my house for dinner?" Tricia asked as they got back into her car.

"No. I just want to go home and be with my dog." Angelica sighed. "If I thought I was depressed earlier, I'm twice as downhearted now."

"The new carpet is to be installed in my shop tomorrow. That means I have most of the day free—probably Thursday, too. I wondered if we could spend the time together."

"Doing what?" Angelica asked.

"Well, if it's not too upsetting, putting the finishing touches on Stonecreek Manor. I'm not sure I'm up to doing much in the gardening department, but I guess I could rake flower beds or vacuum or dust or . . . whatever needs to be done."

"Right now, I'm inclined to wash my hands of the place."

"You know you don't mean that. You love that old house."

Angelica eyed her sister. "Have *you* fallen in love with the house?"

"Well, maybe a little . . . by proxy. David certainly has fallen under its spell. I think he might like to tackle such a project—on a much smaller scale one day," Tricia amended.

"And you'd like to be a part of such a project?" Angelica asked.

Tricia started the car and pulled away from the curb. "I can't deny the allure. But I don't think I'd have the stamina required should a rehab take more than a few months."

Angelica nodded and muddled over what her sister had just said. "Would you be willing to bankroll him on such a renovation?"

Tricia's gaze narrowed. "Why do you ask?"

Angelica pressed her lips together, looking smug. "Because there's a little house on the edge of the village that's currently a hot mess. It needs someone with vision to bring it back to life. Once rehabilitated, it would make a great short-term rental."

"Why wouldn't you take on the project yourself?" Tricia asked, turning onto Main Street.

Angelica shook her head. "It's much too small for me. But for someone who wanted to get his hands dirty, it could be the perfect venture."

Tricia thought back to the little house she'd stayed in after the arson at her store. She'd lived above the temporary home of the Stoneham Chamber of Commerce for six months and adored that space. Pixie and Fred now owned the home.

"What are you proposing?" Tricia asked.

"That you and David inspect the property with an eye for commercialization. If he's interested, it could be a fun project for you two to work on."

Tricia knew David would jump at such an opportunity. The problem was, they both had full-time jobs and didn't see each other nearly enough. Also, did Tricia *want* to be a landlord? She knew she could palm off the maintenance of such a property on a management company. After expenses and because Booktown was a tourist destination, it wasn't likely she'd lose money. She'd probably make back her investment in a relatively short period.

"I'll think about it and ask David if he has plans along those lines."

"If you think that's best," Angelica said in obvious disappointment.

Tricia steered the car to her former parking space. The sisters exited the Lexus and walked toward their places of business in silence. "Would you like me to stay with you for a while?" Tricia asked.

Angelica shook her head, retrieving her keys from her jacket pocket. "No. Call me in the morning, and we'll figure out what we want to do."

"Will do." Tricia hugged her sister. Angelica hung on for longer than Tricia expected.

"Thanks for being with me this evening. I don't think I could have handled it on my own."

Of course you could, Tricia thought but didn't say it aloud. "What are sisters for? Now, go hug your dog."

"You bet I will. See you tomorrow."

Tricia waited for a few moments as her sister crossed to the Cookery and turned out the lights before she walked the few feet to her own store and entered. Angelica may have lost her appetite, but Tricia was starving. She had enough food for two, so naturally, she invited David over to either help her eat it or keep her company while she ate her dinner. As usual, David was accommodating and arrived at Tricia's place just fifteen minutes after she'd arrived.

The pitcher with two martinis was still chilling in the fridge, but David was a beer man, so Tricia figured she would pour one once he arrived. She chilled a clean glass for herself and put the chicken and vegetables back in the oven to reheat.

David used his key to enter Haven't Got a Clue, and upon hearing his footsteps on the stairs to the apartment, Miss Marple positioned herself in front of the door, waiting for the new man in hers and Tricia's life. Miss Marple seemed to like David much more than any of the others who'd darkened her door, which Tricia took as a positive sign.

Upon entering, David first greeted the cat and then studied Tricia's expression before holding out his arms for a hug. "You look like you need it."

"Yeah," she admitted. "I do."

Once David shed his jacket, and after pouring herself that martini and David a beer, they settled onto the couch in Tricia's living room, with a purring Miss Marple sitting between them, as effective as a chastity belt.

"What's wrong?" David asked.

Tricia sighed before telling him everything that had transpired since Angelica got Cleo's call about Bunny's demise.

David let out a long breath. "That's . . . tough."

"Yeah," Tricia agreed.

"Do you really think either of your parents are capable of murder?" he asked. His tone bordered on skepticism with more than a touch of alarm.

"I wouldn't have thought so a year ago. Now?" She shrugged. "It seems like anything's possible."

David let out a sigh. "Boy, do I feel lucky that my parents are so boring and loving. I can only remember one time when they argued in front of me and my brother, and that was over what color to paint the kitchen. Mom wanted white, and Dad wanted blue."

"How did they compromise?"

"By painting it beige. Talk about bland."

Tricia smiled but quickly sobered. "I'm worried that I may have told an inadvertent lie to the chief."

A Perilous Plot

"How's that?"

"Because I said Angelica had an iron-clad alibi. But she was late getting to my place. I was about to text or phone her when she finally showed up—and with no real explanation for taking so long."

"Couldn't she just have been taking her time getting ready? Or walking Sarge or any number of things. Maybe she washed a few dishes or swept her kitchen floor before she left."

"I suppose," Tricia said, and sipped her drink. "And I don't blame her for not immediately surrendering her phone, although if she's innocent . . ."

"Are you doubting her?" David asked, sounding skeptical.

"No. Angelica's no killer, even if she was upset with Bunny for cheating with Daddy."

"Chief McDonald might think differently. She makes a good suspect," David pointed out.

Yes, she did.

"They might think the same of you," David continued. "As far as the chief's concerned, you've got a gap of unaccounted time from when Pixie and Mr. E left Haven't Got a Clue until Angelica arrived here. You see his point about wanting to check the phones, right? It could clear both of you in an instant. Refusing to give up that information paints you as potential suspects."

Tricia reluctantly agreed and decided that she'd volunteer to let McDonald check out her phone the very next day. But did that mean she'd have to give it up for a few days?

The stove's timer went off, and Tricia got up to check on their dinner. She'd drained her glass and wondered if she ought to indulge in the last of the martini mix still in the fridge. Nope. She didn't want her thoughts clouded more than they already were.

She doled out portions on plates and set them on the counter she'd set for two hours before. "Come and get it."

David appeared, empty beer glass in hand, and sat down at his usual spot at the kitchen island. "Smells great."

"Would you like another beer?" Tricia asked.

David shook his head, picked up his fork and knife, and attacked the food on his plate.

Their conversation lagged until Tricia remembered what her sister had suggested an hour before.

"Angelica was telling me about a little house on the edge of the village that she thinks you could reimagine. She thinks highly of your abilities."

David smiled. "I'm flattered."

Tricia nodded. "She suggested I buy it as a project we could work on together with an eye to make it a short-term rental. It could be a great investment. What do you think?" Tricia asked.

David's eyes were wide with what Tricia deemed anticipation. It was obvious the idea of refurbishing a house appealed to him. But then she watched in puzzlement as his expression underwent several permutations.

"So?" Tricia prodded.

"I love the idea. I love that you would give me that opportunity . . ." His voice trailed off.

"But?" Tricia asked.

David sighed, his features falling into a defeated pose. "There's a lot to unravel. I absolutely love the idea of being given a blank slate to upgrade a home and make it into my pride and joy . . . but if the goal is not to live there, then it *wouldn't* be mine—or even ours."

Tricia frowned. "What do you mean?"

David looked thoughtful. "First, there's the whole gentrification problem." They'd discussed that before. "Living in the village is already out of reach for a lot of the people who work in Stoneham. Since it's become a tourist destination, home values have skyrocketed, with a lot of them turning into short-term rentals. Where are the people who work here supposed to live?"

That was a good question.

"But to keep people coming to our village, we need to provide accommodations—and the more upscale, the better," Tricia pointed out.

"That's true. So why doesn't the Select Board allow a hotel to be built within the village limits?"

Again, that was a good question.

"You've been happy working with Angelica on Stonecreek Manor," Tricia remarked.

"Yes, but unless one is a multimillionaire, there's no way in this day and age that a regular person could pay the kind of taxes New Hampshire is imposing on such a property."

It was only *because* the man who'd built the house in the first place had gained that distinction that the house was built at all.

"So, a historical home is fair game when it comes to rehabilitation, but a single-family home isn't?" Tricia asked.

"If it isn't you who buys it, someone else will, and they'll also likely turn it into a short-term rental. But I wouldn't want to be a part of that scenario."

Tricia looked away. "I'm sorry I suggested it."

"No!" David protested. "Don't take it that way. I'm flattered that you'd give me that kind of gift to treat such a renovation as a blank canvas. It *would* be fun. I'd absolutely love it, but then if I couldn't live in it . . ." He shook his head. "That's not what I want to do."

Tricia nodded. "I get it," she said, although she wasn't exactly sure that was true.

What he'd said about home values was true. Angelica had given Pixie and Fred the deal of the century with the little house they'd purchased from Nigela Ricita Associates, selling it to them below market value because of Tricia's friendship with Pixie. Otherwise, they'd still be living in that horrible apartment building at the north edge of the village.

Since that discussion had soured, Tricia changed the subject. "I've got tomorrow off."

"The new carpet's going in?" David asked.

Tricia nodded. "I'm trying to talk Angelica into going to the manor to help Cleo get everything in order for the weekend shakedown."

"Will she want to do that after what you guys have been through this evening?"

"I don't know. But I hope so. It would take some pressure off her to see things settled."

David's gaze dipped. "I envy you."

"I might end up only mopping floors and vacuuming."

"Let's hope she comes up with more appealing tasks than that."

Tricia watched with enjoyment as David finished his dinner with gusto. Just being with him brought her a feeling of contentment, something she hadn't always experienced in past relationships.

"Will you be staying the night?" she asked.

David shook his head and waited to swallow before answering. "I wish I could, but I've got to get to work early to prepare for an eight o'clock meeting."

Tricia nodded, disappointed but accepting.

"It's just as well. I've also got to finish the packing we didn't manage to get done before Pixie and Mr. Everett had to go home."

David glanced at the clock. "I'm afraid I'm going to have to eat and run."

"That's okay. Maybe we'll have more time to share later in the week." Tricia sighed. "Why does it seem like all we get are stolen moments?"

"I graduate in three weeks. After that, I'll have a lot more time to spend with you."

At that moment, twenty-one days seemed like an eternity. But Tricia knew it would pass in a heartbeat. Well, maybe more than a few heartbeats.

Then again, with everything that was going on, maybe she shouldn't try to think too far into the uncertain future. Someone had killed Bunny Murdock. The thought that it might have been one—or perhaps both—of her parents sent a chill down her spine.

The touch of David's hand on hers caused Tricia to look up. "Maybe I could just get up a little earlier tomorrow morning. That is, if you still want me to stay."

Tricia chewed at her lip. She had her big-girl panties on. She didn't *need* to have someone hang around just to hold her hand.

"You don't have to."

"I want to. After what you've been through today, I don't think you should be alone tonight."

Tricia thought about her sister in the building next door, alone with her dog. Angelica had no one to hold her hand—or snuggle up with. Perhaps she should have insisted on staying with her sister.

Feeling like three different kinds of a rat, she said, "Please stay."

David didn't bother with breakfast the next morning and left Tricia's home before seven. The carpet installers were scheduled to show up at nine. That gave Tricia only a couple of hours to finish packing the stock in her store. After a quick breakfast of a toasted English muffin and coffee, she donned jeans and a sweatshirt and trundled down the stairs to her store with Miss Marple trailing behind her.

She was dismantling the beverage station when she heard a knock on the shop's door and saw Pixie.

Tricia unlocked the door. "What are you doing here? You've got the day off."

"We didn't finish. I didn't want you to struggle to get it done on your own."

"But—your day off."

"Hey, you're paying me for that time off. And besides, the thrift shops in Nashua won't open for another couple of hours anyway. I'd just be killing time at home."

"You are a gem," Tricia said, smiling.

"Maybe a diamond in the rough," Pixie retorted, unzipping the aged bomber jacket she wore over a Betty Boop sweatshirt and fashionably torn and faded jeans. "Now, let's get to work." Pixie began by assembling a couple of boxes. "I heard there was some excitement at Angelica's new inn last night," she said nonchalantly.

"Well, if you want to call it that," Tricia answered slowly.

"Yeah, I had the police scanner on and heard the call for a DB."

Tricia assumed she meant a dead body. "Yes."

"And, of course, you guys were there, right?"

Tricia nodded, her lips pulling together into a thin line.

"So, who bought the farm?" Pixie asked, her tone light.

"My aunt Bunny."

Pixie's eyes widened in horror. "Oh, I'm so sorry. I would never have made light of it if I'd known."

But she *had* rather dismissed the idea of a death before Tricia identified the victim. Then again, it was a bad joke among Booktown's citizens who'd proclaimed Tricia as the village jinx just because she seemed to be the nucleus when it came to deaths that happened thereabouts.

A Perilous Plot

"She wasn't my biological aunt," Tricia went on. "Just my mother's best friend."

Pixie nodded knowingly. "Yeah, I had one of those, too. Only it turned out she was the partner of my mother's pimp. She was never a real friend to my mom or me."

Trisha noted the sadness in Pixie's tone and agreed that Bunny may have been her mother's friend at one point, but cheating with her father made her persona non grata in Tricia's opinion. And now that the woman was dead, it was all moot . . . unless it was one of her parents who'd killed the woman. And if that was so, she didn't know what to think.

"Do you need time off to grieve?" Pixie asked, her concern genuine.

"Thanks for asking, but no, I think it's better that I stay occupied."

Pixie nodded. "And how is Angelica doing? I assume she also had feelings toward this woman," Pixie said.

Oh, yeah, she did. And they were more profound than Tricia's. "I'm not sure," Tricia answered honestly. "She was much closer to Bunny than I ever was. But certain circumstances have recently given her a more jaundiced view of our pseudo aunt."

Pixie nodded but didn't ask for a more in-depth explanation. "So, what are you going to do today and tomorrow?"

Tricia looked blankly at her assistant manager. "That depends on Angelica. Otherwise, I suppose I'll be here, of course."

"And underfoot during the new carpet installation?"

Tricia's phone pinged. She retrieved it from her pocket. "Ah, it's Angelica."

Pixie waited as Tricia read the text. "It looks like she's taking my suggestion that we work on getting Stonecreek Manor ready for the upcoming shakedown."

Pixie grimaced. "After finding a body there last night?"

Tricia shrugged.

"To each her own," Pixie said.

Tricia answered the text, and they agreed to meet as soon as the carpet installers arrived.

Pixie moved the last of the boxes to the back of the shop just as the workers showed up.

"Good luck at the antique shops," Tricia said.

Pixie grinned. "I'll let you know on Friday if I got a good haul."

"See you then," Tricia said. She then spoke with the two-man crew of installers before taking her cat up the stairs to her apartment and leaving for the day.

Tricia called her sister and waited outside the Cookery until Angelica emerged. "Will Sarge be okay for the day?"

"I took him out just before you got here. June will let him out at lunchtime and later in the afternoon if I'm not back first."

Tricia nodded. "Did you mention to Cleo that we'd be volunteering at the manor today?"

"Antonio took care of that. We shouldn't have any problems."

Tricia wasn't so sure, considering what had occurred the previous evening.

"What's new?" Tricia asked as the sisters walked toward the municipal parking lot.

Angelica sighed, looking distinctly unhappy. "By 'new,' do you mean anything concerning Aunt Bunny's death?"

Tricia nodded.

"Then, no. There was to be an autopsy, although I can't figure out why. The knife wound as a cause of death would seem pretty obvious to me."

And to Tricia, too. "Anything else to report?"

Angelica frowned. "I'm not sure."

"What does that mean?"

A Perilous Plot

"Remember Cleo said she went to the kitchen to take out bacon to thaw for Bunny's breakfast?"

Tricia nodded.

"Well, apparently it disappeared."

Tricia scowled. "Is she sure she took it out to thaw?"

Angelica nodded.

"Well, if there was only one person in the manor—Bunny—where would the bacon go? I'm assuming there were no workers there during her stay."

Angelica nodded again, then shrugged. "I'm sure Cleo just misplaced it."

How would one misplace a pound of frozen bacon?

"Was anything else missing?"

"Not that I know of. I could sneak a peek in the freezer. I'm the one who stocked what's in there. Cleo will probably start buying food for the guests any day now."

"Then you'd better look today."

They arrived at Tricia's car. Angelica rode shotgun once again. It took only a couple of minutes to arrive at Stonecreek Manor. Tricia parked her car in front of the manor's front door. Surely, they—and Cleo—would be the only people in the house that day.

The sisters found Cleo in the kitchen stocking the pantry shelves with staples delivered by the same restaurant supply company that serviced the Bookview Inn, the Dog-Eared Page, and Booked for Lunch.

"Good morning," Angelica called cheerfully.

Cleo turned. "Oh. Hello," she said, her voice rather flat.

"Anything wrong?" Angelica asked as she and Tricia stripped off their jackets and hung them on pegs across the way.

"Well . . ." But then Cleo merely shrugged and went back to stacking the shelves.

Tricia wondered if Cleo was still upset by the murder the evening before. But then, she hadn't seemed too bothered when it happened, which still seemed strange to Tricia. And though she knew they were coming, Cleo hadn't put on a fresh pot of coffee or attempted to welcome them.

Angelica grabbed the carafe to fill it with water, and Tricia jerked a thumb in Cleo's direction.

Angelica nodded in understanding. "Is it okay if I start a pot of coffee?"

Cleo didn't even turn. "Sure."

If Tricia had been in Cleo's position, she might have felt a bit miffed at having two people blunder in to potentially interfere with how she'd decided to run the manor. Taking the lead, Tricia spoke up. "Do you have a list of tasks you need us to tackle?"

"Not specifically. The window washers are coming later this morning, and I'll be interviewing the potential kitchen staff members this afternoon."

"Oooh! Can I sit in on that?" Angelica asked.

Tricia threw her sister an annoyed glance.

Cleo eyed Angelica coolly. "I'd prefer not."

Angelica blinked. She'd obviously forgotten that Cleo was officially in charge of the manor and that she and Tricia were merely "friends of the owner." Tricia wouldn't be surprised if Cleo contacted Nigela with a list of complaints about how her supposed helpers tried to take over. And how would Angelica handle that?

"Why don't we figure out how to best help Cleo?" Tricia suggested.

"Oh . . . well, yes," Angelica finally acknowledged. She finished measuring the coffee and flipped the maker's switch.

"Where do you want us to start?" Tricia asked the innkeeper.

"When you've finished your break," Cleo began with disdain, "the bedrooms need to be dusted, vacuumed, and the beds made."

"Yes, ma'am," Tricia said meekly.

A Perilous Plot

Angelica pursed her lips. Tricia got the feeling she'd anticipated arranging bric-a-brac, hanging pictures, and adding the toiletries to the guest bathrooms. Angelica opened the cupboard where she'd previously placed the mugs with the manor's logo, only to find a stack of plates. "Um . . . what happened to the mugs?"

Cleo grabbed a box cutter from the counter and slit the tape on the carton she'd just emptied and collapsed it. "I moved them." She didn't volunteer the info on where to find them, moving to take the box into the pantry.

Angelica started opening cupboards until she found the elusive mugs. "Do you get the feeling Cleo resents us being here?" she hissed.

"Definitely. I'd probably feel the same in her shoes," Tricia whispered. "We'd better drink up and get out of Cleo's hair."

Angelica frowned. "It sounds like she expects us to do *all* the heavy lifting."

"And why wouldn't she? *You* are not the innkeeper. *We're* the volunteer help."

Angelica's glower was blistering.

Cleo returned with a couple of dry mops and two caddies filled with cleaning supplies. She set them on the floor. "Here's everything you'll need except for the vacuum cleaner. That's in the main closet near the Morrison Suite."

"I know where it is," Angelica deadpanned.

The look that passed between the women was icy.

As it looked like Angelica was about to explode, Tricia intervened. "We'll have all the rooms looking shipshape in Bristol fashion in no time," she quipped.

Cleo stared at her blankly, apparently having never heard that old saw. "I've got work to do in my office. Check in with me when you've finished your tasks, and I'll see what else I can assign you." And with a curt nod, she left the sisters alone.

Angelica looked distinctly unhappy. "I may just fire that woman," she grated.

"You need to give her a chance to prove herself. Remember, at first, I wasn't sold on Pixie but you encouraged me to give her a chance."

"That's right. But I was right about her. And now I feel I'm right about getting rid of Cleo."

"That's not how you felt when you hired her. You sang her praises on high."

"Rare as it is, sometimes I *do* make mistakes," Angelica said, and poured herself a cup of coffee, belatedly retrieving half-and-half from the industrial-sized fridge to doctor their brews.

"We made a bad impression on Cleo by starting out having coffee," Tricia said.

"Which Cleo should have had waiting for unpaid help. A couple of doughnuts wouldn't have hurt, either," Angelica muttered. "Cleo *should* have welcomed us with open arms."

Tricia refrained from commenting. Instead of sipping her coffee, she gulped it. If Cleo was going to report bad behavior to her boss, Tricia didn't want any negativity attached to her name.

Placing her empty cup in the sink, Tricia ran water into it so there'd be no coffee stains, and she'd make sure to place it in the dishwasher before she exited the premises. "I'm heading upstairs," she announced.

Angelica's gaze roamed all the closed cupboards. "I'll be along in a few minutes," she muttered. Her cup was still nearly full.

Tricia picked up her cleaning caddy and dry mop and headed for the grand staircase. Once topping the stairs, she noted all the guest room doors were open. She entered the first bedroom on the left.

The room wasn't particularly dusty, but she sprayed furniture polish on a microfiber cloth and attacked all the flat surfaces. Next, she

A Perilous Plot

retrieved the professional vacuum cleaner from the supply closet and vacuumed the newly laid carpet. Angelica had sprung for wool—and there was no telltale odor of formaldehyde—always a good sign. Tricia had purchased something similar for her store. No way did she want to expose herself, her cat, or Pixie and Mr. Everett to anything toxic.

After turning off the vacuum, Tricia heard Angelica rattling around in the room across the way. She left the vacuum in the hall so that Angelica could access it, then turned to make the bed before moving to the next room.

When she entered the suite, Tricia immediately noted crumbs on the carpet. Upon further inspection, she saw the remnants of potato chip shards in the wastebasket. She frowned. Angelica said she'd tested the beds in the manor to see how comfortable they were. She also said she'd covered her tracks so no one would know she'd ever been there. And yet, there were clear signs of someone inhabiting the room. Could Bunny have eaten in the room before returning to her own to be killed? Had the killer had a snack while waiting to ambush Bunny? If so, surely the police would have noticed traces of food and asked about it. Had Cleo been queried and not reported it to Nigela or anyone else at NR Associates?

Tricia searched for her sister, but Angelica seemed to have disappeared.

Returning to the kitchen, Tricia found a box of sandwich bags in one of the cupboards and returned to the room to collect the evidence. As she did so, Tricia wondered what she could do with it or what it would prove. The idea that Bunny's killer had gained access to the manor bothered her. Angelica had installed their aunt at the manor only hours before Bunny had been murdered.

That led to only one conclusion: Bunny must have let her assailant enter the manor.

That meant she'd trusted him . . . or her.

Tricia was about to dump the wastebasket's contents into the sandwich bag when she paused. Doing so might be looked upon as tampering with evidence. She pondered the situation momentarily before texting Angelica to ask where she was and received no reply. With no number for Cleo, Tricia again descended the stairs, called for the home's new innkeeper, and got no answer.

Unable to obtain guidance from the manor's management, she went with gut instinct. Pulling her phone from her slacks pocket, she consulted her contacts list before she tapped Ian McDonald's personal cell number, surprised when he quickly answered. She explained the situation.

"I personally checked every room in the mansion after the ME took the body away. There was no sign of habitation in any of the rooms."

"Would you like to see what I've found?" Tricia asked.

"Definitely. I'll be there as soon as I can. Don't disturb anything."

"Okay."

The connection was broken.

Supposedly, Bunny had been the only living person staying at the manor. After her death, no one—save Cleo—should have had access to the building.

So, who had snacked in a room across the hall from where Bunny Murdock had died?

ELEVEN

Angelica was furious—and she wasn't above letting anyone know it. She'd left the floor without telling Tricia, ostensibly to check out the fridge and freezer. She'd returned just as McDonald arrived, and she was more than a little annoyed. "How could you call Chief McDonald without consulting me first?" she hissed at her sister.

"If you hadn't disappeared without telling me where you'd gone, I might have had a chance," Tricia whispered. "Maybe the next time you won't leave me in the lurch." She wasn't about to take Angelica's sass.

"So, what have you got to show me?" McDonald asked Tricia upon entering the manor, his voice neutral. He followed her up the stairs to the bedroom she hadn't yet had a chance to clean and listened to her theory, frowning before he commented. "I assure you, I personally made a recon of all the rooms. These crumbs and other debris weren't here last night."

Tricia swallowed and nodded. "Do you think the killer returned to the scene of the crime?"

"I'm saying you *may* have a squatter. It may or may not be the person or persons responsible for Ms. Murdock's death."

"And your recommendation?" Tricia asked.

"Change the key code for the electronic lock on the front door regularly."

The fact that he hadn't said that the innkeeper should do so let Tricia know that McDonald was onto Angelica's not-so-secret other identity. "And set up more security cameras—and more closely monitor those already installed to see who might be coming and going."

"A squatter," Angelica muttered, her gaze turning toward her sister. And who might that be? Their father? Their mother? Both of them?

Tricia didn't want to believe that.

And yet . . .

Suddenly, Cleo arrived on the scene. "Excuse me," she said, sounding profoundly annoyed, "but what is happening here?"

Tricia began to explain, but Cleo cut her off. "I'd prefer to hear about it from the voice of authority," she said stridently. Her words, along with her tone, had Tricia suddenly agreeing that Angelica should fire the woman at her earliest convenience.

"I did look for you before I called the authorities, but you were nowhere to be found," Tricia said, keeping her tone neutral.

Cleo merely glared at her. "Please explain what's going on," she said, her inquiry aimed at McDonald, not the Miles sisters.

He explained.

"Well, I certainly haven't seen any evidence of a squatter," Cleo said tartly.

"In the three days you've been innkeeper here," Angelica muttered.

Cleo glared at the eldest Miles sister. "Nothing's gone missing, and all the bed linens have been accounted for."

A Perilous Plot

Tricia bit her tongue to keep from saying *Except that pound of frozen bacon!*

"Ladies," McDonald admonished. "We all have the same goal: to see that Ms. Murdock's killer is brought to justice."

"That's right," Cleo said smugly.

"We never said otherwise," Angelica grated.

Tricia sighed. "What needs to happen going forward?"

McDonald scowled. "Keep an eye out for anything untoward—and then report to my office should anything seem amiss."

"I most certainly will," Cleo remarked. "And I'll speak to Mr. Barbero today about setting up more cameras around the property. Will you be checking the building for evidence of this supposed squatter?"

McDonald glanced at his watch. "I've got a meeting with the cemetery trustees in ten minutes. I can come back later and have a look if that would make you feel better."

"It certainly would."

"Fine."

Before he left, Chief McDonald took photographic shots of the evidence, although Tricia wasn't sure what good it would do. She was advised to throw away the crumbs and potato chip shards.

McDonald nodded a good-bye and saw himself out.

The three women exchanged tense glances. It was Cleo who broke the quiet. "Well, now that we've handled that unfortunate situation, I hope you ladies will continue with your work. I'm sure Ms. Ricita will appreciate it. Speaking of which, what have you accomplished so far?"

Tricia shot her sister a look. Angelica did not look pleased.

"Uh, I finished with the first bedroom and was about to start on my second when I noticed the crumbs."

Cleo turned a jaundiced eye in Angelica's direction. "And you?"

"Well, I *started* on my first room, but . . ."

Cleo glared at Angelica before turning to face Tricia once again.

"I'll be sure to tell Ms. Ricita how helpful you've been. I'm sure she'll want to reward you in some way."

Once again, Tricia had to hold her tongue before answering. "There's no need for that. Her friendship is my reward," she said sweetly.

Angelica rolled her eyes and muttered, "Oh, please."

"I'll definitely tell her of your devotion," Cleo said. Long moments of silence followed that declaration before Cleo spoke again. "Now, I must get back to work. I assume you ladies will take a break for lunch at noon."

"Well, of course," Angelica said.

"Fine. Text me when you leave and return so I can ensure the manor is secure against any intruders."

"Yes, ma'am," Tricia said contritely, determined not to laugh.

"Oh, yeah, we'll do so," Angelica grated.

Cleo gave the sisters a disingenuous smile and left the manor's second floor hall to do heaven only knew what.

"I despise that woman," Angelica whispered.

"I repeat: *you* hired her."

"Not for long."

Tricia adopted a crooked smile. "And how will Nigela react when Cleo checks in later today to give me a glowing review and report you as AWOL?"

"I'm *not* her toady," Angelica answered tartly.

"Well, where did you go?"

"Outside to have a private conversation."

"With whom?"

Angelica's glare was icy. "None of your business."

Tricia scowled. "Are you sure you want to be so secretive when a murder happened on your property less than twenty-four hours ago?"

Angelica glowered but didn't reply.

A Perilous Plot

A stare-off continued for long seconds before Tricia spoke again. "And what do you think about a possible squatter?"

"I'll talk with Antonio about it after we finish here."

"But we've made a significant find."

"*You* did," Angelica remarked.

Tricia ignored the gibe. "Unless you want Nigela to hear what a horrible person you are, you'd—*we'd*—better get back to work."

Angelica glowered.

"How *are* you going to handle speaking with Cleo later today?"

"With tact," Angelica said in a tone that made Tricia doubt its veracity.

Tricia's gaze wandered toward the end of the hall, where she knew the back staircase to the home's attic resided. "I'd have felt better if Ian could have checked out the upper floor before he left. Wouldn't that be the best place for a squatter to hide during daylight hours?"

Angelica frowned. "I suppose you want to go look."

Tricia nodded.

Angelica looked distinctly unhappy. "Okay. Then we should go up there with a weapon in hand—just in case."

"What kind of weapon? Because neither of us has a gun."

"Are you sure?" Angelica asked.

Tricia took a step back.

Angelica shrugged. "Well, we don't have that kind of a weapon here. What do you suggest we arm ourselves with?"

"I'm not sure we need to arm ourselves at all."

"And why not? Someone killed Bunny. If they're in the manor's attic, why wouldn't they attack us, too?"

"Because the only ones who had a grudge against Bunny were our mother or father."

"A grudge that we suspect," Angelica clarified.

Tricia nodded. "You're right."

"And would you really want to bludgeon Mother or Daddy?"

Tricia had to think about that question. If Sheila Miles was behind Bunny's death . . . well, she might be willing to understand the retaliation of a woman scorned . . . but that didn't mean she would approve of such a thing.

"What kind of weapon do you think we need to take on this attic quest?" Tricia asked.

"Oh, I don't know. Some kind of club?"

"And where are we likely to find one here?"

Angelica looked thoughtful. "The garden shed?"

Tricia shook her head. Her gaze traveled into the open bedroom doors. "What about one of the complimentary irons that are in each of the guest rooms?"

Angelica's eyes widened. "Sounds like a plan."

So, Tricia retrieved the brand-new, never-been-used iron that had been stashed away in the room she'd already prepared, and the sisters traveled to the end of the hall, where narrow stairs led to the attic.

They stared at each other.

"You should go first," Angelica said, giving Tricia a little shove forward.

"You're the building's owner," Tricia countered. "It's *your* responsibility. And anyway, if there *is* a squatter, it's probably Mother or Daddy."

"They aren't likely to hurt us."

"Speak for yourself," Tricia muttered.

Angelica knew perfectly well why Tricia had no good reason to trust their mother.

As Angelica didn't look like she was going to take the lead, Tricia started up the dark, narrow stairwell, holding the rail with her right hand and the iron with her left, hoping she wouldn't trip over the dangling cord. She paused at the closed door. "Have you been up here before?"

"Only once. It was used for storage and the servants' quarters."

Before insulation became the norm, the people who lived and worked in the house probably froze in the winter and broiled in the summer.

"There's a light switch on the left as you enter," Angelica whispered.

And how was Tricia supposed to flip it while holding an iron?

The antique brass handle turned easily, the hinges singing as the door swung open. Tricia peered into the darkness before groping for the switch with her right hand. A naked bulb glowed off in the distance.

"What do you see?" Angelica hissed.

"Boxes, stacks of various lengths of wood, and assorted junk." Tricia stepped forward, hearing only the sound of her own footsteps on the dusty plank flooring. She paused, taking in the tangle of footprints before her, but there was no way of knowing how recent they were.

"What's your plan?" Angelica asked. She was so close that Tricia felt the warmth of her sister's breath in her ear.

"We should check out the servants' rooms."

"I remember there was furniture in some of them," Angelica volunteered. "Beds and such."

"Point the way."

Angelica did.

They shuffled around obstacles, with Tricia pulling the strings attached to other dim bulbs that randomly dotted the joists overhead. With every step, Tricia felt her insides twisting with anxiety. It didn't help that Angelica had grabbed her by the arm so that it felt like she was towing her sister along.

They stopped at a closed door. "Open it," Angelica whispered.

"You open it."

"You're the brave one."

"Who says I'm brave?"

"Me."

Tricia's angst mingled with annoyance, but she turned the handle and was greeted by more darkness. After fumbling around, she found a light switch. Apparently, the former owners had invested in only 25-watt incandescent lightbulbs, for the light didn't reach into the darkest corners of the small room. Sagging cardboard cartons were stacked floor to ceiling, and it was obvious no one had inhabited the room for decades—possibly a century.

"Did you ever investigate what's in the boxes?" Tricia asked.

Angelica shook her head. "I thought Pixie and David might like to do that some weekend."

"Free labor?" Tricia asked sourly.

"No! But they have a better handle on what could be sold to offset the cost of running this place—and it's not cheap."

Tricia figured that; but then, Angelica had deep pockets.

"I'm sure they'd be thrilled. Do you want me to mention it to them?"

Angelica shook her head. "I have to figure out some kind of reward to offer them first."

"The right of first refusal? Pixie would be interested in any vintage clothes. David's passion is dinnerware."

"I know. I don't want them to think I'm just using them for their expertise."

Tricia suppressed a grin. "But of course you want their expert opinions on what you've bought."

Angelica sighed. "I guess so."

Tricia didn't think less of her sister. She knew David and Pixie would have a howling good time going through everything in the attic. But now it was time to move on.

A Perilous Plot

Tricia backed out of the room, with Angelica following. She closed the door behind them.

They moved on to the next room. When Tricia opened the door, she could tell by the thick veil of spiderwebs that it hadn't been entered in a very long time. No amount of fumbling revealed a light switch, so Tricia shut the door and moved on.

The floor was mottled with more footprints but there seemed to be a lot in front of the last sectioned-off area of the attic. Tricia had a feeling that if they were going to find anything of significance, it would be there. It was with trepidation that she reached for the tarnished brass door handle, turning it and pulling the door open.

"Good grief!" she hollered, and rushed forward.

Lying on the hard plank floor, bound and gagged, was a lifeless-looking Sheila Miles.

TWELVE

"**We've got** to stop meeting like this," Ian McDonald deadpanned.

Angelica glared at him.

Tricia sighed, too downhearted to admonish the local top cop. The glaring fluorescent lights at St. Joseph Hospital's emergency room seemed to sear Tricia's retinas, making her wish she'd grabbed her sunglasses from her car's glove box before entering the waiting room. Or maybe her eyes smarted from seeing her mother so vulnerable—a sight she'd never witnessed before.

Sheila had been unconscious and remained that way on the ambulance ride to Nashua. She'd suffered a blow to the head and seemed to be suffering from dehydration. The rescue squad members had treated her with the appropriate TLC, getting her onto a gurney, down Stonecreek Manor's stairs, and into the ambulance.

Since arriving at the hospital, the sisters had been allowed to see her once, and Tricia was stuck with how old her mother appeared lying on the treatment table with no makeup and disheveled hair.

A Perilous Plot

She'd never seen her in such a state. Not Sheila Miles, who had always been perfectly dressed and coiffed even when she had nowhere to go on a given day. Tricia tried to swallow down feelings of pity, remembering how her mother had treated her in the past, but she had nothing but empathy for someone who'd been treated so brutally.

The sisters waited to be called in again. In the meantime, they needed to tell McDonald about Stonecreek Manor's squatter. He listened quietly before speaking.

"I spoke with the paramedics who arrived on the scene and called in the state forensic team to go over the attic to look for fingerprint evidence. Do you have any idea who could have done this to your mother?"

Tricia and Angelica exchanged uncomfortable glances, neither wanting to state the obvious.

"Are you thinking your father might be a suspect?"

Neither woman spoke.

"Well, we'll get to the bottom of this," McDonald promised.

A nurse poked his head around the doors that led to the ER's inner sanctum. "Miles family," he called.

The sisters popped out of their seats as though they were ejected from a toaster. Tricia looked toward McDonald as Angelica charged forward to acknowledge the nurse. "Will you wait for a bit?" she asked.

McDonald nodded. "Take your time."

Tricia gave him a grateful smile before jogging to catch up with Angelica before the automatic doors closed behind her.

They followed the scrubs-clad man who ushered them back to cubicle 9.

The upper portion of the hospital bed had been cranked to a forty-five-degree angle, and Sheila lay back on the pillows with her eyes closed.

"Mrs. Miles," the nurse called. "Your daughters are here to see you."

It seemed that Sheila opened her eyes with great difficulty. Tricia held her breath as her mother's gaze traveled across her and Angelica's faces.

Angelica leapt forward, capturing Sheila's hand and giving it a squeeze, but instead of accepting the touch, Sheila shook off Angelica's hand, looking up at her in horror. "Please, don't touch me," Sheila said in a voice dripping with disgust.

"Mother," Angelica said, her tone a mix of sadness and disappointment.

"Your daughters have been so worried about you," the nurse explained.

Sheila frowned. "Daughters?"

The nurse nodded encouragingly.

Again, Sheila's gaze traveled to take in Tricia and Angelica.

"I don't have any daughters. And I've never seen either of these people before in my life."

Even Sarge's joyful leaps and barks upon Angelica and Tricia's arrival at the former's home couldn't lighten the darkness that clung to the sisters' souls.

It wasn't long past when they usually gathered for happy hour and dinner, but this hour held nothing that could even approximate merriment. Sarge didn't need to be let out just yet, as June had taken him for a bathroom break just an hour before their arrival.

The sisters shucked their jackets, and Tricia gave Sarge his usual evening snack before she settled at Angelica's kitchen island, feeling desolate.

Angelica went straight to work mixing a pitcher of martinis. It was the least she could do. From the back of a cupboard, she came up with a box of poppy seed crackers—no slices of Brie or cheddar cheese to go with them—and set them on a tray before she served the sisters' usual martinis. She hadn't had time to chill the glasses and drained the concoction from the ice before it could truly cool the liquid, but Tricia didn't care. At that moment, she could have poured straight gin down her throat and wasn't convinced it would erase the memories of what the sisters had endured during the preceding hours.

Angelica shoved a stemmed glass in Tricia's direction. She picked up her own and held it aloft. "To Mother."

Tricia didn't lift hers. "As you say," was all she could muster in response.

Angelica took a fortifying gulp of the cocktail.

"Ange," Tricia began sympathetically, "the doctor said short-term memory loss was common after a head trauma. I'm sure in a couple of days Mother will recognize us." Or at least Angelica. Sheila had never been fond of Tricia.

Angelica gestured toward the living room, but Tricia shook her head. "Now that I'm planted on this stool, I don't want to move."

Angelica shrugged and settled on an adjacent seat. She swallowed a couple of times before she spoke again. "How . . . how could she just forget we're her children?" she almost sobbed.

"Head injuries are often funny that way. But you heard the doctor; it's likely her memory could return tomorrow, and then not only will she remember us, but who hurt her."

"And what if she doesn't?" Angelica said, anguish coloring her voice.

"Then . . . we'll deal with it," Tricia said logically.

Angelica seemed in no mood for rational observations.

"What we need to ascertain is who would hurt Mother and tie her up. She might have died if we hadn't searched the manor's attic."

"I want to know *how* she got up there just as much as I want to know *who* hurt her," Angelica declared.

"Well, we've already figured that Bunny let her killer into the manor."

"*You* did so. I'm not so sure."

"Is that just wishful thinking on your part?" Tricia asked.

Angelica took a brutal slug of her drink. "Maybe. But why would Daddy hog-tie our mother and leave her to die?"

Tricia pursed her lips, thinking long and hard before answering. "What if . . ." she began. "What if this whole ordeal with Bunny and Mother was just some sort of elaborate plot?"

"To what end?"

Tricia shrugged. "I'm just postulating. We know—or at least we *think* we know—that Mother and Daddy were having some kind of financial crisis. What if the three of them were in on the scam, and it all went wrong?"

Angelica's eyes widened. "That sounds like you think someone else was also in on the plot."

"I don't know. Do you think Daddy *could* have had a long-term relationship with Bunny and that Mother knew about it and didn't object?"

"If so, she'd be much more forgiving than me," Angelica remarked. "And even if that was true, who would be the fourth person in the plot?"

Tricia shrugged. "How about the guy whose watch went missing?"

"Why?" Angelica asked.

"Maybe he gave Daddy the watch and made an insurance claim."

"Why was it hidden in Daddy's so-called cremation urn?" Angelica asked.

"And what was the point of faking Daddy's death? Another insurance fraud?" Tricia guessed.

"If that was so, he should have left the country," Angelica pronounced.

A Perilous Plot

"And go where? They'd already dumped their Brazilian and English homes," Tricia reminded her sister.

Their conversation was interrupted by a ringtone Tricia didn't recognize. "Are you going to get that?" she asked.

"It's my Nigela phone. It can only be Cleo. I don't want to deal with her."

"I want to hear what she's got to say," Tricia insisted.

Angelica rolled her eyes and got up to retrieve the phone from the desk in her living room.

"Do you have the voice-altering software on that phone?" Tricia asked.

"Of course." Angelica stabbed the green call-acceptance icon and then the speaker feature so Tricia could listen in. "Cleo?" she said.

"Yes, Ms. Ricita, I'm calling to tell you about the unfortunate events that occurred at the manor today."

"Yes, I see I missed several of your calls. I'm sorry, I was at some *very* important meetings. What did you want to tell me?"

"The Miles sisters were here this morning and—"

"Yes, I've heard all about the happenings at the manor from Mr. Barbero. He keeps me informed about *everything* that happens on my properties."

"Yes, well, he wasn't in attendance during the dreadful events."

"Why don't you tell me everything—in *excruciating* detail," Angelica-as-Nigela encouraged.

Cleo hesitated before answering. "I know the Miles sisters are friends of yours, and I don't want to speak ill of them—"

Angelica mouthed to Tricia, *But she will!*

"Then please don't," Angelica said.

Silence followed that request.

"Oh," Cleo said finally. "Er, then let me just say what a hard worker Tricia is. If she wasn't a bookseller"—she spoke as though the occupation was less than reputable—"I think she'd make a fine innkeeper. She seems to be the sharper of the two."

"Really?" Angelica said. "And what about Angelica?"

"She mysteriously disappeared for a while. And then it was discovered that their mother was the squatter in the attic!"

"As I understand it, the police are still investigating the incident," Angelica remarked.

"That's true, and I don't suppose they'll keep me in the loop."

"What are you doing about improving the manor's security?" Angelica pointedly asked.

"Mr. Barbero and I will be discussing that in the morning. It's too bad that drama had to happen. I hoped to have all the bedrooms ready for the shakedown this weekend."

"Did you step in to make that happen?"

"Me?" Cleo asked, as though vacuuming and bed-making were far beneath her job description.

"Yes, you," Angelica said.

"I'm still working on the breakfast menu."

"What about the notebook full of recipes that was provided for you?"

"Oh, I thought that was just suggestions. I don't want to duplicate anything that's being offered at the Brookview Inn."

"None of them are," Angelica said, an edge entering her tone.

Tricia glared at her sister, raising her hand to make a slashing motion across her throat—a broad hint to cut the call short.

"I understand that you want to make your mark on the manor, but let's see how things go for the shakedown first, then we can talk about you initiating changes."

"As you wish," Cleo said, her voice dripping with contempt.

"In case you were wondering, Mrs. Miles is physically improving, although her memory seems to be impaired."

A Perilous Plot

"Of course, I was just about to ask," Cleo said with what sounded like profound insincerity.

"Yes, I'm sure you were," Angelica said with disdain. "I'll expect an update tomorrow on how things are progressing at the manor, but please don't call me outside of business hours."

"Very well," Cleo said, her tone clipped.

"Until tomorrow, then," Angelica said, and ended the call without waiting for Cleo to respond.

Tricia grimaced. "Wow. That was cold."

Angelica shrugged. "Cleo only has to last through the shakedown before I fire her."

"I really think you should give her a chance."

"I told you I would, but you heard her disparage me."

"Well, you *did* disappear and never finished the room you were supposed to be preparing. And what did you discover when you worked in the fridge and freezer?"

"Quite a bit of the food is missing from the freezer."

"Such as?"

"English muffins. Butter. But mostly meat—bacon in particular. Fred gave the manor a great deal. There had to be ten pounds of it in the freezer. Now . . . nothing."

"Who would steal that much meat? And how could any one person eat that much?"

It sounded ridiculous.

Angelica had no answer.

Tricia decided to introduce another uncomfortable subject. "What are we going to do about Mother?"

"What do you mean—*do* about her?" Angelica asked, frowning.

"If she's no longer in medical jeopardy, they're going to want to eject her from that hospital bed faster than a jet fighter pilot on a downward trajectory."

Angelica blinked, apparently startled by the analogy. "She can come to stay with me."

"And if she doesn't remember who you are, is she likely to want that?"

Angelica scowled. "I suppose we could place her at the Brookview Inn, but the last time we did so, she disappeared the very next day."

"Is there anyone on staff at the inn who could look out for her?"

Angelica looked thoughtful. "I could ask Antonio. I'm sure we can spare someone to do it for a day or two."

"Then do it," Tricia asserted.

Angelica nodded.

"Have you got anyone in mind?" Tricia asked.

Angelica gazed heavenward. "Not really."

A possible solution immediately came to mind. "What would you think about assigning Pixie to shadow her?"

"Pixie?" Angelica asked.

"She's gregarious. She's poised when need be, and she's the eyes and the ears of the world—or at least the village of Stoneham."

Angelica looked thoughtful. "Could you spare her for a few days, and would she even be willing to take on the assignment?"

"Pixie's led such an extraordinary life. She's a former EMT, so she could monitor Mother's health and cognitive ability. I'm sure she wouldn't mind doing something different for a few days—at least until we can figure out what's going on with the current situation."

Angelica shrugged. "I'm game. Now you have to convince Pixie."

"I'll talk to her about it tomorrow."

"You'd better make that tonight."

Tricia nodded, deciding to text Pixie at her earliest convenience.

Angelica looked pensive. "Mother has always been rather . . ." She didn't finish the sentence.

"Judgmental?" Tricia supplied.

A Perilous Plot

"Well, yes. Pixie is a wonderful person—the salt of the earth—but I'm not sure Mother would appreciate that kind of personality. And did she meet Pixie three years ago when she and Daddy visited the village?"

"I don't quite remember. Does it really matter? Pixie is a compassionate soul. If she can get Mother to open up about what's been happening in her life . . ."

"Yes, but Pixie is also pretty tight-lipped when it comes to gossip," Angelica pointed out. That trait hadn't gone unnoticed by others.

"It's something I'd have to discuss with her," Tricia agreed.

"Well, go for it. And if she doesn't agree, then what are we to do?"

That was a question for which Tricia had no answer.

THIRTEEN

Tricia texted Pixie as soon as she returned home, and then they chatted on the phone for a good twenty minutes before they'd decided on a path forward with Operation Sheila. Pixie understood what it would take to cultivate Sheila Miles's trust, so she would dress accordingly. She seemed to process the plan as a lark, a chance not only to play dress-up but also to indulge in an acting assignment. She would use her real name, but she would play the part of a confidant. She made it clear that depending on the level of trust Sheila gave her, she may or may not repeat the information she learned to Tricia and/or Angelica.

"That's all I can ask of you," Tricia said. "Our aim is to keep her safe."

"I get it. What say I start the day at Haven't Got a Clue, and when you get the release forms signed at the hospital, let me know and I'll meet you at the Brookview."

"Great. And I really appreciate you taking this on."

"I haven't had an acting job since playing a bit part in a summer stock production of *Chicago* I did back when I was a teen."

A Perilous Plot

Pixie had had so many weird and wonderful occupations during her life that Tricia wasn't surprised that thespian was another one that could be entered on her résumé.

"Really?"

"Oh, yeah. My mom was doing two months in the county lockup, and nobody knew what to do with me, so I got some kind of scholarship and got shipped to Connecticut. I had room and board, and even got some new clothes out of the deal. Best summer of my life—until I married Fred, of course."

"Of course."

With a tentative plan in place, Tricia thought she might sleep well that night, but she was wrong. She tossed and turned and was forced to add another layer of concealer under her eyes when she did her makeup the following morning.

Pixie and Mr. Everett were to arrive at Haven't Got a Clue at the usual hour to begin unpacking and reshelving the books. Meanwhile, Tricia texted Ginny to postpone their lunch until the next day, before she and Angelica left for visiting hours at the Nashua hospital.

Upon reaching Sheila's room, they found their mother sitting on the only available chair, staring out the window.

"Good morning, Mother," Angelica said brightly.

Sheila turned her head, leveling her icy glare at Angelica. "I'm *not* your mother."

Angelica threw an anguished look in Tricia's direction. She could only shrug. "We're here to take you home."

"I don't know where my home is."

"It could be with me," Angelica said.

Sheila looked horrified. "Why would I want to go with *you*—a complete stranger?"

"Well, then, how would you feel about staying at an upscale inn for a few days?" Tricia said.

Sheila seemed to ponder the question before narrowing her eyes and answering. "How upscale?"

"The Brookview Inn in Stoneham has received great reviews on all the online sites. And the chef was a finalist for a James Beard Award."

"He can't be all that good if he didn't win," Sheila muttered.

"He *will* next time around," Tricia volunteered. The fact that a former felon had risen above his past was reason enough to celebrate.

"What are you doing here, anyway?" Sheila snapped.

"The hospital asked us to help you out until your memory comes back."

"Well, I don't need *your* help," Sheila grumbled.

Tricia had just about had enough. "Would you rather we drop you off at the nearest homeless shelter?"

Sheila looked horrified. "No, I would not."

"Then perhaps you'll accept Angelica's generous offer and come with us to the village's best accommodations."

Sheila's lips narrowed into a thin line as she considered the offer. "Very well. I *will* accompany you to this inn. But once I get my memory back, I'm sure my *real* family will swoop down to rescue me."

Rescue her from what, Tricia wondered. A pampered life in a gorgeous inn where not only were all her meals covered, but her every whim granted.

"What have you got in the way of clothes?" Angelica asked.

Sheila's gaze narrowed. "Apparently what I was wearing when I got here."

Angelica let out a mirthless laugh. "Well, we can help you out in that regard."

And for the first time, Sheila sported a smile. What seemed to Tricia a venomous one, at that.

A Perilous Plot

"Great," Angelica said, smiling. "We'll stop at the nearest big-box store in the area to get you outfitted with a few dynamite outfits."

"Big-box store?" Sheila asked, aghast.

"I'm afraid there isn't anything better in these parts," Angelica assured their mother.

Again, Sheila's lips pursed. "Well, I guess I can live with that . . . for the time being. Before my *real* family comes to fetch me."

"And who might they be?" Tricia asked.

Sheila seemed about to answer, but then her face puckered into a disturbing frown. "I don't know," she confessed. "I just know that I have a family out there who loves me."

Tricia glanced in her sister's direction. Angelica's eyes brimmed with tears. *She* had been Sheila's favorite. That their mother seemed to have forgotten that had to be a blow to Angelica's ego.

The wait for the doctor to sign the release papers seemed interminable, and sitting on the bed for so long in awkward silence was more than a little uncomfortable. The fact that Sheila refused to engage with Tricia and Angelica made the wait even more brutal.

It was nearly noon when the doctor finally signed off. While Angelica retrieved her car, Tricia accompanied Sheila through the seemingly endless corridors until arriving at the hospital's discharge exit.

Once again, Sheila refused to converse on the ride to the discount department store. Upon arriving, Angelica deposited the older woman into an ambulatory shopping cart and pushed her through the aisles of the women's section, picking out underwear, hose, slacks, sweaters, and shirts. Sheila let her contempt for the store and its offerings be known. Tricia fumed during the expedition. How ungrateful could one person be when someone—*anyone*—offered to bail one out of a precarious situation?

It was long past lunchtime when they arrived at the Brookview

Inn, but the dining room staff accommodated the three women. Sheila seemed to think the arrangement was her due.

Tricia's ire was so raw she could barely eat her house salad, let alone the soup that came with it. Angelica hardly touched her slice of quiche, while Sheila tucked into her steak au poivre with gusto.

As Tricia had alerted Pixie upon their arrival, she was pleased when her assistant manager arrived just as the trio finished their lunches.

"Mrs. Miles?" Pixie said, standing formally before the table, dressed in a dark linen suit, her hair newly tinted the color of bleached muslin and twisted into a chignon. Her makeup was minimal, and she held a leather binder tucked under her left arm. "Ms. Poe, at your service."

"My service?" Sheila questioned.

"Yes, ma'am. The inn's owner has asked me to be your personal concierge." Even Pixie's voice sounded different, more sophisticated.

Sheila's eyes narrowed. "And why would she do that?"

Pixie's gaze drifted to Angelica, who said, "Because she's a personal friend of mine and I asked her to do so."

Sheila's expression darkened and she squinted at Pixie. "Have we met before?"

Pixie threw a glance in Tricia's direction. Sheila had visited Haven't Got a Clue three years before, but she hadn't been interested in meeting *the help*. She seemed to consider the services she'd been offered, and her manner changed to acceptance—as though someone waiting on her was justified.

"Very well, Ms.—"

"Poe," Pixie answered with a curt nod. Tricia was surprised she didn't click her heels together with the reply.

Sheila waved a hand in the sisters' direction. "You don't have to hang around any longer. I'm sure Ms. Poe and I can handle things."

A Perilous Plot

"Don't you want us to help you get settled in your room?" Angelica asked, sounding hurt.

"Please have my things sent up. I'm sure Ms. Poe will be more than happy to put them away for me."

Tricia was sure Angelica was about to burst into tears. But after swallowing several times, Angelica braved a smile. "I'll do that," she said, her voice only cracking on the last word.

"Good."

"Now, Ms. Poe, would you please escort me to my room?"

"I'd be happy to," Pixie said. She held out her arm. Sheila grasped it, and Pixie helped the older lady to her feet.

Tricia waited for her mother to say thank you—for the clothes, lunch, and the *attention*—but Sheila let Pixie whisk her out of the room without a backward glance.

"Bitch," Tricia muttered.

"Tricia!" Angelica admonished her sister.

"Not Mother. Me. Because if I let you know what I'm thinking right now, that's exactly what you'd call me."

Angelica bit her lip before heaving a heavy sigh. "Then I guess you'd have to call me the same thing."

Tricia's gaze traveled to the restaurant's exit. Sheila and Pixie were no longer in sight. "I hope to heaven I never feel as privileged as our mother," Tricia grated.

"How did we ever turn out so well when she was our role model?" Angelica asked, and again the anguish in her voice nearly broke Tricia's heart.

"She was never our role model," Tricia remarked. "It was always Grandma Miles. We inherited the best of her."

"And it's too bad it skipped a generation, because Daddy certainly didn't get the best of her. I often wonder what kind of a beast our paternal grandfather was, because neither Grandma nor Daddy ever spoke about him."

"And did Daddy inherit Grandpa's worst habits?" Tricia asked.

"Probably."

"You have to admit, Grandma Miles was the only stabilizing person in our earliest years."

"Yes," Angelica agreed. "I've never not loved Mother and Daddy, but . . . if I'm honest, I always loved Grandma Miles best."

Tricia nodded. She didn't need to say the words aloud. She changed topics. "What are your plans for the rest of the day?"

Angelica shrugged. "To get back to work. I've missed nearly the whole day. I'm sure my inbox and phone are full of messages that need my attention. I turned everything off so I wouldn't have to deal with it during what I knew would be a full day getting Mother settled."

Full day? More like an exhausting day.

By the time Tricia returned to Haven't Got a Clue, there was only an hour left in the workday.

Mr. Everett seemed on edge. "I'm sorry I wasn't able to unbox and reshelve more of the stack."

"I have the whole day tomorrow to work it out."

"I'm more than willing to come in to help you finish the job."

"But it's your day off."

"My plans were to read and have lunch with Grace. I can still fulfill the latter with no problem."

Tricia looked at the old man with affection. "Thank you. With your help, Haven't Got a Clue can reopen on Saturday."

Mr. Everett nodded and seemed to contemplate what he would say next. "Are we to see Pixie anytime soon?"

Tricia shook her head. "But I'm so impressed with how she presented herself to my mother. Talk about the epitome of professionalism."

Mr. Everett smiled. "I thought she looked the part."

A Perilous Plot

It was yet another reference to how they were staging some kind of theatrical intervention. That didn't exactly bode well.

Tricia and Mr. Everett made good progress on the shelving. However, when their usual closing time arrived, Mr. Everett seemed as eager as Tricia to leave the premises.

"See you tomorrow," she said.

"Bright and early," he agreed before slipping out the door.

Tricia gave her cat a snack before she left for Angelica's, eager to connect with her sibling to try to make sense of what they'd experienced that day.

Tricia let herself into the Cookery, but as she mounted the steps to Angelica's apartment, there was no joyful—or otherwise—barking from Sarge.

"Hello!" she called as she turned the doorknob to Angelica's apartment.

Nothing. No sign of Angelica. No sign of Sarge. Had her sister taken the dog for a walk?

"Ange?" Tricia called.

Still no answer.

Tricia moved to the fridge and found no indication that their happy hour drinks had been made. So, she appropriated the glasses from the cupboard, stuck them in the freezer, poured the gin and vermouth into the pitcher, and stirred it, placing the pitcher into the fridge. Then she searched the fridge and the cupboard to come up with some kind of snack and/or dinner idea with what Angelica had on hand.

Tricia decided they'd have omelets for dinner, and plucked everything from the fridge she thought they might want. Afterward, Tricia sat down at the kitchen island to wait for her sister. She could have texted Angelica, but she decided to wait. Angelica had been far more traumatized by the day's events than Tricia.

While she waited, Tricia contacted David, telling him that she didn't think she would be able to see him that evening, but that they should talk in a few hours so that she could update him on the day's events.

And just how could she describe the lows—as there were no highs—during the day?

It was a full twenty minutes later that Angelica arrived. Sarge's demeanor was joyful. Angelica's was not.

"I'm sorry, Trish," Angelica apologized as she hung up Sarge's leash and her coat. "I was just so downhearted I didn't have time to pull anything together for our supper."

"Luckily, I did. Now, sit down, and let's figure out what's going on."

Tricia presented her sister with the nibbly bits she'd found in the fridge and poured their martinis. They carried their drinks and snacks into the living room and took their accustomed seats.

Angelica didn't even propose a toast, just took a big slug of her drink, looking on the verge of tears. "What are we going to do?"

"About what?"

"Mother—who else?"

"I don't know," Tricia answered honestly.

"Pixie is not exactly loquacious when it comes to gossip," Angelica said, and it was true.

"No, but she agreed she *would* report back what she learned, although she wouldn't betray Mother, either."

Angelica scowled and picked up a cracker and a piece of cheese, shoving it into her mouth without thinking. "Isn't that an oxymoron?"

"Well, something like that. Anyway, she knows that Aunt Bunny is dead and that something fishy is going on with Mother and Daddy. She knows what the stakes are."

And there was the whole escapade with the phony cremains and the emotional turmoil it had caused the sisters. Angelica might accept their parents' eventual explanation, but Tricia was far less forgiving.

A Perilous Plot

Tricia's phone pinged. She ignored it, taking a sip of her drink before choosing a cracker and cheese. It pinged again.

"Aren't you going to see who wants your attention? It might be David," Angelica said.

"We already texted. It's probably Becca."

"It might be Pixie," Angelica said anxiously. "You should look."

Tricia frowned but retrieved the phone from her pocket. Her frown deepened when her suspicions were confirmed, her heart sinking. "It's Becca."

"What does she want now?"

"No doubt some Bridezilla commandment or other."

"You're not even going to read her text?"

"Not after the day I've had," Tricia muttered.

It was just after eight, and Tricia was loading the dishwasher while Angelica attacked the stainless steel omelet pan with a Brillo pad when Tricia's phone rang. She looked at the number and grabbed it. "It's Pixie." She accepted the call and stabbed the speaker icon, so Angelica could listen in. She let Pixie know about it, too.

"Your mother dismissed me for the evening but expects me back at ten tomorrow morning."

"How nice of her to let you sleep in," Tricia muttered.

"How did she seem? Confused? Upset?" Angelica asked, her tone conveying her anxiety.

"Not really."

"What did you guys talk about?" Angelica pushed.

"Nothing much. She wanted to know about the village, but decided it sounded like a tourist trap with not much of value to offer."

"Not a good reflection on our hard work with the Chamber of Commerce," Tricia said.

"She didn't want to watch TV—said it was vulgar. She didn't want to read—she said that was boring," Pixie reported.

"So, how did you kill the hours?" Tricia asked.

"Playing gin rummy. It was lucky I threw a deck in my purse before I left home—just in case."

"I hope she didn't fleece you."

"Not a chance," Pixie said, sounding like her old self. "The thing is . . ." she began.

"Yes?"

"Mrs. Miles seemed to be watching the clock. She kicked me out just before eight."

"Interesting. Do you think she was waiting for someone?"

"Well, if what she said was true, she wasn't waitin' for her favorite show to come on."

"Rats," Tricia muttered.

"I could hang around and pull guard duty."

"No, you've already put in a full day—and are likely going to do it again tomorrow."

"There's cameras galore in the joint. Why don't you have Antonio pull the video in the morning? He can tell you if your ma entertains any gentlemen callers."

"What a great idea," Angelica said. "I'll phone him as soon as we get off this call."

"Anything else to report?"

"Yeah, my feet are killing me. I'm wearing flats tomorrow."

Tricia allowed herself the ghost of a grin. "We can't thank you enough for taking this on."

"And thank Fred for being so patient. I hope you both won't mind if this takes a few more days," Angelica said.

"With what Tricia's paying me, we can go on a nice vacation. Vegas, here we come, baby!"

It wasn't Tricia's idea of a vacation but to each her own. "Keep in contact."

A Perilous Plot

"I'll call around lunchtime tomorrow. Mrs. Miles already told me she doesn't eat with the help."

Classy as ever, Tricia thought. "Thanks again. Have a good evening."

"I'm gonna try," Pixie said, and rang off.

Angelica let out a loud puff of air and leaned against the counter. "Now what?"

"I'm going home to my cat," Tricia announced. "You call Antonio and let him know what's going on."

"And what we need to happen," Angelica added.

"Yes." Tricia snagged her jacket. "Sleep well," she wished her sister.

"I won't," Angelica deadpanned.

Tricia had a feeling she wouldn't, either.

FOURTEEN

 Tricia let herself into Haven't Got a Clue and made her way up to her apartment, where she found Miss Marple patiently sitting behind the door. "Are you ready for your dinner?"

Before Tricia could shuck her jacket, Miss Marple rose to all fours and preceded her into the kitchen, where she took up her usual position before her food and water bowls. Tricia picked up both, refilling the water bowl and setting the other in the sink to soak. Then she doled out some gravy-heavy nuggets that looked like tofu in a fresh bowl and set it on the floor in front of her cat. Miss Marple lapped the gravy for a full three seconds before she raised her head, decided she'd had enough, and walked away.

"You like gravy!" Tricia called in frustration to the cat's retreating back. She also knew the bowl would be empty by the morning.

Glancing around the kitchen, Tricia's gaze fell on the envelope containing the manuscript pages McDonald had given her. Why had

A Perilous Plot

she ever said she'd read the tome? It was her experience that most wannabe novelists hadn't put in the time and effort to produce a readable book and yet expected a million-dollar advance and a book tour to glamorous cities accompanied by a fat expense account.

As McDonald wasn't allowed to write about the crimes he'd encountered during his time as a cruise ship's security officer, what else could he possibly write about?

Tricia glanced at her watch; it was still relatively early. She could call David, but she wasn't sure she wanted to rehash the day's events, at least not just then. She glanced at the envelope again, feeling like she'd rather have a tooth pulled than subject herself to dreadful prose.

Heaving a sigh, Tricia picked up the envelope, turned out the lights, and headed up the stairs to her bedroom suite. After getting ready for the night, she fluffed up and stacked the pillows, then climbed into bed, making herself comfortable. Opening the envelope, she settled the typed pages on her lap and began to read, while Miss Marple jumped onto the foot of the bed, kneading the duvet until she made herself a little nest and hunkered down.

It wasn't long before a smile quirked Tricia's lips. She read on and giggled. She continued reading, and then she laughed. Not a mild titter, but a full belly laugh. McDonald had chosen not to write from the point of view of a ship's officer, but of a custodian—and the mishaps and foibles exhibited by the cruising public.

Tricia read on and couldn't contain her laughter the deeper she delved into the manuscript, jostling the bed. Miss Marple glared at her for several minutes before deciding to find somewhere else to sleep—at least until the light went out. But the light didn't go out until after Tricia read the words THE END, and by then it was too late for a chat with David. But what she was sure of was that McDonald's manuscript needed to be read by someone connected to the publishing industry. And that person was Angelica's literary agent, Artemis Hamilton. She wasn't sure he usually represented humor, but it wouldn't hurt to ask.

In the meantime, her spirits had been lifted. It wouldn't last, but she fell asleep with a smile on her lips and her heart lighter. That would change come morning, but she decided laughter really was the best medicine for what ailed one.

Tricia's mood was still high upon waking the next morning, and while making coffee, she called her sister.

"Please don't tell me you've got more bad news to share," Angelica said, despair evident in her tone.

"On the contrary. I read Ian McDonald's manuscript last night and I think you need to send it to your agent."

"It's good?" Angelica asked, incredulous.

"I'm not one to use the word 'hilarious,' as I think the term is vastly overused, but his book is pretty darn funny."

"I'd have to read it first," Angelica said skeptically. "You'd better ask him if that's okay."

Tricia shook her head. "I don't want to get his hopes up, although I do think I'm a pretty good judge of talent. And after the last few awful days, it sure raised my spirits."

She heard Angelica sigh. "Well, okay. You're having lunch with Ginny today, so I guess you can give it to me tonight when you come over for happy hour."

"If you're feeling as depressed as I was last night, I think you should take the time to at least start it sometime today."

"If you insist. You can drop it off with June and she'll make sure I get it. Will that suit you?"

"Yes."

"Good. Anything else?"

"Nope."

"Okay, then we'll talk later."

"See ya." Tricia ended the call. The idea of McDonald's book bringing laughs to a large audience pleased Tricia so much that she felt good enough to bake. She'd make brownies for David; and for Mr. Everett, his favorite thumbprint cookies.

The baking took longer than she anticipated and Tricia ended up forgoing her usual morning walk, figuring she'd make up for it with physical labor moving and unpacking heavy boxes. She made it down to Haven't Got a Clue with a plate of cookies and enough time to drop off McDonald's manuscript at the Cookery and return to make coffee before Mr. Everett arrived. Together, they set up the reader's nook and shared a cup of joe before going back to unboxing and reshelving.

They hadn't been working long when Tricia's ringtone sounded. Retrieving her phone from her apron pocket, she glanced at the number, her heart sinking: Becca. If she didn't take the call, she knew she'd suffer from a barrage of texts she wouldn't want to answer. She tapped the green call icon. "Hello, Becca."

"You are *such* a killjoy!" Becca groused without preamble.

"I beg your pardon?"

"Ian is insisting we have—in his words—a subdued ceremony. Just our closest friends and relatives."

So, he'd finally gotten around to discussing the wedding with his fiancée.

"What's wrong with that?" Tricia asked.

"You know that's not my taste."

"How many people were you thinking of inviting?"

"Just a modest crowd. Maybe two hundred to two-fifty."

Since leaving her job at the nonprofit in Manhattan a decade before, Tricia wasn't sure she even knew fifty people anymore. As a former world-class athlete, perhaps a couple hundred–plus people *was* a modest crowd to Becca.

"Have you investigated reception sites?" she asked, noting Mr. Everett had discreetly removed himself from eavesdropping on the conversation.

"Yes, and nothing local will suffice. Ian wants to be married in the vicinity. I've had my assistant scout the local country clubs, but I haven't seen anything that meets my standards."

Oh, the first-world problems poor Becca had to face.

"I'm sorry to hear that," Tricia said, not in the least remorseful. "When were you thinking of having the ceremony?"

"Early fall. I even looked into some of the mansions in Newport, but everything's been booked years in advance."

"There *are* mansions in New Hampshire that host weddings, you know," Tricia countered

"Probably the same problem," Becca grumbled.

"What about Stonecreek Manor here in the village?"

"Never heard of it."

"That's because it hasn't opened yet. It's one of Nigela Ricita's new business ventures. I can't imagine they're booked that far in advance. Would you like the number of their innkeeper?"

Becca heaved a heavy sigh. "I suppose."

Tricia retrieved the information from her contacts list, glad she'd thought to add it. "Her name is Cleo Gardener."

"Thanks," Becca said, not sounding at all grateful.

"Will you call her today?"

"I might," Becca said listlessly.

"I'm not sure what they've got available in the way of advertising material, but I'll be speaking with NR Associates' marketing manager at lunch. Do you want me to mention you *may* be looking for a wedding venue?"

"You could," Becca said offhandedly.

Tricia bit her tongue to keep from being any more helpful since obviously her suggestions didn't seem to be all that welcome.

"Oh, dear, look at the time. I really need to get back to work. My store has been closed for a couple of days and I need to get it back in shape so we can reopen tomorrow."

"Why did you close?"

"New carpet."

"Oh," Becca said, sounding bored.

"We'll talk again soon," Tricia said, hoping she was wrong.

"Very well." And with that, Becca ended the call.

Tricia placed her phone back in her pocket. How would Cleo react to Bridezilla Becca as a potential client? Tricia couldn't help but smile, feeling just a little evil.

Mr. Everett had already left Haven't Got a Clue to take his lunch break with Grace when Pixie phoned in her midday report. Tricia was glad she had no customers at the time and hoped it would stay that way during the duration of the call.

"I spoke with Antonio this morning and he gave me the lowdown on Mrs. Miles's activities after I left the inn last night," Pixie said.

"Tell all," Tricia encouraged.

"I showed up promptly at ten and found your mother sitting in the lobby reading a magazine. Antonio had someone on staff hit a store and buy up everything current they had in case your mom might be interested. Has she always liked decorating magazines?"

"I wouldn't know."

"Anyway, that's what she was reading when I got there. She'd already gone through all the other stuff."

"Other stuff?"

"Entertainment magazines. For someone who said she doesn't watch TV or movies, she sure thumbed through the lot of them—and pretty carelessly. I wouldn't want to see how she treats a book."

Books and reading had rescued Pixie from a life of crime; it was no wonder she revered them.

"Anyway, she wanted to freshen up before lunch so I walked her up to her room. While she was in the bathroom, I had an idea that I should check Mrs. Miles's laundry bag. In it, I found several pairs of men's boxers, undershirts, and socks."

Tricia pursed her lips. She knew her father had been lurking somewhere nearby. Was this proof, or had her mother hooked up with some other guy? Perhaps the one who owned the Rolex? That seemed preposterous . . . and yet Tricia couldn't rule it out, either.

"Anything else?" Tricia asked.

"Angelica will be footing quite the room service bill."

"Don't tell me; double dinners last night?"

"But only one breakfast this morning."

As Pixie had predicted, it sounded like someone of the male persuasion had spent the night with her mother, only to disappear early the next morning. Like most commercial properties, the Brookview had security cameras located in strategic locations. Pixie's idea to have Antonio pull the video so Tricia or Angelica could watch it to catch their father—or someone else—sneaking in and out of the inn was a good one.

In other circumstances, Tricia would have definitely felt guilty violating her mother's privacy—but Bunny Murdock was dead. Someone had killed her, and probably to keep her mouth shut. That meant all bets were off. No matter what Bunny's relationship status was with the elder Miles couple, if Tricia's mother or father had done the deed, Tricia's own code of ethics would compel her to speak the truth of what she knew. Would Angelica feel the same way? Tricia sure hoped so. And yet . . .

"What are your plans for entertaining my mother this afternoon?"

"A trip to Nashua. Thanks to the corporate credit card Angelica slipped me, we're off on a shoe hunt—or at least a slipper hunt. Apparently, the complimentary ones provided by the inn aren't good enough."

There was more than just a little hint of judgment in her tone.

"'Have I Told You Lately That I Love You?'" Tricia said, quoting a song title.

Pixie laughed. "Well, darlin', you're telling me now."

For a moment—and only that long—Tricia smiled. "Thank you."

"You're welcome." Pixie cleared her throat before speaking again. "I'll call you this evening."

"Okay. 'Til then." The connection was broken.

Tricia set her phone down. She had a feeling Angelica's credit card was going to take a massive hit that afternoon. Of course, she could well afford it—as could Tricia—but the niggling feeling that Sheila Miles was still scamming her children was a bitter pill to swallow.

Tricia sighed. The thought that her parents' foibles had seemed to escalate during the previous months said a lot—about *them*. They were typical of the uninvolved parents of her generation.

She couldn't swallow down the feeling of betrayal—and also what was yet to come.

FIFTEEN

By the time Tricia's lunchtime rolled around, Haven't Got a Clue was looking nearly its normal self again. Most of the shelves were full, and she left Mr. Everett to style the big glass showcase that doubled as a cash desk. They'd finish setting up the shop well before their usual closing time.

All that activity had sharpened Tricia's appetite and she hurried across the street to meet Ginny at Booked for Lunch.

Ginny was already there, which was a switch from how things had been years previous. Ginny was a superb supervisor but had tended to micromanage her team. That changed when she volunteered to help Angelica with Stonecreek Manor's renovation. Best of all, Ginny seemed to have learned to relax, and she appeared a lot happier and much less harried.

"Am I late?" Tricia asked.

"Does thirty seconds count?" Ginny asked with a grin.

Trisha settled herself in the booth, where a menu already sat at her place. "I've been toting barges and lifting bales all morning. I'm so hungry, I could eat my foot—as long as it was covered in barbeque sauce."

"I think the closest you'll come to that is a sloppy joe," Ginny said.

Molly, the server, came by and filled their coffee cups. "Ready to order?"

"We could use a few minutes," Ginny said.

"Just so you know, the special today is Yankee potpie with mashed potatoes and green beans. Just put your menus on the edge of the table when you're ready," she said, and wandered off to fill other cups.

"You seem like you're in a good mood," Tricia observed.

"I got a call this morning from Cleo Gardener at the manor," Ginny said excitedly.

Tricia raised an eyebrow. "Oh?"

"She's speaking to an important client about the possibility of hosting a wedding and reception later this summer."

Tricia cringed. "She didn't mention the name of the bride-to-be?"

Ginny shook her head, lifting her cup and sipping her coffee.

"It's Becca Dickson-Chandler," Tricia muttered.

Ginny's mug hit the table with a dull thunk, her expression darkening. "Oh, no!"

"Yes, and I'm afraid I'm responsible for possibly foisting Bridezilla on you guys."

Ginny let out a breath. "Well, if she does end up booking the manor, it'll be Cleo's problem."

Tricia nodded. "Have you spoken to Angelica lately?"

"Not since Sunday. Why?"

"She's thinking of letting Cleo go."

"Already?" Ginny asked, surprised.

Tricia shrugged.

Ginny frowned, picked up her cup, and took another fortifying gulp of her coffee. "Where are my manners? I should've said first thing that I'm sorry about what happened to your mother. Antonio's kept me up-to-date, but what do you think about the situation? Is she faking amnesia?"

"That's a good question. I'd say yes. Angelica doesn't agree, and she's very upset that Mother apparently doesn't recognize her."

"Oh, dear. I'd better call her as soon as I get back to the office," Ginny said with sincerity.

"I think she'd like that."

Ginny looked contrite. "Am I being too nosy to ask what all happened?"

"Not at all." And Tricia launched into a recitation, something she knew she would have to repeat when she next spoke to David. It was interrupted only when Molly came by to take their orders: the potpie for Tricia and a burger and fries for Ginny.

After Tricia finished her story, Ginny nodded, thinking. "You said there're a lot of boxes in the attic."

Tricia nodded.

"I've never been up there. I wonder if there's any documentation concerning the mansion's gardens."

"Angelica was planning on letting Pixie and David go through it all to see if there was anything worth keeping or selling."

"When?"

Tricia shrugged. "Someday."

Ginny looked thoughtful. "We've hired a gardening team for the manor, and they've drawn up some preliminary plans based on the photos David located and colorized. It sure would be nice if we could find the original garden plans."

"There's a lot of junk up there. It would take weeks—maybe months—to go through it all."

Ginny stared at the tabletop, cogitating. She was still at it when Molly arrived with their lunch plates.

A Perilous Plot

"Earth to Ginny," Tricia said with a laugh.

Ginny shook herself. "Sorry. I was thinking about how we could cut the timing on going through all the attic stuff."

Tricia scrutinized Ginny's face. "And?"

"Well, Antonio and I have this gigantic three-car garage. What if we had movers empty the attic, deliver the stuff to us, and we gathered everybody up on Sunday and went through the boxes?"

"It's an idea," Tricia remarked.

"I can get Juliet"—the children's nanny—"to stay with the kids while we blast through everything."

"Don't you think you should ask Antonio before you start making those kinds of plans?" Tricia asked, digging into her potpie.

Ginny waved a hand in dismissal. "He won't care. He parks in the driveway most of the time anyway."

"That would work, except I have a store to run on Sundays. And Mr. Everett works with me."

"Shoot," Ginny groused, picking up a French fry and absently nibbling on it. Tricia knew Ginny wasn't about to ask her to close the store for a day, especially since she'd already lost too many days due to the carpet replacement.

"It was just a thought," Ginny muttered.

"It's a good one. When you talk to Angelica, mention it to her. I'll do the same."

Ginny straightened in her seat, her expression one of resolve. "Okay. I will."

"Now, we'd better start some serious eating or our lunches will be stone cold."

Ginny grabbed the ketchup bottle and left a puddle next to her pile of fries. "Yes, ma'am." It wasn't long before she spoke again. "Well, if Becca does decide to have her wedding at the inn," Ginny said, picking up on their previous discussion, "she can tell her guests—no kids!"

"You've worked with Angelica on Stonecreek Manor renovation for some time now—"

"And enjoyed every minute," Ginny said.

"I was just wondering how you felt about her no-children policy for the manor."

"Ecstatic," Ginny deadpanned.

Tricia wasn't sure if she was serious. "Really?"

"Yes. Don't get me wrong, I love my kids and I'm a definite mama bear when it comes to protecting them, but I might just sell my soul for one blissful night of sleep after an evening alone with my husband and a bottle of wine . . ." Ginny's gaze seemed to wander—unfocused—as though in a dreamlike state.

Tricia snapped her fingers. "Hello!"

Ginny shook herself. "Sorry. As you can tell, this has been a long-held fantasy."

Tricia frowned. "I'm kind of surprised by your attitude."

"Why? Kids are messy—and people with money don't want to be disturbed by the noise of small children."

"And that doesn't offend you," Tricia stated.

Ginny shrugged. "Okay, maybe a little. But as someone who works in marketing, I get it."

With the subject of children came the memory of Tricia's own childhood. "Do you have an opinion on everything that's gone on with my folks?" she asked, not sure she wanted to know the answer.

Ginny shrugged, her expression neutral. "It's not my business."

"That's not what I asked."

Ginny took a few moments to ruminate before answering. "All I know is that your parents' rejection hurts my husband. He puts up this facade of acceptance—even with me—but I know his heart."

"And what about Angelica's refusal to acknowledge you guys as her family to the world at large?"

A Perilous Plot

Again, Ginny took her time before answering. "Antonio was perfectly okay with it before he had kids. Now . . . not so much."

Tricia frowned. "Has he ever mentioned it to Angelica?"

Ginny shook her head. "He never would. And don't you dare say a word, either. Whether we approve of it or not, Angelica and Antonio made a pact *not* to acknowledge their true relationship. Though it pains me to say it, we have to honor their desires."

"As you wish," Tricia reluctantly agreed. Much as she wanted to confront Angelica on the deal she and her son had agreed upon years before, it wasn't up to Tricia to force them to revisit the agreement. She felt Ginny's gaze settle upon her.

"But, yeah, it's hard. Antonio is so grateful for every opportunity Angelica has given him that he'd never complain."

"So I've seen," Tricia acknowledged. "But that doesn't mean it's right."

Ginny nodded.

"I also know that Angelica had Antonio's best interest at heart by keeping him away from our toxic parents," Tricia added.

"You've alluded to that in the past. Toxic how?"

"It's embarrassing," Tricia admitted, emotion welling within her, and her lower lip began to quiver. They say confession is good for the soul, and Tricia found herself unburdening hers by telling Ginny about the demise of her twin and how her parents—her mother in particular—chose to react. Had she spoken these words to Ginny before? She couldn't remember. But saying the words aloud seemed to lift a weight from her soul.

There were tears in Ginny's eyes when Tricia finished her soliloquy. "Oh, Tricia. I'm so sorry. I can't imagine the pain you've endured your entire life. I assure you, most parents—most *normal* parents—would have embraced their surviving child and probably spoiled the hell out of them. It's so unfair that your mother didn't do that for you."

Tricia cleared her throat. "Well, it was a long time ago. I've—" She was about to say *made my peace with it*, but instead remarked, "Gotten used to it. Sheila"—and at that moment Tricia made the decision to never again give the woman the title of *Mother*; in Tricia's eyes, the woman didn't deserve it—"might just have to fend for herself."

"Oh, Tricia, I didn't mean to—"

Tricia held up a hand to stave off Ginny's rebuttal. "No, Sheila is—or at least was before her injury—perpetrating some kind of scam. I'm not about to cut her any slack."

Ginny nodded. She had a good relationship with her parents, but she had an even better relationship with Angelica and her adopted grandparents, the Everetts. They were chosen family. Sometimes one had to remove themselves from the drama blood relatives brought and embrace the chosen few who warmed the heart.

They spent the rest of their time together gabbing like old friends. But in the back of her mind, Tricia's thoughts kept wandering to the problems that were likely to keep her awake that night. Her mother and whatever scam she was involved in, McDonald's manuscript, and Becca—the Bride from Hell. It was too much to process.

Tricia shook herself, looking forward to happy hour and the buzz of a couple of martinis. And, of course, the desire to reconnect with David.

Tricia glanced at the clock and sighed. "I guess we'd better get back to work."

Ginny nodded. "I'm going to go straight to the office, close my door, and have a long conversation with my employer. As she's also my mother-in-law, I don't think she'll dock my pay," she said wryly.

Tricia smiled. "Probably not."

Another perk of being related to Angelica was the free lunch at the café. They left a large tip for Molly and headed out the door.

Both women had things to accomplish.

A Perilous Plot

* * *

Haven't Got a Clue looked brand spanking new by the time Tricia called it quits for the day, letting Mr. Everett loose hours early. Much as she'd enjoyed her lunch with Ginny, Tricia kept ruminating over the more painful parts of their conversation. After texting to make sure Angelica was home, Tricia locked the door to her store and stepped next door to the Cookery, waving to June before she trudged up the steps to Angelica's apartment, melancholy settling around her heart.

Sarge heard her approach and started barking in what sounded like joy. That such a small soul could feel such happiness raised Tricia's spirits but not enough to counteract the depression that had settled around her like a shroud. She tossed the dog a couple of biscuits from the crystal jar on the kitchen island, and he took them to his cushy little bed to enjoy them. Then she faced her sister, who stood in the kitchen.

"Are you okay?" Angelica asked, concerned.

"I've made it through the day so far, so—yeah—I guess I'm okay."

"Well, you don't look—or sound—it. Is it too early for martinis?"

"Sadly, yes. I'll take a glass of ginger ale, if you have some."

Angelica nodded, took down two glasses, and retrieved the soda from the fridge, pouring it.

"Let's go sit in the living room and dissect the day," Angelica suggested.

Dissect was a good way to put it. When one dissected something, they cut into the heart of the problem—or flesh—and that's how Tricia felt at that moment. Raw and bleeding, metaphorically.

Following Angelica's lead, Tricia picked up her glass and moved toward her usual chair, plunking down with a flourish that didn't feel at all buoyant. "What a day," she remarked, sinking into the chair and kicking off her shoes, something she didn't ordinarily do.

"That bad?" Angelica asked.

"Pretty bad, but with a few highlights."

"Name one," Angelica challenged.

"Mr. Everett. That man worked so hard to get Haven't Got a Clue set up again and ready for tomorrow."

Angelica nodded. "He's a doll all right."

He was, but that wasn't what Tricia needed to discuss.

"What are we going to do with Sheila on Sunday?"

"Well, we could bring her to Antonio and Ginny's home for our usual Sunday dinner," Angelica said.

Rats. Sheila was bound to be a wet blanket, spoiling the day for everyone. Tricia decided not to comment.

"By the way, did you get an update from Pixie today?" Angelica asked.

"Yes. She said you ought to be prepared for a large credit card bill."

Angelica rolled her eyes. "Oh, yeah. I've already received several notifications from my bank about the charges against my card."

Tricia nodded and relayed everything Pixie had told her earlier that day. Angelica didn't look happy.

"I had lunch with Ginny today," Tricia said.

"Yes, she phoned me afterward and asked for my opinion on moving the contents of the Stonecreek's attic to her garage."

"And?" Tricia asked.

"I think it's a great idea. Of course, we need to get Pixie and David on board—"

"I don't think that will be a problem," Tricia remarked.

"Absolutely. I can be available, and I'm sure we can depend on Grace to help us, too."

"I'm seriously considering closing the store so that Mr. Everett and I can be a part of the sorting, too."

"This is probably the best time of year you could do so," Angelica said reasonably. "Sales at the Cookery are dismal. So far this week, receipts haven't been enough to cover June's salary, let alone pay for utilities."

"Well, I'm still planning on opening tomorrow," Tricia said. "Is there a chance you could hire someone to deliver the boxes to Ginny's house before Sunday?"

"Antonio is going to ask a few of the NR Associates' maintenance guys if they'd like to earn a little on the side. I'm sure it could happen," Angelica said, and sipped her drink, then her expression darkened. "By the way, Antonio looked at the Brookview's surveillance video. Mother *did* have a gentleman caller after Pixie left."

Which corroborated what Pixie had said. Tricia schooled her features. "Go on."

"He stayed the night, sneaking out just before dawn."

"And was it Daddy?"

"Antonio couldn't tell. He just said it was an older man. He checked all the cameras and the guy got into a silver BMW."

"License plate?" Tricia said hopefully.

Angelica shook her head, frowning. "The video wasn't that good. Maybe I should upgrade the system."

"Rats! Have you looked at the video?" Tricia asked.

"No."

"Have Antonio send it—or at least a link to it—to both of us. We should be able to tell if it's our father or some other guy."

"Are you suggesting Mother might have been cheating on Daddy?" Angelica asked, appalled.

"Well, we know Daddy hasn't exactly been the most chaste spouse," Tricia countered.

Angelica looked distinctly unhappy with that reminder. "I suppose."

Tricia could tell by her sister's expression that Angelica

acknowledged the pain Sheila—and by not acknowledging that, their father—had inflicted upon her.

Angelica's expression soured and she pushed her glass away. "I'm done." She sighed. "Do you have *any* good news to share?"

Tricia shook her head. "Sorry."

Angelica's lips settled into a frown. She swallowed and took a deep breath before continuing. "We can't keep Mother at the inn long-term. We've got a family reunion and are fully booked."

"Is there room at the Sheer Comfort Inn?"

Angelica shook her head. "Sold out. Sorority sisters weekend," Angelica replied.

"There's always Stonecreek Manor," Tricia said.

"Where someone bonked Mother over the head, leaving her for dead, and causing her amnesia?" Angelica protested.

"Then it's back to your spare room—or a motel room up on the highway."

"She'd never stand for that." Yes, non-amnesia Sheila never would. Funny how post-amnesia Sheila hadn't lost her taste for the finer things in life. "If she won't come to me, would you be willing to take her in?"

"Absolutely not," Tricia said. "I still think Stonecreek Manor is our best bet. Especially since there will be a lot of people there this weekend, all of whom you personally know."

"That's true," Angelica acknowledged, but didn't seem cheered by it.

"What else is going on?" Tricia asked.

Angelica sighed. "Antonio has asked the night staff to keep an eye out for the BMW—and take down the license plate number. That way we can ask Chief McDonald to look it up."

"Speaking of Ian, did you have a chance to have a look at his manuscript?" Tricia asked.

A Perilous Plot

Angelica grinned—it was the first time in days Tricia had seen her sister smile. "I spent the entire morning reading it. I didn't even finish it before I called Artemis and told him about it. He seemed enthusiastic about it, so I went to the big-box store on the highway, copied the manuscript, and had it shipped overnight to him."

Tricia blinked. "Wow. I'm impressed."

"No, *I* was impressed. I never got the idea Ian had a sense of humor, but that manuscript proved me wrong—and in a big way."

"With cruising being so popular, it could find a wide audience," Tricia predicted.

"I agree," Angelica said. "But better than that, I laughed. I can't tell you how much I needed to laugh after what we've been through this past week."

Tricia nodded. "Did Artemis give you an idea of when he could get to read it?"

Angelica's lips took a downward stance. "Well, he said as soon as he had a chance, which could mean days, weeks—or even months. You shouldn't get your hopes up to hear about it anytime soon."

Tricia nodded. "That's too bad. You probably wasted the overnight fee."

"If nothing else, it proved to Artemis that I have faith in the manuscript."

"I appreciate that. And I'm sure if he agrees to represent the book, Ian will, too."

"I'll cross my fingers." Angelica cocked her head, looking pensive. "What do you think would happen if Ian sold the book?"

"What do you mean?"

"I mean, will Becca be open to supporting his literary career?"

"Why wouldn't she?"

"Are you kidding? The woman has an ego the size of Montana. Would she be willing to share the limelight with Ian?"

Tricia thought about it. "That's a good question." She frowned. Should she say what she really thought about the impending nuptials? Oh, heck—why not? "To be honest, my gut feeling is that this wedding isn't going to happen. And if it does, that marriage won't last more than a couple of months."

"And why's that?" Angelica asked.

"Because Becca is too full of herself. Marriage is a compromise and both partners had better be willing to do so."

"Was that how you felt when you were married to Christopher?" Angelica asked.

"Pretty much."

Angelica looked skeptical.

"How about you?" Tricia asked.

Angelica scowled. "Too many of my husbands weren't into compromise. That's why we divorced."

Tricia gazed into her empty glass. So far, she and David hadn't had to compromise on much of anything—usually just the toppings on a pizza.

Angelica rose. "Why don't I contact Antonio about that video footage?"

"Good idea."

Angelica retrieved her phone and Tricia headed for the kitchen to top off her glass, giving her sister privacy while she made the call. A minute or so later, Angelica entered the kitchen with her empty glass. "Antonio came up with a link to the video; he said it was too big to send as an email."

"You pull it up on the laptop and I'll refill your glass."

"No, thanks."

A minute later, Tricia stood over her sister, her attention focused on the laptop's screen. The sisters watched the rather grainy

A Perilous Plot

black-and-white video showing a man in the hallway outside Sheila's room. Unfortunately, his back was to the camera as he headed for the second-floor staircase. The next camera picked him up in the inn's lobby, and they watched as he covered the carpet-covered floor heading for the exit.

"Does he look familiar to you?" Tricia asked.

"Hmmm."

Tricia wasn't sure if that was a yes or a no.

The video changed again, showing the man walking onto the veranda. While the older man's features were totally clear, Tricia was sure he was not their father.

"That's Uncle Leo," Angelica quipped.

Tricia gave her sister a side eye roll. "We don't *have* an uncle Leo."

"Well, we used to," Angelica insisted.

Tricia squinted at her sister. "When?"

Angelica shrugged. "I'm just a tiny bit older than you—"

By five years, Tricia thought, *a bit more than tiny.*

"When we were little, Uncle Leo and Aunt Fern were constants in our home."

"In what way?" Tricia asked.

"Socializing with our parents. They came to dinner a lot. They gave us presents on our birthdays and at Christmas. And then they just disappeared from our lives."

"They had a falling-out?"

"Considering who our mother is, would that be a shock?" Angelica deadpanned.

Tricia shook her head. "Do you remember Leo's last name?"

Angelica shook her head. "It's been so long, you're lucky I remember his *first* name."

"This information isn't at all helpful," Tricia said.

Angelica nodded. "I guess we'll just have to hope one of the staff sees the car and can take down the license number to track him down."

"And if it's a rental?"

"The company who owns it will have all the information we need to track Leo down."

"And if it's stolen?" Tricia proposed.

Angelica frowned. "Then we're skunked." She pushed the laptop aside and plunked down on one of the island's stools. "Looks like we're no better off than we were before."

"Sheila is faking amnesia," Tricia announced with authority.

"What?" Angelica asked, once again appalled.

"Think about it. She claims she doesn't know who she is, but she had to have contacted her gentleman caller for him to know where to find her."

Angelica's eyes widened. "I hadn't thought of that. And why are you calling Mother by her first name?"

"Because it's better than calling her by a nastier name."

By her sister's expression, Tricia was sure Angelica didn't approve of this change in moniker.

Tricia's ringtone chimed. It was Pixie. Tricia tapped the green phone icon, accepted the call, and tapped the speaker feature. "You're on speaker with me and Angelica," she told her subordinate.

"Thanks for telling me. I wanted to let you know I've just been fired," Pixie reported.

"What?" Angelica practically squealed.

"Mrs. Miles doesn't think she needs a keeper."

"Did she say that?" Tricia asked.

"Not in those words. Just that I didn't need to return tomorrow, as she was a capable adult and didn't need a babysitter."

A Perilous Plot

Pixie let the words sink in before she spoke again. "I don't think I can accept the extra pay you promised me."

"Why not?" Tricia asked.

"Because your ma fired me. Obviously, I didn't do a good enough job when it came to pleasing her."

Tricia frowned. "There's no pleasing that woman," she muttered.

"It's not my business, but . . ."

"But what?" Tricia asked.

Pixie paused, as though reluctant to voice an opinion—but then she did, albeit in a quiet voice. "I don't think your mother has amnesia."

Tricia couldn't help but laugh. "I never for a moment thought she did. But what gave you the clue?"

"It wasn't exactly *what* she said, but kinda what she *didn't* say."

"In what way?"

"She doesn't like you, does she?"

Tricia frowned. "You're very astute."

"I can't understand why. I mean, gee, you're a terrific person and the best boss I've ever had."

Tricia felt a blush warm her cheeks. She sighed, making a decision, and then told Pixie the reason for Sheila's dislike—often contempt—of her.

Pixie let out a breath. "Wow. Even my ma wasn't *that* much of a bitch." She seemed to realize her gaff. "I'm sorry—I didn't mean—"

"Don't worry about it. I've made my peace over Sheila. But that said, she's still a problem Angelica and I have to deal with—and protect. Not because we particularly care for her, but because she's a human being and someone did their best to try to kill her."

"You think?" Pixie asked.

Tricia blinked. "She was hog-tied and suffered a blow to the back of her head, causing a concussion."

"Yeah," Pixie agreed, drawing the word out. "But she *didn't* die."

Tricia frowned. "What are you saying?"

"Remember in that Dick Francis book, *Straight*, there was a character who said he knew how to knock someone out but *not* kill them?"

It had been years since Tricia had read the book, but she'd enjoyed it enough that she'd read it more than once and remembered the scene. "Yes."

"Well, what if something like that happened with your ma?"

Tricia's frown deepened. "But who would do that?"

"Someone who wanted to make it *look* like she was a potential murder victim."

Horror rose within Tricia. "But if Angelica and I hadn't found her, she *might* have died."

"A calculated risk?"

Disturbing as it seemed, was Pixie onto something?

"That's a good point," Tricia conceded, something in her gut tightening. But who was making such decisions—and why?

Angelica looked skeptical.

"So, how are you going to move forward with your ma?" Pixie asked.

"Slowly," Tricia remarked. "Angelica and I have a plan for the next two days. After that, I have no idea. But I've got another proposition for you."

"Spill it."

Tricia told her assistant manager about the possibility of plowing through Stonecreek Manor's attic contents.

"Whoa. Do you think there's any treasure?" Pixie asked, her excitement coming through the airwaves.

"More likely a lot of dust. And it depends on what one considers treasure. I know what you like. David's hoping for porcelain, and Ginny wants those garden plans."

A Perilous Plot

"And what would you hope to find?"

Tricia thought about it for a long moment. *The knife that killed Bunny Murdock.* Should she be honest and tell Pixie that? No. Nor would she mention it to anyone else. She shrugged. "I just hope the three of you have fun."

"And what will you be doing?"

Tricia sighed. "Probably looking at a lot of old papers and trying to figure out if they're worth anything."

"And Angelica?"

Tricia eyed her sister. "Knowing her, she'll be cooking. And we'd like to invite you and Fred to join us for Sunday dinner."

"Aw, you don't have to do that," Pixie protested.

"Did I just mention Angelica would be cooking?" Tricia asked, smiling.

Pixie laughed. "I didn't say we *wouldn't* show up, I just said you didn't have to do that," she said and laughed again. "Can I bring something?"

Tricia shook her head. "Just have Fred join us—that is if he hasn't got anything else penciled in."

"Training camp for football doesn't start until the end of July," Pixie deadpanned.

"Great."

When Pixie spoke again, she'd sobered, sounding depressed. "What do you want me to do?"

Oh, dear. What had Sheila put Pixie through? She was tight-lipped about spreading gossip, but would she unburden herself talking about her time with Sheila?

"Are you okay?"

"Me? Sure. Good as gold," Pixie said, with almost her usual cheer. *Almost.*

"Okay. Then I'll text you about Sunday."

"I'm looking forward to it already."

"See you Sunday."

"At the crack of ten," Pixie said, and ended the call.

Tricia eyed her sister. "What do you make of that?"

"Not good," Angelica replied simply.

"We'd better get moving if we're going to cart Mother's butt to Stonecreek Manor this evening," Angelica said with resolve. "Whether she likes it or not."

"What if she refuses to leave the Brookview?" Tricia asked.

"I'll give her an ultimatum: Stonecreek Manor or under a bridge on Route 101. I think she'll change her tune pretty darn quick."

Tricia blinked at her sister.

"What?" Angelica asked.

"I'm just surprised at your attitude. I mean—in the past . . ."

"That's just it. My loyalty to Mother changed that day in Bermuda."

Angelica was referring to the vacation the sisters had taken on the *Celtic Lady* cruise ship and their only port of call. As a surprise—more like a shock—Angelica had invited Tricia to a special lunch, neglecting to tell her the other guests would be their parents. Sheila had said some pretty nasty things one time too many for Angelica's taste. Still, she felt an obligation toward the woman—even if she didn't like her very much.

"Do you need moral support?" Tricia asked.

Angelica's expression darkened. "I don't think so."

"What about when you actually deliver her to the manor?"

"She's going to get the same support as Bunny."

Tricia frowned. "Ange, Bunny ended up dead."

"Yes, and in my book, Mother is a viable suspect in her murder."

"And she's also an old lady," Tricia pointed out. "And whether or not we want to accept how it happened—or by whom—she recently suffered a concussion."

A Perilous Plot

Angelica's gaze softened. "You, dear Tricia, have a good heart. Mother treated you abominably your entire life and you still have sympathy for her."

Sympathy was about all Tricia felt for her mother.

"Well, if you're going to dump Sheila at the manor, someone needs to stay there with her. She shouldn't be left rattling around alone in that big old house."

Angelica shook her head. "I sure wish Mother hadn't fired Pixie."

"Likewise," Tricia agreed. "Who else can we trust to babysit her—besides us? And who of our friends—or employees—do we want to put in danger?"

"Danger of what?" Angelica asked innocently.

"Being hurt or killed!" Tricia cried. "Unless Sheila bonked herself on the head, someone seems to have had it in for her."

Angelica looked thoughtful. "I suppose I could ask Antonio—"

"No!" Tricia said forcefully. "Don't you dare."

"Why?"

Tricia wrestled with her conscience before answering. "Ginny confessed how abandoned Antonio feels when it comes to his extended family."

"Not me!" Angelica protested.

"Don't be so sure," Tricia said, and then realized she'd said too much. "I'm just saying that were it me, I would not like to be relegated to employee status while being part-owner of NR Associations by birthright."

Angelica chewed at her bottom lip. "I hear what you're saying. But Antonio and I have an agreement—"

"Agreements can be amended," Tricia blurted, but then thought better of it. "I've said too much. I've endangered my friendship with Ginny by repeating what she distinctly asked me not to." A bubble of guilt rose within her until Tricia felt like she might choke.

Angelica reached out to touch her sister's hand. "I won't say a word about it—for a time," she amended. Then her head dipped and she heaved a deep sigh. "But now that I know how Antonio feels, I'll have to—"

"Do what?" Tricia asked.

Angelica shook her head. "Do *something*. Right at this minute, I have no clue. But when the opportunity to address the situation arises, I *will* talk to Antonio about it."

A rush of relief coursed through Tricia. "Thank you. Our family has kept far too many secrets over the decades. I know the depth of my own unhappiness. I can only imagine the pain Antonio has felt for years from the same kind of rejection."

"I *never* rejected him!" Angelica cried.

"Didn't you? Letting him think—for his entire childhood and young adulthood—that his mother was another woman."

"But I always made sure I was part of his life," Angelica insisted.

"A *part* but not the *center* of his life when he was vulnerable and needed his mother the most."

"Sofia—" Angelica countered, referring to Antonio's dead father's sister.

"Was a good substitute and she loved him, but she wasn't his mother."

Angelica's eyes filled with tears. "Why are you torturing me?"

"I'm stating facts. You might want to ask yourself why you've tortured your son by not acknowledging him."

Angelica swallowed hard, turned her gaze to the ceiling, but that couldn't dispel the aura of guilt that seemed to hover over her. Angelica knew how Sheila would have treated her if she'd embarrassed her by having a child out of wedlock because she'd grown up aware of how the woman had treated Tricia.

A Perilous Plot

Long seconds ticked by. Again Angelica swallowed multiple times before she spoke. "Antonio and I *will* talk about it, but it can't be now. Not only because of your pact with Ginny, but mostly because of this whole situation with Bunny, Mother, and Daddy. That has to be resolved before I can deal with anything else."

"I agree," Tricia said sadly.

An aura of melancholy settled over the sisters like a smothering cloak.

Tricia broke the silence. "You wouldn't really kick Sheila to the curb . . . would you?"

Angelica's expression hardened, as did her tone. "I am sorely tempted . . . but no." She scowled before remarking, "I'll stay with her."

"And what about Sarge?"

"Of course he'll come with me. There's no better intruder alert than a dog."

"Will Cleo allow it? I mean, the manor is supposed to be a child-free, pet-free establishment."

"Nigela gets the final word on such matters and she's on *my* side."

Tricia nodded. "So, what time are you going to pick up Sheila?"

Angelica shrugged. "When I get around to it."

"But wasn't the Brookview's checkout at eleven?"

"It doesn't matter. I want her out of there tonight."

"And when are you going to break the news to her?"

"I'll tell her when I get there. That way she can't complain—or refuse to leave."

Tricia brightened. "So, we're on for lunch tomorrow?"

"Of course. I must have *some* normalcy in my day."

Tricia nodded.

Angelica's lips curved downward into a frown. "Call me crazy, but at this point, I'd just as soon pour myself a couple of martinis and drink myself into oblivion."

"You don't mean that," Tricia admonished her.

"Are you so sure?" Angelica asked pointedly.

Tricia had no answer.

SIXTEEN

 It was after four and Tricia was putting on her coat, ready to leave her sister's home, when her phone pinged. A message from David.

It's been at least a century since I've seen you. Can I come over?

Don't you have to work until five?

I'm taking off early.

I'll be home in five minutes.

See you then.

Upon returning to her apartment, Tricia lavished attention on Miss Marple, giving her an extra snack and brushing her long fur, which sent the cat into purrs of ecstasy. Then, as usual, David let himself into Haven't Got a Clue and made his way up to Tricia's home above the store. She met him at the door, giving him a kiss she hoped had made his trip worthwhile. By the enthusiasm with which he responded, she guessed she was right.

"Come in, sit down," she encouraged, once he'd taken off his jacket and hung it up. "Would you like something to drink?"

"I'll take a beer if you've got one."

She did. While he sat down on the couch, Tricia grabbed a bottle from the fridge and poured it into an appropriate glass, then handed it to him before taking her seat beside him. Miss Marple joined them, settling on David's lap.

"Did you have a good day?" Tricia asked.

"Fantastic," he said. But then he studied her face. "I take it you didn't."

"It wasn't horrible," Tricia said, and sighed. "But it just wasn't good." She thought again. "There were a couple of bright moments, but the rest of it was pure crap."

"I'm sorry. Why don't you tell me about it," David said, resting a hand on hers.

She did.

David listened patiently, nodding more than speaking, letting her get everything out of her system.

"Wow," was David's reaction. "I'm so sorry you and Angelica are going through this."

"No more than me," Tricia commented. "But there is a possible bright side to the situation."

"And?" David asked, intrigued.

Tricia told him about Ginny's idea to go through the boxes that had been stored at Stonecreek Manor for decades—and possibly a century.

A Perilous Plot

David grinned. "I'm more than willing to take a Sunday off from thrifting."

Tricia smiled. "I was hoping you'd say that." Then she sobered. "It's not a done deal for this weekend, but knowing Ginny, I'm pretty sure between her and Angelica they'll get the ball rolling sooner rather than later."

"Ginny's a firecracker, all right," David commented, sounding pleased. Then he said the words that cast a shadow over Tricia's soul. "And what are you going to do about your mother?"

Tricia sighed. "She's going to Stonecreek Manor."

"But you said she fired Pixie as her overseer."

Tricia nodded. "Angelica has volunteered to be her babysitter."

David frowned. "You've both got so much on your plates. I've handed in the last of my schoolwork. I'm free as a bird. If you want, I volunteer to stay at the manor to make sure your mother is safe. We can go pick her up now."

Tricia's heart wrenched. "You'd do that?"

David looked surprised. "Why wouldn't I?"

Tricia beamed. "There's a reason I love you so much."

David laughed. "I'll always volunteer to be your knight in shining armor."

"It would only be for a night, as Angelica has her most trusted Brookview Inn employees staying tomorrow night for the shakedown."

"That's okay. If Cleo needs me to launder the sheets in the morning, I'm more than capable. And as I'd only be leaving my betta fish alone, it won't be a hardship."

Tricia felt her throat constrict in gratitude. "Thank you for that. It *would* make me, *and* Angelica, feel better to know there's a man on the premises."

David held out a hand. "Whoa! I'm not a macho John Wayne kind of guy. But I can punch nine one one on my phone faster than an Olympic athlete."

Tricia smiled. "Thanks. And we'll take you up on that offer, although Angelica will be bringing Sheila to the manor."

David threw an arm around Tricia's shoulders, drawing her closer. "I can't imagine what you and Angelica are going through."

"You don't have to."

"But if I can do anything to make this situation easier on you, you know I will."

Tricia's heart swelled with gratitude. "We appreciate that."

They sat in companionable silence for a long few moments before David spoke again, a gleam in his eyes. "What do you think we're likely to find in Stonecreek's attic boxes?"

"Ginny hopes to find the original garden plans."

"That would be fantastic. And other than that?"

"I have no idea. Angelica hopes to find enough goods to help offset the cost of the renovation, but I'm not confident she'll get back more than a modest amount compared to her investment."

"From what she's said, she had no such aspirations before this."

Tricia had to agree with his assessment.

"If we intend to install your mother at the manor this evening, then there has to be some kind of evening meal to take care of her."

"I'm sure between us, Angelica and I could come up with something."

"It has to seem like it's a part of the shakedown. But your mother met me back in October. How will you explain my presence?"

That was a good question.

"Maybe she won't remember you. Or at least she'll feign *not* knowing who you are." Even worse—or better—because he'd been introduced as Tricia's friend, perhaps Sheila hadn't even registered his presence.

A Perilous Plot

"I don't think it matters. Especially as Sheila is supposed to have amnesia."

"Do you think she's faking it?" David asked.

"I wouldn't put it past her."

"Wow," David muttered. His mother was a lovely woman who had the capacity to welcome and embrace her son's choice of companion—despite their age difference. Tricia got the feeling that although her ex-husband had had the greatest of credentials, her mother had never really liked him. In retrospect that wasn't surprising, as Sheila had never really liked her daughter, either.

David leaned back and grinned. "I guess I'm going to be part of the shakedown crew after all."

"Angelica was going to stay there with Sarge, using him as an intruder alert."

"If she'd trust me with him, I wouldn't be opposed to that."

Sarge did know David, but Tricia wasn't sure her sister would trust the safety of her dog to David. That she'd trust her mother to a casual acquaintance said something even more surprising.

That was ridiculous. David was *not* a mere acquaintance. But the whole scenario worried Tricia. What if someone was gunning for Sheila? David could be in danger, too. But then, there'd been no threat to her—so far—when staying at the Brookview Inn. Maybe Tricia was just feeling paranoid.

And maybe she had good reason to feel that way.

"If I'm going to play bodyguard, I'd better go pack my duffel for the night," David said. He gave her a quick kiss before getting up and heading for the door. Tricia wasted no time in calling Angelica to tell her the good news. "Have you got a minute to talk?"

"Why not?" Angelica said morosely. "I've been ruminating on how we're going to deal with Mother."

"You seemed to have everything figured out earlier."

"The logistics, yes. Dealing with Mother—no."

"Well, I have some good news in that regard. David has agreed to stay the night at the manor as sort of a bodyguard."

"Oh, we couldn't ask him to do that."

"He volunteered. But he did have a caveat: he wanted to borrow Sarge for the same reason you wanted him there overnight."

"I would miss him terribly, as I'm sure you'd feel about being separated from Miss Marple, but if it's only for a night . . ."

"That's the thing. The shakedown tomorrow *is* only one night, too. Sunday night, we're back in the same boat."

"Oh, you are such a little ray of sunshine," Angelica grumbled.

"I've been thinking . . . we could hire a bodyguard."

"Now, why didn't I think of that? I'll get right on it," Angelica said, perking up. Of course, that meant she'd have Antonio attend to the matter.

"As David pointed out, we still have to feed Mother dinner tonight."

"I suppose so. And we should probably be there with her as well."

"Yes, until bedtime."

"Nine o'clock?" Angelica said hopefully.

Tricia frowned. "Until Sheila says she's ready to turn in for the night."

"As it is, Antonio will have to tell one of our Brookview people that they can't participate in the shakedown due to Mother taking up a room. But don't worry, that person will get a free night in the not-too-distant future to make up for the inconvenience."

Much as she admired David's assurance that he could take care of any situation that arose, Tricia still didn't feel comfortable. "As David's going to be staying at the manor, would you mind if I stayed there, too? I mean . . . Sheila *is* our mother—our responsibility. I don't feel completely comfortable dumping that chore on David."

"I get it," Angelica said. "Would you still want Sarge?"

"Definitely. And he might feel better being left with me than just David."

"You're right. Of course, I know this isn't something you really want to do. And that Mother has never appreciated the wonderful person you've always been."

A lump rose in Tricia's throat. "Thank you for that."

"I'm only being honest," Angelica said sincerely. "So, what kind of meal can I provide that would make David happy?"

Tricia nearly snorted. "Mac and cheese. Burgers. Fried chicken. His taste in food is evolving," she said kindly. "But like most people, he thrives on simple comfort food."

"I'm not sure Mother would feel the same way. I'll figure out something that should please everyone—including us."

"Thanks."

"By the way, I decided to call Mother to tell her about our plan to relocate her."

"I take it that didn't go over well."

"You've got that right. Luckily, I was prepared."

"For what?"

"Her argument. She threatened to call Adult Protective Services and sic them on me."

Tricia's jaw dropped momentarily. "What did you tell her?"

"To go right ahead and do it. And that I hoped she'd enjoy having a roommate while living in a minuscule room in a Medicare-paid nursing home."

Tricia cringed. "And what did she say?"

"That she'd wait for me to pick her up," Angelica answered smugly.

Tricia stifled a grin. For someone who claimed to have amnesia, Sheila seemed to be incredibly informed. "And what time will you do that?"

"Oh, sometime before midnight."

Tricia frowned. "It had better be sooner than that. Will we at least have happy hour?"

"We can. I'm not sure Mother is allowed to drink alcohol so soon after her concussion. I can probably rustle up a bottle of sparkling grape juice or cider."

Would a loopy Sheila be easier to take than a sober one? Tricia wasn't sure. "Anything else?" she asked.

"Would you be a dear and pick up Sarge? I need to rustle up dinner and pick up Mother. You know her opinion about pets."

Did she ever.

"Can do. But what should I bring for him?"

"Oh, I'll pack him a little doggy suitcase with everything he'll need. Just take him out for a pee before you leave."

"No problem."

"Oh, and the Brookview's maintenance guys are definitely arriving at the manor tomorrow morning to pack up the attic and deliver the boxes to Antonio's garage."

"Wow, that was fast."

"Money talks. And the guys were happy for a little overtime."

Tricia nodded. "Who's going to coordinate it?"

Angelica didn't answer right away.

"Me?" Tricia guessed.

"You're terribly organized," Angelica said, her tone encouraging.

Tricia scowled. "I suppose I could have Mr. Everett open my shop."

"Um, you might want to tell him you'll be gone all day. I'm sure he'll understand—such a nice, accommodating man."

Tricia recognized defeat when it arrived. She changed the subject. "Pixie and David are willing to miss their weekly thrifting forays to get a look at the attic's loot."

"They might be greatly disappointed."

A Perilous Plot

"Well, I'm crossing my fingers no one will feel let down."

"We'll see. I'd better pack my own bag and Sarge's and get moving. I'll meet you and David at the manor."

"Right."

They ended the call.

Tricia looked around her empty apartment and let out a breath, her mind awhirl. "I guess I ought to pack a bag to go," she muttered. Miss Marple suddenly appeared. It was almost kitty snack time. Tricia hated the idea of leaving her cat alone, but it should only be for one night. Feeling guilty, she gave the cat double treats and set out fresh food and water to last her little feline friend until morning, then went up to her bedroom to pack a bag.

Once again, a feeling of melancholy shrouded her as she carefully packed her overnight bag, adding her cosmetics, shampoo, and conditioner. She knew the manor would stock all those items but felt more comfortable bringing her own things. It was then she realized she was stalling. She needed to get moving. But first, she texted Mr. Everett, who was more than happy to open the store the next day.

Gathering up her case, Tricia headed down the stairs, pausing just long enough to pet her cat one last time. Miss Marple wound around her legs, leaving her slacks with a ring of loose cat hair. Well, it was shedding season.

"Good night, little girl. Your mama will see you bright and early tomorrow morning."

Tricia just hoped she could keep that promise.

SEVENTEEN

June was still on duty at the Cookery, looking a little disconcerted as Tricia entered the store. "Angelica blew out of here a few minutes ago. She said you'd be arriving to collect Sarge."

Sure enough, Sarge was waiting by the cash desk with his little blue suitcase and leash ready to go.

"What's up? Anything I should know about?" June asked, sounding hopeful.

Tricia waved a hand in dismissal. "Nothing big," she lied. "We're going to do our own little shakedown at Stonecreek Manor tonight."

"Angelica promised me a tour in the next week or so. I can't wait to see it all done up," June said with enthusiasm.

"She's a beauty," Tricia remarked. She glanced down at Sarge, who looked at her with doggy enthusiasm. "Are you ready to go, little buddy?"

Sarge barked happily.

"I let him out ten minutes ago, so he's good to go," June assured Tricia.

"Thanks." Tricia clipped the leash to Sarge's collar, and he barked excitedly. He was always ready for a walk, no matter how short, and the two of them headed off at a jaunty pace for the municipal parking lot.

It was after five when Tricia pulled up to Stonecreek Manor and parked in the back, surprised to find Angelica's car was already there. Tricia got out of her vehicle, tucked Sarge under her arm like a football, and headed for the manor's kitchen entrance. She found the door unlocked, which, considering all that had happened, seemed like a terrible breach of security. Once inside, she locked the door and unclipped Sarge's leash. He was already well acquainted with the large room and went looking for a food bowl, found it and the snack Angelica had left for him, and happily chowed down.

Tricia shrugged out of her jacket, hung it on a peg by the door, and went in search of her sister.

"Angelica! Angelica!"

"Upstairs," came the muffled reply.

Tricia hurried up the stairs and found her sister standing, arms crossed, outside one of the bedrooms—thankfully not the one where Bunny Murdock had met her end.

"Ange?"

Angelica did not look pleased, but her attention was focused on the open doorway and what—or who—was inside. "Are you coming out or not?" she demanded.

Tricia craned her neck to look inside the room. Sheila sat on the bed, her body language mirroring that of her eldest daughter. Tricia knew that angry, stubborn expression.

"I'm not budging an inch," Sheila grated.

"Fine. Then you can sit there and starve."

"Hello, Sheila," Tricia said neutrally.

Sheila's expression darkened even further. "What are *you* doing here?"

Had Sheila forgotten to hide her dislike of Tricia?

"It's *always* a pleasure to see you again, too," Tricia said with irony.

Since it seemed that Angelica and Sheila were at an impasse, Tricia snagged her sister's arm and pulled her aside and out of Sheila's earshot. "Hey, the kitchen door was unlocked when I got here."

Angelica's brow furrowed even deeper. "I specifically asked Cleo to make sure she locked it when she left the building."

"I assume her workday is over."

Angelica nodded. "She wasn't happy to know there'd be three guests staying the night. She said it only increased her workload for the shakedown tomorrow."

"Doesn't an innkeeper's job description include the words 'duties as needed'?"

"Something like that," Angelica agreed. "I told her you guys would wash your sheets and towels and clear up after yourselves, but she looked doubtful—and said as much, too." Angelica looked around. "Where's Sarge?"

"I left him in the kitchen. He found his food and water bowl and the snack you left him."

Angelica nodded.

Tricia tilted her head in the direction of Sheila's room. "What's going on with She Who Must Not Be Named?"

Angelica snorted an impatient breath. "She refuses to leave her room and be sociable."

"I'm fine with that."

"Well, I'm not. She can come downstairs to the parlor and have a

A Perilous Plot

drink before dinner, *and* have dinner with us, or she can bloody well starve."

Angelica was often impatient, but not like this.

"Then let her stew," Tricia advised. "When she gets hungry, she'll likely show up. Meanwhile, the three of us can have a pleasant evening together."

Angelica nodded and sighed. "All right. I brought provisions; liquor for us, and dinner from the Brookview—nothing elaborate. A quart of New England clam chowder, a loaf of garlic bread, and a huge Julienne salad. I figured if Mother was going to harp at you about food, I wasn't going to give her ammunition."

Sheila had been responsible for what Tricia had come to realize was her near lifelong battle with food. For decades, Sheila had berated Tricia into borderline anorexia, although when challenged she'd vehemently denied it.

"David will be here any minute now. Let's go downstairs and enjoy your beautiful new home," Tricia encouraged.

Angelica conjured up a wistful smile. "If only this *was* my home."

"It's too big for you and Sarge," Tricia reminded her.

"But not too big for our whole family," Angelica said with what sounded like optimism.

"You're visiting fantasyland, dear sister. Everyone in our little chosen family wants—needs—their own space."

Angelica frowned. "A girl can dream, can't she?"

Yes.

"Well, think about this: if the manor was closed for the holidays, it could be a magical place for all of us. We could stay here Christmas Eve, wear matching pajamas, and open presents under a tall and gorgeous tree you lovingly decorate. And don't you think Mr. Everett would look cute with colorful drop-seat long johns?"

Angelica actually laughed. "Oh, he's much too prim and proper for that."

"I don't know. He might do it for Sofia," Tricia offered. "Or what if he put on a Santa suit?"

Angelica positively grinned. "That he might." But then her happy expression faded. "I guess we'd better go downstairs and wait for David so we can start happy hour."

"Right," Tricia agreed, and after the day she'd had, she was more than ready.

Angelica stalked over to Sheila's room. "We're heading downstairs for a drink and a snack before dinner. You're welcome to join us."

Sheila said nothing.

Angelica shrugged. "Come on," she told Tricia, and the sisters went downstairs and made their way to the kitchen.

True to her word, Angelica had everything they needed for happy hour, including stemmed glasses, a crystal pitcher, a beer for David, and a snack. She'd also brought the food for their breakfast. Cleo was to hit the big grocery store in Milford to buy what the Brookview crew would consume during the shakedown the next evening and the following morning.

David arrived just as Angelica finished mixing the martinis, and Tricia arranged cheese and crackers on a plate, taking out four small plates to plop the treats on—just in case Sheila showed up. David brought along a six-pack of beer, a bag of chips, and a tub of French onion dip.

"You didn't need to do that," Angelica chided him.

"I felt like I should bring something. And if nobody else wants chips, I *could* force myself to eat them all."

"Oh, you could, could you?" Tricia asked, amused.

"Just to be nice," David said confidently as he took off his jacket and hung it next to Tricia's on a peg by the door.

A Perilous Plot

Tricia pulled out a small bowl for the dip and a larger one for the chips while Angelica carried over a couple of trays and started loading the glasses, pitcher, and snacks on them.

With everything assembled, the trio headed for the front parlor. After setting the food and drinks on one of the coffee tables, they took their seats.

"The one thing we're missing is music," David said. "Would you mind if I chose something to enjoy?"

"Not at all," Angelica said.

David pulled out his phone and scrolled through his list of albums. He liked all kinds of music, but American standards seemed to be his favorite. He hit play. "I think the man known as the Velvet Fog is a good choice."

"Who's that?" Angelica asked.

"Mel Tormé. You've probably sung his most famous song thousands of times—which he also co-wrote."

Angelica looked confused.

"'The Christmas Song.' You know"—and he sang the first two words—"'Chestnuts roasting—'"

"Ah," Angelica said and smiled. "Just a while ago, Tricia suggested it might be fun for us all to gather here for an old-fashioned Christmas."

David's eyes widened in delight. He was a sucker for all things merry and bright. "Sounds perfect."

Angelica poured martinis for herself and Tricia while David cracked open a beer before they each piled chips, dip, and cheese and crackers onto their plates.

"So, what have you ladies been up to all day?" David asked, and took a swig of beer.

Angelica grimaced. "I'm not up to reciting my disappointing day," she said, and plucked another cheese-laden cracker from her plate.

"Ahem!" came a sound from the open doorway. Three heads turned in that direction. Sheila stood there, looking small.

Angelica jumped up, holding out her hand in friendship. "Mother, come join us."

Sheila slowly entered the large room, declining to accept Angelica's offered hand, and choosing a seat closest to David. She eyed him closely. "Have we met before?"

"Yes, ma'am. Back in October. You came to the Barberos' home with an urn and said it contained your husband's remains. That turned out not to be true."

"David!" Tricia protested.

"Why tippy-toe around the truth?" he asked reasonably.

Something inside Tricia seemed to snap. *Yes. Why not?*

"Uh . . . what would you like to drink, Mother?" Angelica asked, her tone tentative.

"Mineral water."

"We don't have any. How about seltzer?"

Sheila eyed the stemmed glasses decorated with colorful frill picks and olives. "Then a vodka martini with a twist."

"We've got gin and olives. Other than that, we can offer you a beer," Angelica said flatly.

Sheila looked horrified at the latter suggestion, but then her sour expression seemed to sag. "I'll take the gin martini," she said, and gave a small shudder.

Angelica scurried to the kitchen, only to return with a large wineglass as, presumably, there were no other martini glasses on the premises.

"Is this a joke?" Sheila asked.

Tricia took in her sister's no-nonsense expression and swallowed. Something not-so-fine, at least by Sheila—was about to unfold.

"No," Angelica declared. "If you don't like it, don't drink it." Then she turned her attention back to Tricia and David, her tone softening.

A Perilous Plot

"Did Tricia tell you that the attic contents are to be moved to Antonio and Ginny's garage tomorrow?"

"That sounds great," David said keenly.

"I've already spoken to Pixie and she's excited to give up her Sunday estate sales to dig through the boxes," Tricia added.

"Count me in, too."

Sheila snorted—something Tricia had never heard her mother do. "Who cares about the junk left behind by dead people?"

"I do," David asserted. "We can learn—and appreciate—a lot from those who came before us."

"You mentioned Pixie. Is that the same woman who was my personal concierge at the Brookview Inn?"

"Yes," Tricia answered.

Sheila rolled her eyes before commenting, "Why does she need to go to estate sales?"

"She's a part-time picker," David said.

"A what?" Sheila asked, sounding confused.

"She looks for vintage books for some of the booksellers here in Stoneham."

"What for?"

"Because the village is known as Booktown," Tricia said slowly, drawing out each word. Surely Sheila had seen the signs posted just about everywhere in the village.

Sheila shrugged. "I guess I did hear someone say that."

No one commented.

Mel continued to sing.

"Uh, how do you like your room?" David asked conversationally, and Angelica leaned forward as though eager to hear the reply.

Sheila shrugged. "It's adequate."

Angelica's lips pursed. She picked up her glass and mumbled into it, "Better than a nursing home."

David ignored the retort. "Tricia and I are staying in the room right across from yours. I think it's fantastic."

"Then you must not have a lot of such experiences under your belt," Sheila said snidely, and took another sip of her drink, shuddering.

"Is your memory starting to come back?" David asked, apparently having taken no offense from her unkind words.

"How would I know?" Sheila said blankly.

"I mean, what *do* you remember?" he asked.

Sheila looked thoughtful and sighed. "My beautiful house."

"Which one?" Angelica asked.

Sheila's brow furrowed. "What do you mean?"

"I mean, until recently, you had five of them," Angelica said.

"What happened to them?" Sheila asked, sounding confused.

"That's what we'd all like to know," Tricia said.

"What about your husband?" David asked.

"I don't have a husband," Sheila remarked.

"And apparently no children, either," Angelica muttered sourly.

"What about the Rolex watch?" Tricia asked in an effort to distract from her sister's bitter comments.

"What watch?" Sheila asked.

"Back in October, you gave us a funeral urn full of kitty litter, and hidden in it was a stolen Rolex watch," Tricia said.

Pink spots appeared on Sheila's cheeks and her expression darkened. "Are you calling me a thief?"

"If the shoe fits," Angelica mumbled into her drink once more.

Tricia ignored the remark. "What were you doing at the manor? How did you get here?"

"I have no idea," Sheila said firmly.

"Did Bunny Murdock let you in?"

"I don't know that name," Sheila said, perturbed.

"Who wanted to hurt you?" Tricia asked.

Sheila's expression darkened. "I've answered all these questions for the police chief. I don't owe you any explanations," Sheila grated, anger tingeing her tone.

"Nursing home," Angelica muttered under her breath once again, and Tricia shot her a dirty look. Those comments weren't helping the situation.

"We're trying to figure out what happened to you so we can return you to your regular life," Tricia told the older woman.

"Don't you think I want the same thing?" Sheila demanded.

"No, I don't," Angelica asserted, abandoning her passive-aggressive retorts.

"Are you insane?" Sheila asked.

"No. You've done nothing but lie to us for decades. Why would you think we'd believe you now?"

Sheila's eyes blazed. "I've never lied to you."

"How can you say that and then tell us you don't remember us?" Angelica asked, her tone a taunt.

"Ladies, ladies," David chided the mother and child. "Losing our tempers isn't going to induce clarity."

"Oh, shut up," Angelica and Sheila said in unison.

Tricia blinked. Too many times in the far past Angelica had sided with their mother against her. And while that was no longer the case, a pang of remorse coursed through her. But she also agreed with David. Interrogating Sheila was getting them nowhere. If Sheila was being honest and her memory was mostly gone, then incessant questioning would only anger and confuse her more. And if she was faking amnesia, nothing they said would entice her to confess.

"David's right," she said, turning a warning glare in Angelica's direction. "We should change the subject."

"And the music," David piped in, which had stopped. Albums

made decades before weren't known to be all that long. "Mrs. Miles, do you have a favorite musical artist you'd like to hear?"

Sheila looked thoughtful. "Well, there is a song I remember. It was by Peggy Lee. It's called 'Is That All There Is?' For some reason, I seem to remember it."

Angelica turned a sharp glance in her sister's direction. They both remembered the song after hearing it countless times during their early years. It was a song of regret. That nothing in life had measured up to its potential. That recalled a life in shades of gray instead of all the colors of the rainbow. That Sheila would remember such a morose song said a lot. A sorry lot.

"Don't you remember any happier songs?" Tricia asked.

Sheila looked thoughtful. "'Dancing Queen.'"

"By ABBA?" David asked.

Sheila nodded. "I remember dancing to it under a glittering disco ball."

"You remember that, but not *us*," Angelica grated, her anger threatening to boil over once again.

"I've read that music—and familiar smells, like cinnamon and perfume—are powerful when it comes to retrieving long-forgotten memories," David said.

Tricia had heard that, too.

"I can download the song if you'd like to hear it."

"No, it's a silly song. I'd rather hear the other one," Sheila said, belatedly adding, "Thank you."

Of course, downloading a large digital file was going to take a few minutes. In the meantime, Tricia changed the subject, turning her attention to Angelica. "So, did Cleo give Becca a tour of the house and grounds this afternoon?"

Angelica glowered. "Yes."

"It didn't go over well?" Tricia asked. Becca was running out of options if she wanted to cement her vows locally.

"Oh, no. Cleo said it went well. Maybe *too* well."

"What does that mean?" David asked, taking the last swig of his beer.

"She liked the house but found the grounds to be lacking."

"That was a given. It's going to take years to re-create the lost gardens."

"Who's Becca?" Sheila asked.

"Just some washed-up tennis player," Angelica replied offhandedly.

"Becca Dickinson-Chambers?" Sheila asked.

The sisters' heads snapped around to face their mother. "You know who she is?"

"Of course I do. Goodness knows we've been introduced several times in the past."

"Name one," Angelica said.

"At her wedding."

"And when was that?" Tricia asked, shocked that her parents had attended Becca's wedding to Tricia's former lover.

Sheila looked thoughtful. "I . . . I don't know. But I also remember watching her play a number of times." Sheila's eyes widened. "One of them was at Wimbledon."

"And who were you there with?" Tricia asked, her tone growing darker.

Sheila frowned and shook her head. "I . . . I don't remember."

"Were you a friend of the bride or the groom?"

"Definitely the bride." But then Sheila looked uncertain.

Becca's father had turned out to be a criminal and the reason the tennis star's first husband had had to go into hiding after testifying against him. It made a sick kind of sense knowing that their father, who had a rap sheet as long as his arm, would know a criminal kingpin. That Becca had been able to rise above her father's sordid reputation said a lot. But had she accomplished that on her own, or did she have a great PR team behind her? And did Ian, as a newcomer to the US, know about Becca's family history?

It wasn't something Tricia was willing to divulge to Stoneham's top cop.

"How come you remember Becca and not us?" Angelica demanded.

Sheila's eyes narrowed. "It's a fluke of the amnesia. The doctor said my memory might come back in dribs and drabs."

Yeah, and Tricia might one day climb Everest in a bikini and Birkenstocks.

Sheila looked uncomfortable. "Maybe she made a greater impact on me than you," she backpedaled.

Angelica's cheeks blushed a bright pink. Before she could explode, David broke in. "The song has completed downloading." He tapped an icon and the tiny speakers on his phone played the song.

No one spoke as they listened to the words chronicling the life of someone who was so bored by it. What a sad commentary that this song was the first one Sheila remembered.

After it finished, three of the four sat there, looking at the floor without speaking. Meanwhile, David's thumbs were in action once again. Instead of downloading, he must have tapped into another site, because in less than a minute the happy sound of the Beatles' "Here Comes the Sun" filled the air. The bouncy tune and cheerful voices were a welcome relief after hearing the previous tune.

Silence reigned again once the song was over. "Any other requests?" David asked.

"Anything you want," Angelica said in a small voice. Tricia nodded in agreement.

David's thumbs went back to work, and the easy-listening voices

A Perilous Plot

of the Eagles issued from his phone: "Peaceful Easy Feeling." Tricia knew the song, but it wasn't one from her childhood—usually one she heard when grocery shopping. But it was gentle and sweet, almost a balm to her aching heart. She hoped Angelica would react to it in the same way.

"What did Becca have to say about the manor?" Tricia asked.

"I heard secondhand from Cleo that she seemed rather iffy about it. She thought the gardens *might* be big enough for a tent to accommodate her modified guest list and she *might* be willing to supplement the poor landscaping with rented potted flowers."

"Where does she think she's going to find them around here?" David asked.

"That's not our problem," Angelica said.

"Why would it be *your* problem? I understand some billionaire named Nigela Ricita owns the place," Sheila said.

"Billionaire?" Tricia asked, stifling a laugh.

Angelica coughed before replying. "Yes, I'm sure my dearest friend Nigela is a billionaire. Why else would I be a slave to her whims?" she asked the room at large.

"Pleasing powerful people keeps one safe," Sheila said grimly, having obviously missed the sarcasm in Angelica's tone.

Tricia considered her mother's words. Amnesia or not, the knowledge of her father's criminal past seemed to suddenly hang over the room like a pall. Tricia was sure that, no matter what acrimony her parents had experienced during their marriage, her father wasn't capable of ever physically hurting her mother.

So, that left one question: Who else did John and Sheila know who could inflict that kind of pain and embarrassment upon them? The phantom Uncle Leo?

Tricia was afraid to find out.

EIGHTEEN

 The soup, salad, and bread Angelica provided made a fine dinner for three of the four gathered around the manor's large dining room table.

"You call this a meal?" Sheila griped, her gaze traveling to the little dog sitting on Angelica's lap who was watching each spoonful of chowder Angelica dished up.

"I love clam chowder," David said. "I like garlic bread even more. I could probably eat an entire loaf."

"I'm glad you're enjoying it." Tricia's gaze turned to her mother, "And sorry you aren't."

"Peasant food," Sheila grated, pushing away her nearly full bowl.

"I'm sorry I've got nothing else to offer you. The manor won't be up and running for another couple of weeks. And for some reason, food seems to disappear from the kitchen. You wouldn't happen to know anything about that, would you?" Angelica asked. It sounded like an accusation.

"Of course not," Sheila retorted.

A Perilous Plot

"If you want some more crackers and cheese to tide you over 'til the morning, I'd be glad to get them for you," Angelica said, which was the most generous thing she'd said all evening.

"No thank you. I don't need any more carbs today." She glanced in Tricia's direction. "I've had enough."

Sheila had harped on Tricia's weight for most of her life. Another reason why Tricia didn't believe her mother suffered from amnesia. As though in defiance, Tricia reached for another slice of garlic bread, took a bite, and chewed with a broad smile covering her lips.

"It turns out the guys cleared out the boxes from the Stonecreek's attic this afternoon and delivered them to Antonio's garage," Angelica remarked.

"And?" Tricia prompted, grateful she wouldn't have to coordinate the task after all.

"We're all set for the unboxing on Sunday morning."

Tricia frowned, disappointment dragging her down. "I wish I could be there."

"No one's stopping you," Angelica quipped.

"I do have a store to run," Tricia reminded her sister.

"Mr. Everett could run it for you. At this time of year, it's not like he'd be overwhelmed with customers."

That was true.

"And," Angelica continued, "one of us could go fetch him when dinnertime rolled around."

"I volunteer," David quipped.

"You're a good guy," Angelica praised him.

Tricia bit her lip, sorely tempted. "First, I'd have to talk to Mr. Everett about it."

"You do that," Angelica said pointedly. "Meanwhile, I've already spoken to Pixie about the unboxing and she sounded as happy as a pig in poop at the prospect. And, of course, I'll pay her for her time.

I'll have the Brookview's kitchen whip up something special. Or maybe we could have a picnic. Antonio cooks a mean steak on the grill. What do you think?"

"I'll enjoy whatever you come up with, as I'm sure the rest of the gang will, too," Tricia said.

"I love steak—especially with horseradish mayo," David said.

Angelica nodded, looking satisfied.

"Red meat cooked on a grill is full of carcinogens," Sheila remarked sourly. Talk about a wet blanket!

Tricia sipped her drink before changing the subject. "You didn't finish telling us about Becca's reaction to the manor," Tricia pointed out.

"Oh, yeah," Angelica said sourly. "She wasn't at all pleased."

"She hated it?"

Angelica scowled. "*Hate's* a strong word. She was *disappointed.*" She said the last word in a simpering tone.

"And why's that?"

"Because the gardens haven't yet been restored. Because not all the furnishings are in place. Because we don't yet have a catering staff on the premises."

"I thought the Brookview was going to cater those kinds of events," Tricia said.

Angelica nodded. "Apparently that's a detriment. Also, she's chagrinned that we only have six guest rooms."

"But you have plans to renovate the attic space at a later date."

"Yes, but it won't be in time for Becca's nuptials."

Tricia shrugged. "Well, easy come, easy go."

"I'm more annoyed by her criticisms than her not booking the venue. I hate to think how she might abuse the staff hired to take care of the reception."

Tricia nodded. "So, she's still looking for another locale."

"Apparently."

A Perilous Plot

Sheila looked wistful. "What I wouldn't give to lob a few balls over a net with her."

"You don't have anything but the clothes we bought you," Angelica reminded her.

"I meant that figuratively," Sheila replied. "What is such a gifted athlete doing here in the sticks?" she asked.

"Becca has business interests here in Stoneham. She inherited a retail establishment, liked the area, and decided to build her first tennis club here, something she intends to franchise throughout the world," Tricia explained.

"And she's engaged to the village's most eligible bachelor," Angelica added.

"Who's that?"

"The chief of police. We met him on our ill-fated trip to Bermuda. You remember that disaster, don't you, Mother?" Angelica asked. Again, an edge had crept into her voice.

"No, I don't," Sheila deadpanned. She served herself a small portion of salad, choosing the bottle of raspberry vinaigrette dressing to accompany it. "When can I meet with her?"

"I'll text her tomorrow," Tricia promised.

"Why can't you do it now?" Sheila pressed.

"Because it's a Friday night, after working hours. I don't want to intrude on her time with her fiancé."

"Then will you contact her *first thing* tomorrow?"

"Probably not," Tricia said. They needed a reason to keep Sheila in the village until they could determine what the heck was going on. She needed to stall and this was the perfect opportunity. "I'd be willing to text or call her on Monday during regular business hours. Our relationship *is* strictly business," Tricia said, not confessing that Becca had asked Tricia to be her maid of honor at the upcoming nuptials.

Sheila glowered. She wasn't used to being put off when it came to fulfilling her whims.

The music issuing from David's phone petered out and he selected something else from his playlist. This time it was the big band sounds of Glenn Miller.

Sheila grimaced. "Aren't you a little young to be listening to such *old* music? My father listened to that crap."

"It's not crap at all," David said defensively. "Pixie and I listen to these tracks all the time—and we sing along while on our thrifting adventures."

"What do you want with a load of old junk?" Sheila asked with disdain.

"We're not only saving stuff from landfills but recycling and upcycling items that still have a lot of life left in them."

"Junk," Sheila reiterated.

Tricia and David exchanged sour glances. She could almost read his mind: *I can't wait to meet your father*, with a real sarcastic bent.

At last, Sheila finished her salad, pushing the plate away. "I saw this place's library. It's empty. There's no TV in my room. How am I supposed to amuse myself this evening?"

"Why, with our sparkling conversation, of course," Angelica quipped.

"I've brought a couple of vintage mysteries with me. Would you care to read one of Agatha Christie's titles?" Tricia offered.

"No!" Sheila said emphatically. She turned her gaze toward Angelica. "I need a phone. There isn't even one in my room."

"Who would a person with amnesia call?" Angelica inquired.

It took a few moments before Sheila answered. "I . . . I could tune into the news of the day. I could look up things like . . . like . . ." But she couldn't seem to come up with that kind of subject matter.

"I'd be happy to get you an Android phone from Walmart," Angelica said.

A Perilous Plot

Sheila glowered. "You two have iPhones."

"Yes, and we're on the family plan."

"Why can't you put me on it?"

"We've reached maximum capacity," Angelica answered, but Tricia knew better. They didn't want Sheila to have unfettered access to the World Wide Web, not until they could trust her—and trust was not something they'd enjoyed in the past.

"The manor will be subscribing to several magazines, but we haven't decided just what yet. Do you have any suggestions?"

"*We?*" Sheila asked.

"Uh, that's what my friend Nigela Ricita told me. It's a question that'll be on the survey given to the people who participate in the shakedown tomorrow night."

"Shakedown?" Sheila asked.

"Yes. Nigela has invited members of her staff at the Brookview Inn to stay the night and evaluate what's on offer to guests."

"The help?" Again, Sheila said the word like it was a slur.

"They are the lifeblood of the Brookview Inn. They give tremendous service on every shift. They are the ultimate guinea pigs."

"Pigs is right," Sheila said.

A royal flush rose up from Angelica's neck to stain her cheeks. "Some of those people may not have been born in this country, but they are the hardest, most loyal employees on the face of the planet."

"How would you know? They don't work for you," Sheila sneered.

Angelica breathed in deeply through her nose before answering. "Antonio told me so."

Sheila rolled her eyes. "Another immigrant."

Angelica jumped to her feet. "Dinner is done," she announced. "Why don't you go up to your room, *Mother*."

Sheila glared at her older daughter. "I'm *not* your mother."

"Then retire for the night, *old* woman," Angelica declared.

Tricia and David had remained silent through the discord. After all, what could they say?

"I think I will," Sheila said defiantly. She pushed her chair back, rose to her feet, and walked out of the room.

Silence settled over the room like a shroud. It was Tricia who finally broke the quiet. "Well, that was . . . something," was all she could come up with.

"What'll you do? Get her a burner phone?" David asked Angelica.

"Yes. I want to limit her contacts. But the truth is, I wouldn't be surprised if she already has a phone hidden here in the manor. I mean . . . how did she get in here in the first place? Did Bunny let her in? And who else has had access to the place?"

Tricia didn't like to think about it. After all, she and David would be staying the night in the manor. And there was still the specter of the man Angelica had called Uncle Leo. Who was he and what was his relationship with Sheila and/or John Miles?

Tricia wasn't sure she wanted to know.

After tossing and turning for more than an hour, Tricia reached over and switched on the bedside lamp. She knew from past experience that doing so wasn't likely to affect David, who would instinctively turn over to avoid the light. They'd discussed it on more than one occasion, and he was so pro-reading, he didn't care who did it where or when. They were simpatico on that.

Tricia sat cross-legged on the bed, her book nestled between her knees, and after about half an hour she felt drowsy enough to place her bookmark between the pages and close the book, when suddenly the light winked out. The lamp's bulb hadn't suddenly brightened before expiring, so the power must have given out, which sometimes happened in a village as old as Stoneham.

A Perilous Plot

Tricia placed the book on the floor next to the bed. She hunkered down, pulling the duvet up to her chin, closed her eyes, and hoped sleep would come sooner rather than later.

Tuning in to a favorite memory—the champagne tea on the *Celtic Lady* cruise ship that she'd shared with Angelica—Tricia tried to remember each and every moment, from the white tux–clad servers to the lovely little cakes and crustless sandwiches.

Tricia was melting into that memory when a woman's scream pierced the darkness. As Tricia was only one of two women in the mansion, that meant it was Sheila who made the sound.

Suddenly wide awake, Tricia poked David hard enough to rouse him.

"Get up! Sheila just screamed!" she cried, and threw off the covers, grabbed her phone, pawing through the apps before she tapped its flashlight feature and stumbled out of the room into the hall.

Something—someone—barreled into her, knocking Tricia to the ground and sending her phone flying. Righting herself, Tricia crawled to recapture her phone before climbing to her feet and finding her way to Sheila's room, where she found her mother cowering in her bed, the covers drawn up to her chin.

"Are you okay?" Tricia demanded as she approached the older woman.

"Of course I'm not!" Sheila wailed. "Someone just tried to choke me."

Tricia stepped forward and Sheila lunged at her, capturing Tricia in a near stranglehold.

"What's going on?" David asked from the doorway, outlined in silhouette.

"Someone was in Sheila's room," Tricia managed above her mother's wails.

"Where's Sarge?" David asked. "Why didn't he bark?"

"I don't know." Had something happened to the little dog? "The security system's been breached. Someone's in the house."

"I'll go look," David said, and disappeared from the doorway in only his underwear, taking the light from his phone with him.

"He tried to kill me!" Sheila cried, still hanging on to Tricia for dear life.

"Who? Who tried to kill you?" Tricia demanded, but Sheila gave no answer and just continued to sob uncontrollably.

Tricia found herself patting her mother on the back, trying to soothe the woman while feeling nothing but resentment. At no time in her life did she ever remember Sheila comforting her.

Time dragged. It must have been five minutes or so since David left them before Sheila's sobs dwindled and she pulled away. The lights came on—at least in the room across from Sheila's. Tricia's ringtone sounded, startling the women.

Sheila grabbed the bedclothes, pulling them up to her chin once more as Tricia accepted the call. "David?"

"I found the breaker box. Someone tripped the main switch. And Sarge—"

Sudden panic coursed through Tricia. "Please don't tell me—"

"He's alive but unresponsive. I think someone may have drugged him."

"If anything happens to that dog Angelica will kill me!"

"Don't panic. He's as limp as a dishrag, but he's still breathing. Siri tells me there's a twenty-four-hour vet in Nashua. I'll get him in the car and call them on the way. I just need to get my wallet and clothes."

"I can bring them down to you," Tricia said.

"Don't leave me alone!" Sheila shrieked.

"Call nine one one and get the cops out here. Once you do that, bring my stuff down," David advised.

A Perilous Plot

"Okay," Tricia agreed, her mouth dry, feeling like the earth beneath her was shaky.

The connection was cut.

With a trembling hand, Tricia reached out and turned on the bedside lamp. Then she hit the call button on her phone and tapped the numbers 911.

"Nine one one. What is your emergency?"

"Someone broke into Stonecreek Manor."

"The what?" asked the dispatcher.

"The old Morrison Mansion in Stoneham." She gave the woman the address.

"Are you safe?" the disembodied woman's voice asked.

"I think so. I think we scared him away—at least away from his intended victim."

"I'm not a victim!" Sheila declared, and began to wail once again.

"Someone's on the way," the dispatcher said.

"Great."

"Stay on the line."

"Can do," Tricia replied, but she set the phone to mute. "Lock this door and don't let anyone in. In fact, wedge that chair"—she pointed to the seat under the desk—"against the door handle and wait for me to tell you it's safe."

Sheila nodded, still looking terrified.

Tricia pulled the door closed and waited to hear it lock, and the chair being dragged across the floor and shoved under the handle.

"I'll be back as soon as I can," Tricia told her mother before dashing across the hall and stuffing her feet into her slippers. She found David's wallet in his jeans, grabbed them, his discarded socks and shirt from the day before, and his shoes before flying down the mansion's main staircase and heading for the kitchen.

She found David wrapping Sarge in a towel. He laid the limp dog on the counter. Tricia handed him his clothes and stroked the dog's fluffy head. "Poor little guy." He was breathing, which was a good sign.

"The back door was open. Let's hope that means whoever broke in has left the house," David said as he got dressed. Finally, he donned his jacket. "Follow me to the car and open the door," he said.

Tricia nodded and wished she'd thought to don her robe before running down the stairs. The air was chilly—probably in the forties—but Tricia got to David's Jeep and yanked open the passenger side door, letting him settle the unconscious dog onto the seat before shutting it once again.

"Go back in the house," David ordered.

"The cops are on their way," Tricia said.

"Lock yourself in and make sure it's the police before you open the door."

"Will do."

He gave her a quick kiss before she darted inside, locking the door. She watched as he jumped in the Jeep, started it, turned on the headlights, and pulled out of the manor's small back lot.

Tricia's heart sank, worried about how she could ever explain what had happened to her sister. She eyed the clock. It was just after two. There was no sense in waking up Angelica when they didn't know if the pup would make it.

That was wrong thinking. Sarge *would* be okay. He *had* to be.

Tricia realized she was dressed in only a nightshirt and decided she'd better grab her robe before the police showed up. But it was too late. The officer hadn't used the vehicle's siren, but she could already see the flashing lights and grabbed her jacket from the peg, wishing it was longer, and hurried to open the front door.

And wondered what would happen next.

NINETEEN

 David arrived back at Stonecreek Manor around eight that morning. He'd already texted that he was on the way and had a buddy riding shotgun. Tricia hurried out to meet the Jeep. Once the vehicle came to a complete halt, she wrenched open the door and Sarge jumped up, happy to see her. She picked him up and he went crazy licking her face and yipping happily.

"So, what do you think about the little guy?" David asked, rounding the front of the Jeep to join Tricia.

"He seems as good as new," Tricia said, still being smothered in canine kisses.

"The vet said he should be good to go. No one would even know he was drugged a few hours ago. Maybe you shouldn't even mention it to Angelica."

"Oh, no," Tricia said firmly. "I have to tell her. She's going to be extremely upset, but I'd rather have her upset with me now than risk her wrath if she finds out later. It would be a terrible breach of trust."

David nodded, walking a step behind Tricia as they entered the house.

She set the dog on the kitchen floor and he trotted over to his food bowl and looked at her hopefully.

"He really must be on the mend if he wants to eat." Angelica had packed a breakfast of cooked chicken, rice, and green beans for her boy, and Tricia retrieved it from the fridge. But first, she rinsed Sarge's bowl before she dumped the food into it and put it in the microwave for a few seconds to warm, testing its temperature with her pinkie before serving it to the little guy.

They watched Sarge eat for long seconds before David spoke again. "And how did things go with your mother after I left?"

Before Tricia could answer the question, the kitchen door handle rattled and Angelica came into the kitchen. "Morning!" she sang. Sarge immediately abandoned his breakfast and was ecstatic, jumping up and down, eager for his dog mom to pick him up. Shoving a bulging brown paper bag in Tricia's direction, Angelica scooped up Sarge. "Did my little man miss his mama?" she asked in baby talk.

"Oh, yeah," Tricia said.

"Well, his mama missed him, too," Angelica said, giving his head a kiss. She endured a few more doggy kisses before setting Sarge back on the floor. "Mama has work to do, baby boy. We'll play later." She turned her attention to Tricia. "I got up early and made some jumbo blueberry muffins. I thought you guys might be hungry." She didn't wait for a reply and went straight for the coffeemaker. "Did you sleep in late?" she asked, and took the carafe to the sink to fill it.

"Um. Not really," Tricia said.

"Did everything go well?" Angelica asked, and pulled out a fresh filter and a container of coffee.

"Um, we had a couple of little snags," Tricia admitted.

A Perilous Plot

"Yeah, really just too minor to even mention," David said. "Um, I need to go upstairs and, uh, you know—get ready for the day."

Chicken, Tricia mouthed.

Angelica eyed his jacketed form. "Oh, well, hurry back. You don't want the coffee to get cold."

"No, I sure don't," David said, and quickly escaped the kitchen.

Angelica finished her task and finally took off her jacket, hanging it up on a peg. She turned toward her sister, studying her face. "Boy, you look tired. Didn't you sleep well? Was the mattress too hard?"

"Um, no."

Angelica frowned, looking perturbed. "There's an awful lot of *umming* going on. Did something happen I should know about?"

"Uh, yes," Tricia admitted, not knowing how to start. "Maybe we should wait for the coffee and sit down before I explain."

"And maybe you should just stop stalling and tell me what's wrong."

Tricia knew that tone. She took a deep breath before replying. "We had a break-in last night," she said simply.

Angelica's jaw dropped. "What?"

"Well, it wasn't exactly a break-in because no windows were broken and no doors were forced. The lights went out and then Sheila screamed."

Angelica's eyes widened.

"Apparently someone tried to strangle her."

Angelica's eyes were now bulging.

"Not only that but . . . whoever got in, cut the power. But before they made it upstairs, they sort of . . . drugged Sarge."

Horrified, Angelica stooped to grab the little dog at her heels, clutching him to her chest. "Oh, my darling boy, are you all right?"

"He's fine. Now. Um . . . David wrapped him in a towel and rushed him to the emergency vet in Nashua. They only returned just before you arrived."

Sarge rewarded his human mom by giving her more frenetic kisses.

Angelica burst into tears.

Interesting, Tricia thought, that someone trying to kill their mother hadn't had as great an impact as the threat to Angelica's dog, but for some reason, Tricia couldn't blame her sister for her reaction.

"He's okay," Tricia assured her sister. "David can tell you what the vet said when he comes downstairs."

"I want to know everything—and in minute detail," Angelica grated.

Tricia nodded. She contained her recitation of the night's events with how the power went out, about Sheila screaming, bumping into the would-be killer, David's dash out the door with Sarge, and the police arriving to find the intruder was long gone, and everything under control. Angelica listened without comment until Tricia finished her recitation.

"Did Mother have any idea who tried to kill her?"

Tricia shook her head. "It was pitch black—I can attest to that. I didn't see who knocked me over."

Angelica chewed her bottom lip. "Whoever it was knew where to find the circuit breaker."

"That hadn't escaped me," Tricia admitted. "Perhaps someone who worked on the restoration?"

Angelica scowled. "Maybe. But if it was the squatter, that person had plenty of time when the house was unoccupied to scope things out."

"Do you think it was Daddy?"

"He's my prime suspect."

"And what about Uncle Leo?" Tricia asked.

"Another suspect." Angelica let out a breath. "Where was Cleo during all this?"

A Perilous Plot

Tricia blinked. She hadn't given a thought to the innkeeper. "She never showed up."

"Did the police make a lot of noise—sirens and such?" Angelica asked.

"No, but their strobing lights sure lit up the street."

Angelica nodded with a bland expression.

"I suppose there are blackout curtains in the carriage house," Tricia mused.

"In the bedroom."

"Perhaps she just slept through all the trouble."

"Perhaps," Angelica said neutrally, but Tricia had a feeling Cleo was going to be interrogated by Nigela Ricita at Angelica's earliest convenience.

Tricia abandoned that subject and moved on. "I'll speak to Ian later this morning. How soon is that security upgrade going to be made?"

"Not before midweek. But money talks. I'll get Antonio on it right away." Angelica wiped her tears, still holding on to her dog, who had settled comfortably in her arms, gently licking her hand. "And how is Mother this morning?" Angelica finally asked.

"She hadn't emerged when I finally gave up on sleep and came downstairs a couple of hours ago. I'm not sure she's going to want to stay here tonight."

Angelica sighed. "The only option she has left is my place."

"You could put her up in a hotel," Tricia suggested, wondering if the county jail might have an empty cell. At least there Sheila would be safe—at least from whoever was trying to kill her.

"Without an armed guard standing outside her door, it wouldn't be safe."

"And do you want that kind of trouble knocking on *your* door?" Tricia asked.

Angelica seemed to ponder the question. "Not really. Do you have any better suggestions?"

Unfortunately, Tricia did not.

It was nearly ten o'clock when Tricia got to her store. Her first priority was to connect with her cat, who demanded to be picked up and purred louder than a motorboat. She rubbed her head against Tricia's chin, marking her, as though to say *You belong to me*.

Tricia glanced at the clock. There was no time to bake cookies for Mr. Everett or her customers. It would be a lean day for extras at Haven't Got a Clue.

Mr. Everett arrived just minutes before opening. "Hello, Ms. Miles. I wasn't expecting to see you here this morning."

"I had a change of plans."

Mr. Everett scrutinized her face. "And how are you today?"

"We can talk about that in a while, but first, let's make a pot of coffee."

Mr. Everett's expression darkened. He was a happy soul at heart. Unhappy news tended to weigh on his soul.

Once they were seated in the reader's nook, Tricia explained what had transpired the night before.

"I'm so sorry. Your sister must have been beside herself at the threat to not only her mother but sweet little Sarge."

"She was," Tricia said, not confiding where most of Angelica's concern lay. She then told him about the attic contents and how their family group planned to go through the contents the next morning and afternoon. She asked if he'd mind missing out on the "fun" and minding the store.

Mr. Everett frowned. "May I say that I don't envy the task and

A Perilous Plot

would prefer to spend the day here with Miss Marple, taking care of customers and, if there's time, reading in peace."

Tricia suppressed a smile. "I thought as much. Thank you."

Mr. Everett arched an eyebrow. "And what treasure do you think you'll find?"

Tricia shook her head. "I don't think I'll find anything that particularly interests me, but I'd be happy if Pixie and David found items that allowed them to experience the thrill of the hunt. Often, David will return from his Sunday thrifting with Pixie with nothing to show for it but a big smile. Those two get along like two peas in a pod."

Mr. Everett nodded. "Grace and I are fond of them both." That was high praise coming from such a reticent man.

They finished their coffee just as the first customer of the day entered the shop. Mr. Everett stood to greet the woman, politely telling her to ask for help if she needed it.

Tricia's ringtone sounded. She checked her phone to see that it was Angelica calling. "Hang on," she told her sister, and mouthed to Mr. Everett that she would take the call down in the shop's basement office, then left to head there.

"Okay, I'm back. How did things go with Sheila after I left the inn this morning?"

"Swimmingly," Angelica deadpanned.

"So, what did you guys decide about where she's going to stay next?"

"It looks like I'll be stuck with her." And from the tone of her voice, Angelica was distinctly unhappy about the situation.

"Did you have a conversation with Cleo about why she didn't know anything about the break-in?"

Tricia could imagine her sister's eyes blazing. "She said she's a heavy sleeper."

"Did you believe her?"

"Well, I can hardly prove her wrong, can I?"

Tricia decided not to press the issue. "Anything else?"

"Artemus called."

Tricia's jaw dropped. "So soon?"

"He found the FedEx package on his doorstep this morning, made a pot of coffee, and devoured Ian's book."

"And, and?" Tricia prodded, almost dreading the answer.

"He *loved* it."

Tricia's heart swelled. "Does he think he can sell it?"

"It won't be a blockbuster, but he thinks it will quickly find a publisher and it should do well."

"Has he got any houses in mind?"

"He might even put it up for auction," Angelica said.

Tricia couldn't help but grin. "Wow."

"Yes. Now all he has to do is speak to Ian about it. The thing is . . . I think you should break the news to him first."

"Me? But Artemus is your agent."

"Yes, but Ian trusted the manuscript to *you*. He doesn't even know I read it, let alone Artemus."

Tricia couldn't help but cringe. "Yeah, that could be a sticky subject," she agreed. "But I can't see how he'd be angry. I mean, sometimes it takes years to find an agent to rep a manuscript, let alone sell it."

"It hasn't sold yet," Angelica reminded Tricia.

"Should we wait to tell him?"

"No. Artemus can't move forward presenting it to potential publishers without Ian's permission—and a signed contract."

"When do you want me to speak to him?"

"As soon as you can—that is, if you can track him down."

"It shouldn't be hard. He *is* on duty today—at least, as far as I know. I think this kind of news should be delivered in person."

"Agreed."

Tricia considered their next topic of conversation. "What did you think of Pixie's theory about Mother's injury?" Tricia reminded her sister of the scene in the Dick Francis mystery.

"I can't imagine Mother approving of something like that," Angelica said, sounding doubtful.

"Who says the perpetrator asked her?"

Angelica didn't comment.

"This whole situation doesn't make sense," Tricia remarked. "I still can't fathom what Sheila and Daddy were thinking. Daddy didn't have any problem asking you for financial help in the past. Why not ask now?"

"We may have had a discussion about that some time ago," Angelica admitted.

Tricia raised an eyebrow. "And how was that received?"

"Not well," Angelica said tersely. "It may have been me who suggested they sell the house in Rio. I mean, they hadn't lived there in a couple of years. Of course, I never for a minute thought they'd sell the flat in London—especially without asking us about it first."

"Did you happen to mention that to Daddy at the time?" Tricia asked.

"Yes."

If John Miles had protested the sale, his wife obviously ignored his objections. "Sheila is perfectly capable of doing—and saying—things out of spite."

"Yeah," Angelica reluctantly agreed. "But both of those properties would have brought them a considerable amount of cash. Where did it go?"

Tricia scowled. "That's a good question."

Leaving Mr. Everett in charge of Haven't Got a Clue, Tricia stopped by the Cookery to retrieve McDonald's manuscript. Pages in hand,

Tricia crossed the street at the crosswalk and headed toward the Stoneham police station, her thoughts awhirl. How was she going to broach the subject? Just blurt out how she'd allowed others to read the manuscript, which might upset the chief? Then again, the happy news that an agent loved the book and was confident he could sell it *should* negate any anger the chief might feel.

Maybe.

Oh, don't be such a worrywart, Tricia chided herself and picked up her speed, determined to present her news with hope and cheer.

Tricia entered the station. As usual, Polly was behind her desk, but unlike the previous time Tricia had encountered the woman, Polly didn't seem as depressed. "What can we do for you today, Tricia?"

"I'd like to speak to Chief McDonald."

"Official business?" Polly asked. Was she going to revert to type and deny Tricia access to the village's top cop?

"Uh, no."

Polly's eyes widened and she waggled her eyebrows. "Something about the wedding?" Had McDonald mentioned that Becca had asked Tricia to be their maid of honor?

"Sort of," Tricia hedged. She was sure the subject would probably arise, especially if she brought it up, so then her answer wouldn't be an out-and-out lie.

Polly touched the intercom key. "Tricia Miles here to see you, Chief."

"Send her in."

Polly waved a hand in the direction of McDonald's office. "Go right in."

Tricia smiled. "Thanks."

"My pleasure," Polly said sweetly.

Tricia stepped over to the door and knocked.

A Perilous Plot

"Come in."

Tricia turned the handle and entered. McDonald stood. "I was wondering when you'd stop by. I heard all about what happened at Stonecreek Manor last night."

Come to think of it, Tricia wondered why McDonald hadn't shown up in person. He always had in the past. Perhaps he'd been otherwise occupied . . . probably with Becca.

It wasn't her business.

"I assume you'd like an update on your mother's case."

"Yes," she said eagerly.

McDonald waited for her to take a seat before resuming his own. "Unfortunately," he began gravely, "there isn't much to tell. We haven't found a weapon, and our APB on your father hasn't so far been successful. It's only been a couple of days. These things take time."

Tricia nodded. "I wanted to let you know that the contents of Stonecreek Manor's attic were moved and a crew of volunteers will be going through the boxes. I highly doubt there'll be anything to help in your investigation. We're primarily looking for documentation to help restore the mansion's gardens."

"I hope you find it. We have a lot of beautiful public gardens in Ireland. I miss visiting them."

"I've seen pictures of the mansion's grounds. They were pretty spectacular a century and a half ago."

McDonald nodded. "My bride will be returning to the manor sometime today. It seems the best venue she's checked out so far."

From the way he spoke, it was obvious McDonald didn't know it was Tricia who'd suggested the site. "That's lovely. You've seen it for yourself, so you can vouch for the place."

"I've seen it—and not under the best of circumstances. Becca doesn't know there've been two murders and a violent assault there in the last six months. That might taint her assessment."

"Are you going to tell her?" Tricia asked.

"If the innkeeper doesn't, yes."

Well, easy come, easy go for that booking. Still, knowing Becca could be difficult, Tricia was sure not many tears would be shed over her picking another venue.

"There's another reason for my visit here today," Tricia began.

"I figured as much," McDonald said, eyeing the familiar envelope. Tricia handed it to him and McDonald schooled his features, as though expecting the worst. "And?"

"I thought it was marvelous," Tricia said, smiling.

McDonald showed no emotion, but she could see him visibly relax—if only a little.

"I'm pleased to hear that."

"I thought it was so good," Tricia continued, "that I let my sister read it."

McDonald's lips pursed. He was not pleased.

"She thought it was so good, she sent a copy of it overnight to her literary agent."

McDonald's eyes widened, surprise replacing annoyance, but he said nothing.

"Her agent thought it was so good, he'd like to represent you and it. He thinks he can sell it—and quickly."

McDonald stared at her blankly for long seconds.

"Ian?"

McDonald still said nothing.

"Are you okay?" Tricia asked, concerned.

Finally, McDonald let out a breath. "I'm—I'm gobsmacked."

"So you aren't angry with me?"

"Angry? If I weren't an engaged man, I'd kiss you."

"Then I guess it would be okay if the agent—his name is Artemus Hamilton—contacts you?"

A Perilous Plot

"Yes, yes! Of course." And then McDonald laughed—a real belly whopper. "I can't believe it. How can I thank you and your sister?"

"Despite it not being a mystery or a cookbook, you could do a signing at either of our stores."

"I'd love to."

"Because so many Chamber members and their families went on that memorable cruise on the *Celtic Lady*, I'm sure we could give you a great reception."

It was rare that McDonald showed much in the way of emotion, so it was apparent he was overcome by it. "Thank you. Thank you so much."

"You've got a lot of exciting plans to make," Tricia said.

Suddenly, McDonald looked confused. "What do you mean?"

"Talking to booksellers, traveling to promote the book—possibly on cruise lines, although probably not the Celtic line. They may not like one of their own spilling the tea about what goes on belowdecks."

Her words seemed to hit him like a sucker punch. "I hadn't considered that when I wrote down my anecdotes."

"Of course, you could release it under a pseudonym, but without that personal pitch, it might not do as well. And you *want* it to do well to earn back your advance, which could be quite substantial if I'm any judge of what sells."

The joy McDonald might have felt moments before seemed to seep out of him. He frowned. "You've given me a lot to think about."

Tricia decided to ask a brutal question. "Have you got more stories to fill a sequel?"

"Yeah," he muttered.

"Wonderful." Then she sensed his pleasure had turned to concern. "These are the kinds of questions Artemus is going to ask you."

"Thanks for the warning."

Warning? Such a descriptor meant harm, not a heads-up. What had Ian expected when he'd written the manuscript, let alone asked

Tricia to have a look at it? By putting it in front of Angelica—and Angelica showing it to her agent—Tricia had potentially saved Ian years of frustration. Apparently, he had no idea how difficult—and often heartbreaking—the journey could be to become an author with a big-name publishing house. Of course, he hadn't yet been offered a contract, but Artemus Hamilton had impeccable credentials and he never took on an author if he didn't think he could propel them to a bestsellers list.

Tricia decided to bite her tongue. She hadn't wanted the responsibility of reading the manuscript and had done it in the spirit of friendship. Would McDonald appreciate her efforts or now condemn her for them?

Tricia stood. "I'd best be getting back to my store."

McDonald didn't object.

"You'll probably hear from Artemus in the next day or so."

"I'll look forward to it," McDonald said, the enthusiasm gone from his tone.

"We'll talk soon," Tricia said.

"Sure."

Tricia left the office, closing the door behind her.

"Get everything you needed?" Polly asked, sounding mildly curious.

"Oh yeah."

"Have a good afternoon."

"You, too," Tricia said and headed for the exit.

The sidewalk was devoid of other pedestrians as Tricia made her way back to Haven't Got a Clue. There'd been a spring in her step on her way to the police station; now she plodded along.

How had her good news so quickly turned sour?

TWENTY

 While there wasn't a steady stream of patrons, Tricia and Mr. Everett found enough to keep them busy until Mr. Everett's lunch break. During her alone time—and without a customer in sight—Tricia had a lot of time to think about what had gone on in the past and how it might relate to the present situation. At least part of the situation. When Mr. Everett returned, it was Tricia's turn for sustenance and she hurried across the street to meet Angelica at Booked for Lunch.

It was a pretty good crowd for a day in late April, but nothing like during high tourist season. Tricia made her way to the back of the café and took her usual seat across from her sister. Angelica looked up from her phone. "Hi."

"Hi yourself."

Marcie, the weekend server, arrived with a coffee carafe in hand and filled their waiting cups. "Have you decided on what you want?"

"What are the specials?" Tricia asked.

Marcie dutifully recited them and the sisters ordered: a patty melt and fries for Angelica and fish tacos for Tricia.

"Did you speak to Mr. Everett about the unboxing tomorrow?" Angelica asked once Marcie departed to put in their orders.

"Yes. He's content to spend a quiet day at Haven't Got a Clue with Miss Marple."

"Perhaps the idea of all the dust that's sure to come from those boxes was a deterrent as well. We're all going to be filthy by the time we finish going through them."

"Maybe we should take a break for the last hour so everyone can go home and shower and then come back."

"If I left to shower, I'd probably never return. No, I think we'll have an early dinner and go with a picnic theme. It'll just be easier."

Tricia nodded. Speaking about food gave her the perfect opening for her next line of subject matter.

"Remember when Daddy visited three summers ago and cleaned out Booked for Lunch's fridge?"

"You mean *stole* hundreds of dollars' worth of cold cuts and cheese and then just threw them in a dumpster when he couldn't convince Fred Pillins to sell them for him?" Angelica grated.

Tricia nodded. "What if he's the one responsible for the missing food at Stonecreek Manor?"

Angelica looked skeptical. "How is he getting inside? The place is locked. The security system is in use . . ."

"As I mentioned this morning, no windows were broken and no doors forced. Someone has a key."

Angelica's eyes widened. She'd been so concerned about Sarge's welfare that she apparently hadn't taken in that information. "So, some food has gone missing. What would the intruder do with a pound of bacon here, and some frozen dough there? We're talking raw food. Where would he go to cook it?"

A Perilous Plot

Tricia's brow furrowed as she thought about the problem for a moment. "What about the Bookshelf Diner?"

"What about it?"

"It's been empty for months. Could Daddy—or someone else—be squatting there?"

Angelica looked skeptical.

"I mean, you've only owned it for a few days. You haven't even done a walk-through since you were handed the keys, right?"

"With everything that's happened, I haven't had time," Angelica remarked.

"Maybe we ought to make time to visit it."

Angelica's frown deepened. "There're no utilities. They were shut off months ago. How would the intruder cook? Where would he sleep? Good grief, there's no water on. How would he flush the toilet?"

Tricia grimaced. She wasn't sure she wanted to know the answer to that question.

Angelica sighed and her shoulders slumped. "I suppose we ought to go look."

"And bring reinforcements?" Tricia suggested.

Angelica blinked several times. "Why? Do you think Daddy would shoot us or something?"

"I'm not sure what to expect from our father. He's definitely not the man we thought he was while we were growing up."

"Neither was our mother," Angelica muttered. "How did we grow up to be so sane when our parents are so flawed?"

That was a no-brainer. "Grandma Miles." Their paternal grandmother had been the one grounding presence in their lives. And, in retrospect, she'd been around only when their father was absent—in jail—and their mother had absconded for months, and at one time for more than a year. Grandma Miles had fed the girls, sent them to school on time, and kept in order the beautiful home they resided in.

And once their parents reappeared, just as suddenly as they'd exited from their lives—much to their sorrow, Grandma Miles was gone.

"Let's finish our lunch and visit the diner," Tricia suggested.

"If you insist," Angelica said, "but I think we'd just be wasting our time."

"And if we find Daddy there?" Tricia asked.

Angelica glowered. "I just might kill him."

TWENTY-ONE

When Tricia and Angelica approached the old Bookshelf Diner, nothing looked amiss through the restaurant's large (and very dirty) front picture window. It seemed as though time had stood still during the months the eatery had been closed, from the empty coffee cups on the table in front to the out-of-date month of the calendar behind the register. Circling around to the alley, the sisters found a different story. The back door had obviously been kicked in and was now secured with a bungee cord. Why hadn't anyone from the neighboring businesses noticed—and reported—the break-in?

"We should call the police for backup," Tricia said somberly.

"On Daddy?"

"We don't know he's the one who broke in."

"You seemed pretty confident about it not half an hour ago," Angelica remarked.

That confidence had waned upon seeing the splintered doorjamb. Angelica gave her sister a nudge. "Go on."

"Go on what?"

"Go on inside."

"You go first," Tricia said, taking umbrage. "It's *your* restaurant."

Angelica glowered, yanked the bungee cord loose, and flung open the door. Before she stepped inside, however, she activated the flashlight on her phone. Tricia did likewise and followed her sister into the diner's darkened kitchen. The grill hadn't been cleaned before the place shut down, and there was evidence of mice having taken up residence. What was also in evidence was a small, rusty charcoal grill that was situated not far inside. "What the?" Angelica said with a gasp.

"What?" Tricia asked.

"Someone has been using the grill *inside* the restaurant."

Tricia blinked, not understanding.

"Carbon monoxide," Angelica explained. "Under no circumstances should anyone use a charcoal grill in an unventilated space like this."

Since their father's body wasn't lying dead on the floor, Angelica's dire prediction hadn't (yet) taken place. Or had John Miles simply opened the door when he'd cook on the grill?

Looking around the dirty kitchen, they saw other examples of recent habitation: discarded water bottles, food wrappers—like the missing bacon package and other items missing from Stonecreek Manor.

The sisters ventured farther into the building and found that the restaurant's office sported an old leather couch that had seen happier days. On it was a ratty old blanket and a disgusting sweat-stained pillow. Was that where their father laid his head at night for who knew how many days—or weeks?

"What are we going to do?" Angelica asked, her voice an anguished hush.

"I don't know," Tricia said, reluctant to voice the fear that gripped her heart. "Our parents are obviously in over their heads. If Sheila does have her wits about her, she isn't willing to level with us; and

A Perilous Plot

with Daddy hiding from us, there's nothing we can do to help him get out of whatever situation he's in."

Angelica nodded, her expression grim. Then she seemed to shake herself and became all business. "The first thing I need to do is secure the building."

"And shut Daddy out?" Tricia asked.

"Yes," she said with determination. "It's what I should have done the day we closed on the deal. I'll speak to Antonio about getting the power back on and a security system installed."

"And then what?"

"We'll see," was all Angelica could offer. Next, she took out a notebook and pen from her purse and began to take notes, muttering to herself as she walked around the empty restaurant. Tricia caught snippets. New point-of-sale computer system. Reupholster banquettes. Rip out carpet; replace. Angelica took even more notes when they returned to the kitchen. Whoever she hired to man the grill would be working with a spanking brand-new setup. And if Tricia knew her sister, it would all happen extremely fast.

Next, she listened as Angelica contacted a company known for securing buildings after a fire—the same one that had come to board up Tricia's building several years ago. They were used to delivering fast turnaround times and promised to be there within four hours. Four. Long. Hours. That meant if there was no one available to guard the site, John Miles—or whoever else was using the building as a place to squat—could come back and resume residency.

That wasn't about to happen on Angelica's watch.

Tricia leaned against the side of the building as she watched her sister become the almighty Nigela Ricita and speak with Antonio to arrange for the Brookview's security team to come and secure the building.

"I feel bad that Antonio has to give up his day off to take care of the situation," Tricia said.

"These are extraordinary circumstances," Angelica asserted.

Tricia was reminded of one of their previous conversations. "You need to talk to Antonio about revealing all—and soon. He goes above and beyond what anyone should do to make NR Associates work."

"He's part-owner," Angelica reminded her sister.

"Yes, but he has a family."

Angelica stopped dead on the sidewalk. "He's a man."

"Yes," Tricia agreed to the obvious.

"Tell me that you, as a childless cat woman, never had to work more than your fair share of hours because someone else had a family and pulled that card to screw you out of time off, or was forced to work overtime because *you don't have a family.*"

Tricia couldn't refute that. From the first job she'd ever held to the very last when she was the head of a very important and powerful nonprofit organization, she'd always had to work harder, smarter, and longer than anyone else—especially a man.

"But he's your son," Tricia insisted.

"When we're on the clock, he's my partner. I don't ask him to do more than I do myself."

Tricia nodded. What she said made sense. But making sense didn't always feel good. And yet . . . how many holidays had she toiled while others got to enjoy their time off, all because what life had handed her didn't include offspring?

Life isn't fair, Tricia thought.

And had she ever thought it would be?

The sisters hung around until Antonio arrived, along with the same Brookview maintenance guys who'd moved the boxes earlier in the day, and they secured the premises. Angelica gave no orders until the men were out of earshot, and then she and Antonio discussed what else needed to be done to keep the building squatter-free.

"The security company will be sending NR Associates a very large bill," Antonio predicted.

Angelica nodded. "If that's what it takes."

Antonio pulled out his phone and stepped aside to make a call.

"What's next on your agenda?" Tricia asked her sister.

Angelica looked at her watch. "I was supposed to meet Ginny twenty minutes ago at the manor to make sure everything is set up for the shakedown tonight."

"Shouldn't that be Cleo's worry?"

"So far, I'm not at all impressed with her—or her work ethic. I'd hate for the manor to get a bad review from the Brookview staff, but it might give me the out I need to replace Cleo. That would just be one more slot to fill when it comes to hiring personnel."

"Well, good luck with that," Tricia said.

"The bigger challenge will be to collect Mother from Stonecreek and bring her to my place. Somehow, I think I might have to drag her out of the manor kicking and screaming."

"I wish I could help with the former, but not the latter. The thing is, I feel guilty having left Mr. Everett alone for so much of the day—and all of tomorrow."

"If he'd had a problem, he would have called or texted you. I'm sure he's fine," Angelica said reasonably.

"You're right, of course," Tricia said. She looked down the alley toward Hickory Street. "I'm heading for my store, then. See you tonight at your place?"

Angelica nodded and sighed. "Now to figure out something to feed Mother and hope she won't complain *too* much."

No sooner had Tricia greeted Mr. Everett and hung up her jacket than the little bell over the door at Haven't Got a Clue rang. But instead of a customer, it was Becca Dickson-Chandler, looking like she'd stepped out of the pages of *Vogue*. Was she going to some kind of fancy party that afternoon?

"Tricia, Tricia, Tricia," she said by way of a greeting, sounding exhausted.

"What's up?" Tricia asked, tying her shop apron over her clothes.

"That inn you sent me to . . ." Becca began, her gaze dipping to the new carpet—not that she'd notice.

"I'm sorry you didn't care for it."

"Oh, I liked it. I'm just disappointed that it's not *finished*."

"Well, of course it's not. It won't open until next month. In fact, they're going to have a soft opening in a couple of weeks after they've done a shakedown and hired staff. But what does that matter since you said you weren't tying the knot until the fall?"

Becca sighed, looking desolate. "That's true."

"I'm sure by then it'll be up to your very high standards."

"They *are* high," Becca agreed. "And the Brookview Inn is very nice. As the Stonecreek is owned by the same people, I'm sure it'll be fine." Her gaze narrowed. "Eventually."

Tricia had no patience to spar with Becca. "Well, I'm sure you have lots of other venues to check out between now and the fall."

"That's the problem. I have to find something soon because things are either already booked a year in advance, or closing out their dates for early autumn—and I have my heart set on a September wedding date," Becca simpered.

Tricia was in no mood to be a cheerleader to bolster Becca's lack of reasonableness. Instead, she changed the subject. "What did you think about Ian's big news?"

Becca blinked. "News?"

Tricia cringed. *Uh-oh!* "He didn't mention it to you?"

A Perilous Plot

Becca's expression hardened. She did not like being kept in the dark about anything. "It depends on what you mean."

"I . . . I should probably let him tell you all about it. I wouldn't want to spoil the surprise." And why hadn't Ian told her about the possibility of his book being sold? Did Becca even know he'd written a book—or hadn't he wanted to take the chance of upstaging her?

Tricia thought fast, desperate to change the subject. "My mother's in town."

"How nice," Becca said, sounding bored.

"Yes. Apparently, she's a big fan of yours. She met you briefly at your wedding to Gene and saw you compete several times. She's dying to speak to you."

"Yes, well, so are thousands of others."

Ooh! That stung. "Oh, well. I'll just tell her you're far too busy to speak to someone who cheered you on for years. I'm sure she'll understand."

"I didn't say I *wouldn't* meet her," Becca griped.

Yes, that Becca's reputation around the village was being *difficult* was putting it mildly. She'd found no sycophants in Stoneham and her ego probably needed to be stroked on a regular basis. Tricia was sure her mother was up to the task.

"Would you be willing to have lunch with her and me at the Brookview Inn?"

Becca shrugged. "I'm sure I could pencil her in."

"Great. If you could check your schedule and let me know when you're free, I'm sure it would be the thrill of her life." Especially since Sheila said she had no memory of her former existence.

"Yes, yes, of course." Becca extracted her phone from her purse, pulled up the calendar app, and paged through it. "Would Monday at noon do?"

"Yes, thanks. I'm sure she'll be elated. And, of course, lunch would be on me."

Since Becca regularly stiffed when it came to paying for such things, that was a given. And now it was yet again time for Tricia to change the subject.

"That's a lovely dress you've got on under that raincoat. Are you going to some kind of big occasion?"

"I'm meeting with someone in Nashua for drinks and dinner who may become a new business partner. He wants to meet at an ungodly early hour—probably because of his age. But he seems to have deep pockets, and although my first tennis club isn't quite finished, I'm already seeking out franchisees. It just makes good business sense to think ahead," she said reasonably.

Tricia supposed it did.

"After the last couple of days, I could use some good news."

"Oh?" Tricia asked.

Becca looked chagrined. "A lot of petty inconveniences."

"Like what?" Tricia asked out of politeness.

"Someone threw a rock at my car—cracked the windshield. It was lucky I didn't crash."

Tricia frowned. "Anything else?"

"Just some overturned pots on my balcony. I wouldn't have thought the wind was strong enough to do that."

"Is that all?"

Becca looked thoughtful. "Trespassers at the tennis club construction site—but that's nothing new. More than once, we've caught teenage boys trying to get in and vandalize the place."

"Have you reported any of these things to Ian?" Tricia asked, concerned.

"He has his officers drive by the site on a regular basis. They're good at chasing away anyone they find lurking around."

Tricia nodded.

Becca looked at her watch. "I suppose I should hit the road."

"Ian's not going with you?" Tricia asked.

"Why would he? The meeting is *my* business."

And if that were the case, then perhaps not keeping him in the loop was why Ian hadn't mentioned a potential book deal to his soon-to-be life partner.

Tricia gave herself a mental shake. A couple keeping secrets so early in their relationship did not bode well for the health and length of such a partnership. Tricia felt sorry for Ian. If the couple parted, she had no doubt Becca would soon find another someone to warm her bed, if not her heart.

"I'll probably want a second walk-through of Stonecreek Manor—after they pull their act together," Becca said, and brushed a hand across the shoulder of her coat, as though standing in a lowly retail establishment had caused her clothes to accumulate dust—or maybe something worse: cooties!

"We'll talk again soon," Becca said—or was it a threat? Tricia wasn't sure.

"Have a great evening," Tricia said as Becca turned and made her way to the exit, throwing a good-bye wave over her shoulder.

Once the door closed behind Becca, Mr. Everett wandered up to the cash desk, looking pensive. He'd probably heard the whole conversation. He looked like he wanted to say something, but his determination to always remain neutral ruled him.

Tricia decided to test his resolve. "What did you make of my conversation with Becca?"

"I wasn't trying to eavesdrop," Mr. Everett defended himself.

"You couldn't help but hear," Tricia said.

Mr. Everett nodded and let out a breath. "Despite all the accolades that woman has received, I think she must be a very lonely person who needs constant attention to bolster her insecurities. The same could be said about a lot of celebrities."

Mr. Everett, who'd lived his entire life in a small village, had a great understanding of the world at large.

"I think you're right. Becca has asked me to be her maid of honor, and though I've begged off, she doesn't want to take no for an answer. Although we met almost two years ago, we've never really bonded as friends. I suggested to her that someone from her life before she came to Stoneham might be better suited for the job, but she insists it be me."

"And you don't feel comfortable in that role?"

"Not at all," Tricia answered. "I'd feel better standing up for her groom as his best woman, but in the end . . . I don't see this wedding ever taking place. They're just too different."

"Sometimes we have to let people make their own mistakes," Mr. Everett said.

"I agree. But when you can already see the messy aftermath, it's hard. Because at some point, I'm going to have to choose between the two of them, and the other is going to be terribly angry *and* offended."

"You couldn't be neutral?" Mr. Everett asked.

Tricia considered the question. "It would be difficult."

The older gentleman nodded. "I see your dilemma."

Tricia straightened, not content to dwell on that mess. She had too many others that topped her list of concerns.

It was yet another quiet afternoon at Haven't Got a Clue. Several customers came and went, generating modest sales—which wasn't unexpected at that time of year. In between, Tricia and Mr. Everett caught up on some of the daily chores. Finally, Tricia glanced at the clock. It was almost closing time. How had the day gotten away from her?

"So, you're good to go about opening the shop tomorrow?"

"I'll be here at noon. Grace will drop me off, but I will need a ride to Ginny's place for dinner."

Why Mr. Everett and Grace—who were not short of funds—shared one vehicle was beyond Tricia's scope. Maybe it had to do with using fossil fuels. Who knew? "One of us—perhaps David—will pick you up at closing. No way do we want you to miss out on dinner."

Mr. Everett ducked his head. "I must admit, our Sunday evenings are the highlight of my week. Grace feels the same way."

His words warmed Tricia's heart. "Mine, too."

They shared a sweet smile before Mr. Everett once again became all business. "Grace said she's happy to help out with the unboxing tomorrow. Do you think you'll find anything of note?"

Tricia shrugged. "Maybe, maybe not. But if nothing else, we should have a fun day of bonding. I'm just sorry you won't be there to join us."

Mr. Everett shook his head. "That sort of thing isn't my cup of tea. But I will be happy to join you all at dinnertime, and especially to spend time with the little tykes."

And Sofia was always ecstatic about spending time with her Papa. "Have you got any plans for this evening?"

Mr. Everett blushed. "It's date night. Grace and I are going out to dinner at the Brookview Inn. We do it once a month. Other times we cook together or stream an old movie. Last week we streamed *The Philadelphia Story* with Jimmy Stewart. A crackerjack of a film."

Tricia had watched it as a child with her grandmother. Those were the best times of her childhood, snuggled under a quilt, Tricia on one side and Angelica on the other. They made a Grandma sandwich, with a big bowl of buttered popcorn on their grandmother's lap that the three of them shared, and Tricia was allowed to eat as much as she wanted without fear of being fat-shamed. Yes, the best of times.

"Keep me posted on your next movie choices. I think watching them could be something David and I would enjoy on our date nights, too."

"I'll do that." Mr. Everett looked at the clock. "Time to close for the day."

As if on cue, the Everetts' car, with Grace at the wheel, pulled up to the curb outside of Haven't Got a Clue.

"Have a great evening and give Grace my love," Tricia said.

"I will," Mr. Everett replied, and said good night before heading out the door.

Tricia stood in front of the plate glass and waved to Grace, who waved back and blew a kiss, the gesture warming Tricia's heart once again. What she wouldn't give to have had parents like Grace and Mr. Everett. But that evening she had to face her own mother.

Her warm heart turned cold at the thought.

Sometimes life just sucked.

TWENTY-TWO

  Tricia ascended the stairs to Angelica's apartment with a heavy heart. That Sarge's joyful barking didn't announce her presence seemed completely unnatural. Tricia knocked on the door. "It's me," she called.

Still no barking.

"The door's open," Angelica called.

Tricia turned the handle and crept into the apartment. Still no Sarge.

She hung up her jacket and ventured into the kitchen. "Is everything all right?"

"What do you mean?"

"Where's Sarge?"

Angelica nodded toward the little dog bed and the canine who rested his head on the pillowed edge. "He's sulking."

"Why?"

Angelica nodded toward the ceiling. "We have company and he doesn't approve," she said simply.

Neither did Tricia. She grabbed a couple of dog biscuits from the jar on the island's counter, crossed the room, and offered one to the little dog. Sarge lifted his head, ignored the biscuit, but licked her hand in gratitude. "You poor little beast," Tricia said, and crouched down to pet his soft, curly head. "I feel the same way." Tricia resisted the urge to kiss the dog's head, left the biscuits on the side of his bed, and straightened.

Angelica waited for Tricia to join her at the island. The pitcher of martinis was already out, along with the frosted glasses. She quickly poured and held her glass aloft in a toast. "I deserve this."

Tricia lifted hers and they clinked glasses. She hadn't had to put up with Sheila for the better part of the afternoon, but she felt nearly as weary. She glanced down at the evening's snack and frowned. Crudités.

"The dip is made from fat-free Greek yogurt. It's not horrible," Angelica assured her sister.

Tricia might beg to differ.

"I didn't want to give Mother an opportunity to pick on you."

"And what's our dinner to be? Steak and baked potatoes smothered in butter for you and Sheila and a celery stick for me?"

"Don't be ridiculous," Angelica said. "It's celery for all."

Tricia glared at her sister.

"I'm joking. We're all having the same thing."

"Which is?"

Angelica frowned. "A Cobb salad."

Tricia eyed the crystal jar on the counter. "Maybe I'll join Sarge and gnaw on a couple of his dog bones."

"Ha-ha," Angelica said flatly. "Come on, let's go sit in the living room and have a snack. Thanks to fresh herbs, this dip isn't all *that* bad."

A sterling recommendation if Tricia ever heard one.

A Perilous Plot

They brought their drinks and the tray with the veggies and dip to the living room and took their usual seats.

"Did Antonio ever turn over the video footage of Uncle Leo at the Brookview to Chief McDonald?" Tricia asked.

"Yes."

"I don't suppose you asked Sheila what that was about."

Angelica hesitated before answering. "Nobody likes to think of their mother as a—"

"Slut?" Tricia provided.

"That word has more than one meaning," Angelica pointed out. "In the UK, it means a slovenly woman. In the US it means—"

"I know what it means," Tricia cut in.

Angelica looked at her sister with a hooded gaze.

"I assume you haven't confronted Sheila with what we know."

"No," Angelica admitted sheepishly. "It's . . . hard."

No matter how many times their parents had disrespected them, and how they'd abused the sisters' trust, Angelica clung to the hope that things might one day change. She might speak to either of them with snark, but she desperately wanted them to one day be capable of unconditional love.

Tricia knew from bitter experience that that wasn't ever going to happen.

Tricia's gaze traveled to the staircase across the way to the upstairs bedrooms, where Sheila had apparently barricaded herself. As a child, Tricia had often crept from her bed and positioned herself at the top of the stairs to listen to what was going on in the living room down below. (At least when her parents were in residence.) Too many times harsh words were spoken—not that Tricia heard enough to understand what was going on. It was the tone that frightened her. Often, she'd scurried back to bed to have vague nightmares where she was abandoned by the people who were supposed to love her most. But then, when they did leave for months on end, she knew that her sweet grandmother would arrive to take care of her and Angelica. Those times were the happiest. When Grandma Miles was in residence, she and Angelica got along—or at least open warfare didn't break out. Stories were read, cookies baked—and eaten without guilt—and they had fun watching movies like *The Parent Trap*, where twins, separated at birth, had the opportunity to reconnect. The idea had appealed to Tricia. During those times, she liked to pretend that she and Angelica were twins and their one goal was to reunite their parents and be part of a happy family.

How pathetic was that?

Practical matters needed to be discussed.

"What are we going to do with Mother tomorrow morning? Do you want to bring her to Antonio and Ginny's home?"

"What else can we do?"

Tricia nodded. "She isn't going to like it."

"Maybe we can sit her in front of a TV and give her the remote to while away the hours."

"And if she doesn't want to do that?"

"Without a nickel to her name, she can't go anywhere or do anything."

"So, she's basically our prisoner."

"That sounds crass."

"How else would you describe it?" Tricia asked.

Angelica sipped her martini.

"Ahem," came the sound of someone clearing her throat from the stairwell. How long had Sheila been listening to their conversation?

Sheila entered the loft's living room, dressed in a robe and slippers, after apparently having made herself feel truly at home. She eyed their martini glasses. "Am I to be excluded from having a drink with you?"

"You're perfectly welcome to join us," Angelica said, rising. "Vodka martini?"

"With a twist, please," Sheila said.

Please? Tricia had hardly ever heard that word issue from her mother's mouth.

As Angelica started for the kitchen, Tricia waved a hand toward the large sectional. "Come. Sit down."

Sheila did so, but far from where Angelica had perched.

"Are you okay with your room?" Tricia asked.

"I would be if I was a toddler," Sheila groused.

"Is the bed comfortable?" Tricia clarified.

"How would I know? I haven't yet slept on it."

Tricia frowned. "I thought you might have tried it out."

"Well, you thought wrong."

Why do I try? Tricia wondered. She thought about it for a long few seconds before she replied—and after so many years of abuse, she wasn't about to hold back.

"Have you *ever* had a pleasant experience in all your life? Have you ever tried to be a friend to anyone without a thought about how it might enrich you? Have you ever, ever done one kind thing?"

Sheila's eyes widened with anger. "How dare you speak to me like that."

"Why not? You say you have no memory of the past. Why should it bother you?"

Sheila opened her mouth to protest . . . but then backed down. "Where's that drink?" she grated.

Tricia shook her head. At that moment, she felt nothing but contempt for the woman who had birthed her. And, truth be told, it wasn't for the first time.

Angelica arrived on the scene with a stemmed glass and set it before their mother. "I hope you approve."

"We'll see," Sheila said, picking up the glass and taking a sip. She wrinkled her nose. "I've had better."

"When?" Tricia pressed. "As someone with amnesia, how could you tell?"

"Are you always this obnoxious?" Sheila asked.

Tricia proffered her glass in the air. "No. But I think I could get to like it."

Sheila shot daggers at her.

"What were you people talking about when it comes to tomorrow?"

"We have work to do," Angelica said, "and we don't feel it would be safe for you to be here alone."

"Why not?" Sheila asked, her tone grating.

"Because someone has twice tried to kill you. That means you know something that someone doesn't want you to reveal—to us or anyone else."

Sheila seemed to think over that statement. "I appreciate your concern."

Ha! A compliment.

"But"—the older woman continued—"I hardly think it's necessary."

"Unless you want to die, I think you ought to rethink that idea," Angelica offered.

Sheila stared at the drink in her hand. "Dying would not be my first choice."

"Aha!" Angelica quipped. "Then you're coming with us. And we're leaving early in the morning, so you should get a good night's sleep."

"It's not even dark out. Do you expect me to go to bed now?"

Angelica bit her lip, trying to hold on to her patience. Tricia was glad she hadn't had to endure as many hours with their mother as her sister had that day—or during their lives. In that regard, Tricia was the lucky one.

"Anything interesting happen this afternoon?" Angelica asked, directing her question to her sister.

Tricia shrugged. "Becca came by to visit."

"Good grief," Angelica muttered, taking another sip of her mighty fine martini. "And what did she want?"

"To tell me the shortcomings at Stonecreek."

"Of course. And what were they?"

"I could tell you a few," Sheila muttered, but the sisters ignored her.

"Mostly that things are not up to snuff."

"In what way?"

"Finished. The last of the furnishings, the gardens. Mostly that it isn't yet ready to open."

"Well, duh!" Angelica said. "The initial shakedown is only tonight. And by the way, did you and David have any criticisms?"

"Why should *her* opinion count more than mine?" Sheila grated.

"Because I like her better than I like you," Angelica said, which caused Tricia *and* Sheila to blink in surprise.

"Thank you," Tricia said, smiling inwardly. "By the way, Sheila, Becca said she'd be delighted to have lunch with us at the Brookview on Monday."

Sheila's eyes widened. "Do *you* have to be there?"

"It's a deal-breaker," Tricia deadpanned.

Sheila frowned. "Then I guess that's the way it *has* to be."

"Angelica, would you like to join us?" Tricia asked.

"I'm sure I'll be terribly busy, but thank you for the invitation." It sounded more like she was grateful to have dodged a bullet.

They drank their drinks in silence before Sheila finally spoke. "So, what is it you've got in store for me tomorrow?"

"*We'll* be opening the boxes that were stored in Stonecreek Manor's attic, looking for treasure."

Sheila rolled her eyes. "I can't imagine you'll find much."

Angelica shrugged. "One never knows."

The three of them sipped their drinks, looking in different directions. Finally, Sheila spoke.

"Tell me all about Becca Dickson-Chandler. What's she like? How does she spend her days in this backwater? Is she as rich as they say?"

That last question raised a red flag in Tricia's mind. "Why would you care how much money she has?"

"Don't you wonder about such things?"

"Never," Angelica answered for both sisters.

Sheila shrugged. "I was only trying to make conversation." She reached for a celery stick. "Why do I have to wait until Monday to meet Becca?"

"Because she leads a busy life. If you want the truth, she only agreed to do lunch because she wants me to be her maid of honor when she gets married this fall."

Sheila's gaze narrowed. "She's got a fiancé?"

"Yes."

"Does *he* have money?" Sheila asked.

"Why are you so obsessed with how much money people have?" Tricia asked.

"Because social status is important in my circle."

"I thought you didn't remember anything about your past, let alone your social circle."

Sheila positively glowered. "The thing I remember is that money talks. Without it, you're a nobody."

"Like Grandma Miles?" Tricia asked. Sheila had never appreciated the woman or her gifts.

A Perilous Plot

Sheila's expression soured. "I have no idea who you're talking about."

"The woman who was a better mother to us than you," Angelica said, causing Tricia to wince—not that she didn't agree.

"You are a spiteful person," Sheila accused. "I don't know why I ever agreed to let you bully me into coming here."

"Because someone has tried to silence you on two occasions," Tricia reiterated. "What is it you know that could incriminate someone?" Tricia asked.

Sheila's glare could melt steel. "Nothing."

"Tell us about Uncle Leo," Angelica said casually, eyeing their mother over the top of her stemmed glass.

Sheila seemed to school her features. "I have no idea who you're referring to."

"Really?" Angelica asked. "Then why was he caught on video coming out of your room at the Brookview Inn three days ago?"

Sheila's eyes widened in offense. "I do *not* entertain strange gentlemen!"

"Then how about men of long acquaintance?" Tricia asked.

Sheila's gaze dipped. "I don't appreciate being disparaged by two complete strangers."

Angelica's eyes rolled heavenward. "Oh, if we only were."

Tricia decided to change the subject. "I wonder what Daddy's doing tonight now that his squatter's rights have been squashed."

Sheila looked at the sisters askance, but she said nothing.

"Now that the Bookshelf Diner property has been secured, I wonder where he'll go," Tricia continued. "It gets pretty cold at night."

"Especially now that security has been tightened at Stonecreek Manor, too. And the locks changed," Angelica emphasized. Someone had to have a key to enter the building. Or was John Miles a lockpick, too?

"I suppose Daddy could sleep on the deck of the village's gazebo, but hypothermia is a real threat to life," Tricia commented.

"I wonder if he has appropriate cold-weather clothing," Angelica mused. "I don't suppose he has a sleeping bag, either." She tsk-tsked. "Imagine poor Daddy wandering around the area like a homeless person."

"Well, as he and Sheila have sold off at least two of their residences, I suppose he had nowhere else to go," Tricia said.

As the sisters postulated about their father's situation, Sheila's chin kept descending until it hit her chest and had nowhere else to go.

"Well," Angelica said, nodding in Sheila's direction, her voice rising in what came off as almost merriment. "Isn't it lucky you'll have a nice clean, warm bed tonight? That this building has a formidable security system, and that the police station is only a block away should someone threaten you here. They can respond in less than a minute."

That was a lie, because although the station was nearby, the two village police cruisers could be as far as a mile or more away at any given time.

Tricia changed tacks. "What are you afraid of?" she asked their mother.

Sheila scowled. "I'm not afraid of *anything*."

Oh, yeah? Then why were her shoulders slumped? Why wouldn't she look Tricia and Angelica in the eye?

"Well, maybe you ought to be," Angelica said.

Sheila drained her glass. "What's for dinner?"

"Hot dogs and macaroni salad," Angelica said flatly.

Again, Tricia winced. While she enjoyed picnic food, she knew her mother believed the lowly hot dog should be consumed only by those of a lower class.

Tricia recovered and sported a smile. "My favorite summertime treat."

"Sounds revolting," Sheila grated.

"Oh, no," Angelica insisted. "I've got condiments up the wazoo. Ketchup, mustard, sweet pickle relish, onions, and hot sauce. The world's your oyster—except I have no oysters to offer," she said, and laughed. Then she sobered. "We're having a cobb salad. You can pick out the protein if you choose."

Sheila's gaze drifted to the floor. Long seconds later she muttered, "I want to go home."

"And where is your home?" Tricia asked.

Sheila pursed her lips and offered no reply.

TWENTY-THREE

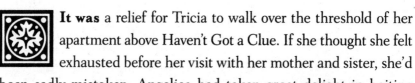**It was** a relief for Tricia to walk over the threshold of her apartment above Haven't Got a Clue. If she thought she felt exhausted before her visit with her mother and sister, she'd been sadly mistaken. Angelica had taken great delight in baiting Sheila. She'd reverted to the Angelica of Tricia's childhood. Snarky and—as Sheila had accused—mean-spirited, which was just not the Angelica Tricia knew in adulthood. If anyone had a bigger grudge against Sheila, it was Tricia, but then during their interactions with their parents in the past three years, Angelica had been focused on forcing them—and particularly Sheila—to make amends. How that was to happen was a mystery. And while Tricia was prepared to let the past go, Angelica hadn't yet reached that level of acceptance. Maybe she never would.

David called—instead of texting. "How did things go with your mother?"

Tricia sighed.

"That bad, huh?"

"Worse."

"Do you want to talk about it?"

"Not tonight. I want to take a long hot bath, and then crawl into bed and not have to think about anything for at least eight hours."

"Well, I'm disappointed," David began, "but not surprised. We'll see each other at Antonio and Ginny's tomorrow morning, right?"

"Right." Tricia winced. Having to spend a good part of the day with Sheila would be pure torture. Still, the woman wouldn't want to be trapped in the garage with piles of dusty boxes, so maybe they could just park her in front of a TV and leave her to her own company. Juliet would be there with the children and could keep an eye on her while the rest were busy looking for treasure.

"What time will you arrive?"

"Early," Tricia said. "And my mother will be in tow."

"Oh." David seemed as happy about the news as Tricia was. "Well, I think I'll let you hit the hay and we can talk tomorrow, right?"

"I love you."

"I love you more," David said.

Tricia had said and heard those words before. This time, she meant it and hoped David did, too.

"Until tomorrow."

The call ended.

Tricia took her bath, went to bed, and slept like the proverbial log. She was up bright and early baking her grandmother's snickerdoodle cookie recipe to take as a midmorning snack for the kids and adults.

The sisters decided that Tricia should drive, and pick up the other two, as Angelica didn't think Sheila would be amenable to walking to the municipal parking lot.

The April weather was typically wet and raw, so Tricia had to juggle her purse, the container of cookies, and an umbrella while hiking to fetch her car. Angelica, Sarge, and Sheila were waiting outside the Cookery when Tricia pulled up to the curb. Angelica reached for the back door and opened it.

"Why do I have to sit in the back?" Sheila groused.

"Pretend you're the Queen."

"She's dead."

"Oh, up on current events, are you? Then pretend you're the Queen Consort. It's an honor."

Sheila didn't seem pleased by the explanation but got into the car. Angelica climbed into the front passenger seat, settling Sarge on her lap before buckling up.

"And I don't see why you had to bring that *animal*."

"Because I don't want to have to clean up pee and poo because I'm leaving him behind for hours on end."

Sheila shuddered.

"Onward!" Angelica commanded, and then giggled.

"You're in a good mood," Tricia remarked.

"It's because I'm going to spend the day *with my chosen family*." She made sure to emphasize the end of that sentence.

"Hear, hear. I made cookies for a coffee break."

"What kind?"

"Snickerdoodles."

"Oh, God, no!" came a disgruntled voice from the back seat.

"You don't like snickerdoodles?" Tricia asked.

"I can't stand the smell of cinnamon. I've always hated it. Especially when—" But then Sheila stopped speaking.

"Sounds like you were on the verge of recovering your memory," Angelica quipped. "They say that smell is a great way to unlock recollections. I'm sure Ginny has a jar of cinnamon. Why don't you take a whiff and—"

"I will not."

A Perilous Plot

"That's too bad," Tricia said. "But on the bright side, there are more cookies for the rest of us."

Again, Angelica giggled.

The Miles women showed up at the Barberos' home at just after nine on Sunday morning and although it was exactly the time Ginny told them to arrive, maybe it was a little *too* early for someone with a baby and a toddler. Ginny was still dressed in her jammies and robe, and Antonio looked bleary-eyed, staggering around, clutching a large mug of black coffee, after a rough night with baby Will. "Sorry, Ma— uh, Angelica," he said.

"Don't worry about it," Angelica said.

"Coffee?" Antonio offered.

"No, thanks. We're ready to work," Angelica assured him. "Just point us to the garage."

"I do not work in garages," Sheila said flatly.

"You remember Antonio and Ginny, don't you, Mother?" Angelica asked.

"No."

"Well, this is Ginny, and this is Antonio."

Ginny forced a smile, which looked more like a grimace. "Hello, Sheila. Nice to see you again."

Antonio merely raised his mug in salute.

"Sheila is going to watch TV while we work. Is that a problem?"

Ginny gestured toward the family room.

Sheila glowered. She removed her coat and handed it to Angelica before striding away. They watched as Sheila took a seat on the sectional, taking in the children's scattered toys with disdain. Ginny stepped forward and offered the TV's remote. "Just press the green button and—"

"I know how to work a television," Sheila said coldly.

Ginny frowned, set the remote on the coffee table, and took a step back. Several decorating magazines were piled nearby and Sheila picked up the top copy, relaxing in her seat.

"Just holler if you need anything."

Sheila flipped open the magazine's cover, ignoring Ginny's hospitality.

Ginny backed away.

Tricia felt like giving her a hug. Angelica *did* hug her daughter-in-law. "Never mind," she whispered. "Hopefully she'll be gone in a couple of days and we can all get back to real life."

Ginny looked skeptical. "I'll be out to help as soon as I get dressed."

"Right."

"We know where the garage is," Tricia said. "We'll see you in a few."

Ginny nodded and returned to the kitchen to attend to her children.

The sisters found that the garage was just as cold and raw as the yard beyond it.

"This is a bad idea," Tricia said after they'd both opened only one box. "It's too cold. There's no way Grace can sit out here without being chilled to the bone. And we're asking Pixie and David to do the same."

Angelica frowned. "There must be something we can do to keep everyone warm and comfortable."

"Well, it should have been thought about *before* we arranged this little get-together," Tricia said.

Angelica bit her lip, looking thoughtful. "I'll take care of this."

Ginny had pulled out a number of patio chairs, along with several folding tables to be used to place the contents of the boxes to be sorted, as well as pristine cartons from the big DIY store up on the highway.

Tricia hefted one of the old and faded sagging cartons onto a table, unfolded the flaps, and found it was full of yellowing papers, newspaper clippings, and old ledger books. With resignation, she pulled up one of the chairs and sat down. This was not going to be the fun-filled day she had envisioned. Maybe Pixie and David would be enthralled with the task, but now she had a feeling she would have been better off spending the long day with a few customers and Mr. Everett. *He* was the lucky one.

After a long discussion with someone on her phone, Angelica rejoined her sister. "Nigela has been in contact with her maintenance team. They're going to arrive within the hour with some kind of portable heating system called a salamander."

"Great," Tricia said, her spirits rising. She scooped out a load of paper, and although she'd been taught cursive as a child, the beautifully scrolled handwriting was difficult to decipher. None of it seemed to have anything to do with the manor's former gardens.

"It's going to take months to read all these documents. You might want to enlist the volunteers at the Historical Society to go through some of these papers," Tricia advised.

"That's a great idea. I'll have someone on the staff contact them about it." Angelica looked thoughtful. "I wonder if I could get a tax write-off by offering them to the Historical Society."

Perhaps, but it wasn't Tricia's problem. She'd started on her second box when the door to the garage opened and David entered. "Am I too late for the fun?" he asked as he approached Tricia, paused, and gave her a sweet kiss.

"I hope you've worn your winter woolies. If not, you're going to freeze your butt off," Tricia opined.

David laughed. "Don't worry about me. I came prepared. I looked up the weather forecast last night. I'm wearing a couple of layers and should be fine."

"Heat is on the way," Angelica assured him but then frowned. "It just might take an hour or so to get here."

David plucked a carton from the pile and opened it, taking out an object wrapped in yellowing newsprint. He removed the paper and whistled before brandishing a pretty, yellow, and rather angular art deco teacup, decorated in red geometric shapes. "Nice."

"But not nearly as old as you'd expect to find in a house as old as the manor," Angelica said.

He rummaged through the box, finding a chipped matching saucer. "There could be much older stuff in some of these boxes. Do you want me to unwrap everything and assess what you've got?"

Angelica shrugged. "May as well. If it's not worth selling, we can donate it to charity."

David was halfway through unwrapping the contents of the box when Pixie arrived. "Good morning, everybody!" she called, rubbing her hands. "What goodies have you found so far?"

"Paper, paper, and more paper," Tricia said ruefully.

"Some cool dishes," David said.

"Any sign of vintage clothes?"

"Not so far," Angelica said. "Grab a box and start looking."

Pixie's box contained books. "Just what we need in Booktown. Wonder if we'll find anything interesting—maybe a first edition," she said, removing several tomes.

"Fiction?"

"Yeah." She looked at the title page. "Copyright 1903."

"Still too new," Angelica griped.

Pixie riffled through the box calling out author names. "James Fenimore Cooper, Nathaniel Hawthorne, Louisa May Alcott, but they all appear to be reprints."

"That's too bad."

"Someone will want them," David commented.

"The manor has an entire library to fill," Angelica remarked. "They

A Perilous Plot

can go straight back to the house, although they look like they could use a thorough dusting."

They'd gone through half a dozen boxes by the time Antonio and Ginny arrived, each carrying a box. Antonio's contained a coffeemaker, cups, and everything needed for a klatch, while Ginny held a large bakery box filled with muffins and pastries.

"Sorry it took so long for us to come out. Juliet was running late and the kids took their time with breakfast."

"Don't worry about it. Grab a box and cross your fingers you find something worth keeping."

They'd worked steadily for half an hour or so when Grace Harris-Everett arrived at the same time as the workers with the heater.

"Thank goodness. My feet are freezing," Ginny quipped.

They stationed Grace near the heater, handing her a sheaf of papers. "Can you read them?" Ginny asked. "The rest of us are having a hard time."

Grace studied the top page. "My great-grandfather's handwriting was just as ornate. I still have some of his letters to my grandmother from when he was a soldier."

David struck gold again with a box filled with ironstone platters. And Pixie finally found a box filled with vintage clothing. Sadly, they weren't from the era she was interested in. Most of them were moth-eaten wool mourning dresses that went straight into the trash.

Tricia had finished with her third or fourth box when she grabbed another heavy one and placed it on the table. "More books," she predicted, and unfolded the interwoven flaps. Her heart skipped a beat as she gazed at the object on top of the dusty books within.

A bloodstained steel butcher knife.

Had it been the instrument that caused Bunny Murdock's death?

It was exactly what Tricia had hoped to find, but now that she had, she felt colder than the garage's temperature warranted.

"We've got to stop meeting like this," Chief McDonald told Tricia as he looked into the carton that contained the possible murder weapon. He wasn't joking.

Upsetting as it was to find the knife, the rest of the gang kept working at emptying and inspecting the contents of the cartons. Was that what was bothering McDonald, or was he still perturbed about what selling his novel might mean?

"Would you like a muffin, Chief?" Ginny asked, and offered the box of pastries.

"We've also got homemade snickerdoodle cookies," Tricia offered. "I baked them myself."

"No, thank you."

"Coffee?" Antonio asked.

"No. Thanks." Instead, the chief retrieved a pair of black nitrile gloves, donned them, and gingerly picked up the knife and examined it before placing it into an evidence bag.

"What are the chances there'll be fingerprints on it?" Tricia asked.

It was then Sheila wandered into the garage, her arms crossed over her chest as though to ward off the cold—which no longer existed.

"We won't know until it goes to the lab."

"And how long until you get the results?" Tricia asked, already knowing the answer.

McDonald shrugged. "Weeks. Maybe a couple of months. The lab is pretty backed up."

Of course.

"I'm sure Bunny will rest in peace knowing that her killer might get away with it because the state lab doesn't have the manpower or equipment to work on her case," Angelica grumbled.

McDonald said nothing. No doubt he'd heard it all before. "On a more personal note, have you spoken to Becca today?"

Tricia shook her head. "No."

"When was the last time you did?" McDonald asked.

"Yesterday afternoon. She came by my shop to tell me her opinion of Stonecreek Manor."

"And?" McDonald prodded.

"She didn't seem impressed but was willing to give them a chance once—or so she said—they got their act together."

"And did she say where she was going?" McDonald asked.

"No," Tricia answered warily. "Why?"

"It's just that she's gone radio silent. I haven't been able to reach her."

"Has that ever happened before?" Tricia asked, noting that Sheila seemed to be hanging on to their every word.

"Unfortunately, yes. That's why I'm not too worried."

For a man who claimed not to be bothered, Tricia detected a note of panic in the guy's voice.

"She was dressed to the nines and said she was meeting with a possible new business partner," Tricia repeated.

"Did she say where she was going?"

Sheila stepped closer, not bothering to hide her eavesdropping.

"Not specifically. Just that she was going to a restaurant in Nashua for drinks and dinner."

McDonald stroked his ginger beard and nodded. "Did she say anything else?"

Tricia shook her head. "No. But she has seemed to have a string of rotten luck lately."

McDonald's eyes widened. "In what way?"

"Didn't she mention her car's cracked windshield and the overturned pots on her balcony?"

"No, she didn't." And from the look on McDonald's face, his anxiety level had shot up several degrees.

"We're supposed to have lunch tomorrow at the Brookview Inn. My mother"—Tricia waved a hand in Sheila's direction—"is eager to meet her. Apparently, she's quite a tennis fan."

McDonald turned toward Sheila. "I thought you had amnesia."

"Yes, that's what we were led to believe," Tricia said glibly.

Sheila blinked, a caricature of innocence. "I may not remember a lot of things about my life, but I do remember some things. Like music—"

"And smells," Tricia added.

"And tennis," Sheila amended. "I saw Becca Dickson play several times."

"Why remember that and not your own name?" McDonald asked.

Sheila shrugged. "I gather that's the nature of a head injury like mine."

It sounded like a convenient excuse to Tricia.

"I'm sure Becca has just gone off on one of her tangents," McDonald said, although without real conviction. "But please let me know if you hear from her today, won't you?" It almost sounded like a plea.

"Of course," Tricia said, her heart aching just a bit. She wasn't sure of Becca's commitment to Ian, but she felt he was totally smitten—and extremely worried when it came to Becca's welfare. But then her thoughts turned back to her last conversation with Becca. Too many little incidents seemed to have accumulated into an amalgam of problems.

"I'll text you if I hear from her."

"I'm sure she'll contact me soon, but I'd appreciate it nonetheless."

Tricia nodded.

A Perilous Plot

McDonald nodded in the direction of the garage. "Please let me know if you find anything else that might pertain to Ms. Murdock's case."

"So far it's mostly papers, books, and china, but will do."

Tricia walked McDonald to the door. "We'll talk again soon," he promised, and left the house.

Tricia shut the door, turned, and found Sheila standing uncomfortably close. "What?"

"I was just wondering how *you* ever became friends with a world-class tennis player."

"It's a long story."

"Evidently I have nothing but time."

"Well, I don't." And with that, Tricia headed for the kitchen and the door to the garage. Before she entered, however, she looked back at her mother. Sheila stood in the kitchen, arms crossed, apparently evaluating her younger daughter.

Evaluating . . . what?

TWENTY-FOUR

 On the whole, the unboxing didn't take long; it was the sorting that took time. But at the point David left to pick up Mr. Everett, the decades of stuff had been divided into three piles. Keep, trash, and donate. Sadly, the trash pile was the largest.

Pixie was disappointed that none of the clothes were salvageable, but she found some pretty brooches and Angelica let her pick a couple as a reward for all her help. They'd found enough old books, most in good condition, to fill at least one of the Stonecreek library's sets of shelves. Whether anyone would care to read them was another story. And David found enough crockery to keep him smiling, some of which would be used in the manor's kitchen and/or as serving pieces. Best of all, the original plans for the gardens were discovered and Ginny was over the moon.

Once the work was done, Antonio manned the grill, cooking steaks, burgers, and a hot dog for Sofia—her most favorite food. Sheila seemed relieved to be served rib eye instead of tube steak, but her sour mood had not improved.

A Perilous Plot

Afterward, Tricia helped Ginny to clear the dining room table. Once in the kitchen, Ginny crooked her index finger, beckoning Tricia closer.

"What's up?"

Ginny grimaced. "I put my phone down in the kitchen and forgot about it for an hour or so while I was in the garage working with everyone. Juliet said that Sheila picked it up and went into the bathroom. She was there for at least fifteen minutes before she returned to the kitchen and put it back where she found it."

Tricia's stomach tightened. "Did Juliet confront her?"

"No. She didn't feel comfortable doing that to a guest in our home, but she told me about it before she left for the day. What do you make of that?"

Tricia's discomfort level ratcheted up a few more points. "I don't know, but I've got a bad feeling in my gut."

"I hope it wasn't the macaroni salad," Ginny quipped, and then seemed to regret her little joke as Tricia's expression darkened. "What do you think Sheila's up to?"

"No good," Tricia said gravely. "If you don't mind, I think Ange and I better take her home and see if we can get her to talk truth."

"You think she's been lying to you all along?"

"I'm surprised she hasn't got third-degree burns on her butt from her pants being on fire for days on end."

Ginny didn't even smile at that description.

"I'll help you finish here in the kitchen—" Tricia began.

"No," Ginny said firmly. "Go. You guys need closure and the sooner you get it, and Sheila goes home, the less tension we'll all feel."

Tricia nodded and mouthed *Thank you.*

"I'll get your coats," Ginny said, and headed for the mudroom. Meanwhile, Tricia made a beeline for the dining room.

Angelica was in an animated discussion with Pixie and Fred when

Tricia stepped up and tapped her sister on the shoulder. "We've got to go."

Angelica turned and frowned. "But I'm not ready."

Tricia's gaze traveled to their mother and back and Angelica got the unspoken message.

Angelica turned back to face Pixie. "Sorry, girlfriend, but when Tricia says 'Jump,' I say 'How high?'"

Pixie gave a dutiful laugh before catching Tricia's gaze and giving her a knowing nod.

Ginny arrived with the coats, handing them out. "Call me later?"

"You bet," Tricia said.

David rose from his chair, moving to stand beside Tricia. "Is everything okay?"

Tricia rolled her eyes in Sheila's direction.

"Gotcha," he said knowingly, and lowered his voice. "We'll talk later."

Tricia nodded.

Hugs and kisses were exchanged and Sarge was collected before the three women left for home.

"Thank goodness that's over," Sheila muttered as they approached Tricia's car.

"What do you mean by that?" Angelica asked tartly.

"I've never been so bored in my entire life."

"Granted, the day was tedious for you, but it was a wonderful dinner with good people."

"Strangers," Sheila said before Angelica closed the car door on her.

"What's going on?" Angelica asked Tricia.

"Apparently, Sheila locked herself in the powder room for fifteen minutes with Ginny's phone."

"Oh, no! It wasn't locked?"

"Apparently not."

A Perilous Plot

"Who do you think she was talking to? Daddy?"

"Maybe. But I don't think the car is the right place for an interrogation. I'll drop you off at the Cookery, park, and meet you. Then we'll talk and hopefully get Sheila to open up."

"Right."

The ride back to Main Street was silent. Only Sarge seemed to enjoy the journey, eagerly looking out the passenger side window at the sights.

Tricia let her passengers out, waiting for them to safely get inside before she parked the car. But as she was about to get out, she noticed a wrinkled white business-sized envelope on the passenger seat. Angelica must have sat on it without realizing it was there.

Tricia stared at it. It hadn't been there hours before. With trepidation, she picked it up. It wasn't sealed. No, that would leave a DNA signature.

Why she had that absurd thought was beyond her. Still . . .

Tricia removed the tri-folded sheet of paper. Like a prop in an old movie, the message had been put together by cutting the letters out of a magazine and newspaper.

> **We have Becca Dickson. Bring one million dollars in cash to the Booktown gazebo at midnight tomorrow. Don't call the police or you will never see her alive again.**

Tricia breathed out a long rush of air.

Well, now she had even more fodder for discussion with Sheila Miles.

It was with a heavy heart that Tricia trudged up the stairs to Angelica's apartment. Again, Sarge did not happily greet her.

Angelica was alone in the kitchen, puttering around.

"Where's Sheila?" Tricia asked, shucking her jacket and settling it onto the back of one of the island's stools.

"In the bathroom."

"With access to a phone?"

"Who knows."

Tricia sat. "I need a drink." They'd had wine with dinner—just a glass—but this conversation was going to require something stronger.

"What's going on?" Angelica asked.

Tricia handed over the envelope and watched as her sister's eyes widened and her jaw dropped.

"Where did you get this?" Angelica asked.

"It was in my car. You sat on it."

Angelica's jaw fell a second time. "Now *I* need a drink."

Once the martinis were made, the sisters settled in their regular seats in the living room. There was no toast. The sisters took a deep slug and stared at the ludicrous-looking sheet of paper that now lay on the coffee table.

"I don't have access to a million dollars in cash," Tricia muttered.

"I do," Angelica said, "but not on the timeline they're asking."

"And who do you suppose is asking?" Tricia wanted to know.

Angelica scowled. "Daddy . . . Uncle Leo?"

Tricia shook her head. "What gave them the idea to kidnap Becca?"

"Daddy probably thought it would be easy money," Angelica opined.

"He who's spent time in jail for petty crimes," Tricia deadpanned.

"What do we do now?" Angelica asked.

Tricia chewed her bottom lip. All the little things Becca had complained about during the previous week added up, leading Tricia to believe they were dealing with amateurs. That said, they could still be as dangerous as criminal masterminds.

Sheila entered the room. Tricia turned her wrath on the woman.

A Perilous Plot

"What do you know about Becca Chandler being kidnapped?"

"About what?" Sheila asked innocently.

"You made a number of phone calls from the Brookview Inn while you were there. You entertained Uncle Leo there, too. Then you made a very long call this afternoon after Ian McDonald left Antonio's house. Who would an amnesiac call when they say they can't remember anyone?"

Sheila frowned. "That's a pretty cynical point of view."

"Who?" Angelica demanded. "Was it Uncle Leo?"

"Why are you working with him?" Tricia asked.

"*I'm* not working with anybody," Sheila asserted.

"You *do* realize that even if nothing happens to Becca, that kidnapping is a federal crime. And it looks like *you* could be charged as an accessory."

"It's a crime that comes with a very stiff sentence," Angelica added.

"You'd be looking at a *life* sentence." Tricia decided to hit Sheila where it would hurt most. "No more manicures or pedicures. A wardrobe that consists of a starched orange jumpsuit. Group showers with convicted murderers."

"And don't forget the prison slop that passes for food," Angelica put in.

Sheila leveled a nasty glare at her daughters. "And how would you know all that? Have *you* gone to prison?"

"No, but we know plenty of people who are currently guests of the state's penal system."

Sheila looked away and muttered, "Following in your father's footsteps, I see . . ."

"Aha! I knew you were faking amnesia," Angelica accused.

"You'd better tell us everything," Tricia said, "so that when we hire an attorney to defend you, we can let him or her know what they're getting into."

Sheila bit her lip before letting out a sigh. "Oh, all right. The original plan was to kidnap Angelica."

"Me?" Angelica squealed in horror.

"Well, you *are* Miss Successful with all your business ventures. Tricia only has one," she said with disdain.

And that failure in her parents' eyes had kept her safe from a possible nasty end. Tricia did not feel particularly grateful that the original plan had been directed at her sister. "What changed?" Tricia asked.

"When they heard Becca Dickson-Chandler lived nearby, they figured a big sports star would have to be worth a lot more than a bookstore owner."

"I'm *not* just a bookstore owner," Angelica cried.

This wasn't the time for Angelica to list her résumé.

"And what's the plan now?" Tricia asked.

"Collect the money and flee," Sheila stated.

"Where?" Tricia pressed.

"Rio, of course," Sheila said with a casual shrug.

"But you sold the house in that city," Tricia protested.

Sheila leveled an ugly glare in her second daughter's direction. "There are other places to live."

"What did Bunny have to do with any of this?" Angelica asked.

"Nothing. She just got in the way."

"In what way?"

"Leo's way." She said the words so coldly. The murder of her best friend didn't seem to have made any impact on the woman. "Bunny didn't think it was right for Leo and John to be hiding in the house," Sheila continued. "She said she was going to tell the innkeeper." Sheila's mouth took a smug turn. "She'd still be alive if *you*"—she pointed at Angelica—"hadn't enticed her to come to Stoneham."

"She invited herself. I merely called her looking for *you*," Angelica protested.

A Perilous Plot

"Well, you should have minded your own business."

Tricia didn't want to dwell on that point. "Who hit you over the head and left you for dead?"

Sheila scowled. "Leo wasn't supposed to hit me that hard. I could have suffered a skull fracture!" she said indignantly.

"So, you *were* working together!" Tricia accused.

"No, I came to Stoneham to save your father's bacon." Sheila lowered her voice. "For the thousandth time."

"So, it *was* the three of you working together," Tricia persisted.

Sheila said nothing.

"Where's Daddy now?" Angelica asked.

"I don't know. Leo has him stashed somewhere."

"Daddy wasn't squatting at the Bookshelf Diner?" Angelica asked, sounding confused.

Sheila shook her head. "That was Leo. You don't think your father would willingly stay in a rathole like that, do you?"

"I don't know what Daddy's capable of," Angelica muttered.

"We have to contact Ian," Tricia said firmly.

"No! If you do, Leo is just mean enough that he'd kill Becca *and* your father. And if he got the chance, me, too!" Sheila cried.

Tricia exchanged a look with her sister. At that moment, she wasn't sure how she'd feel about Sheila's last prediction. *Ambivalent* seemed apropos.

"What are we going to do?" Angelica asked.

Tricia eyed her mother. The woman had been feeding Leo information for days. She'd known the original plan included kidnapping her own daughter. She'd probably been in on the plan from the beginning.

Tricia's contempt for the woman couldn't be greater.

"Trish?" Angelica pressed.

"I don't know. I just don't know."

TWENTY-FIVE

Tricia had no time to consider the options—what options? There was no way she or Angelica could come up with the money to pay Becca's ransom. Their only course of action was to contact Ian McDonald. He'd know what to do—or would he be too emotionally involved? He was a professional. If he couldn't handle the situation, Tricia was sure he'd call for reinforcements—including the FBI. She said as much to Angelica before she turned to face her mother. "You are well and truly screwed."

"What do you mean?"

"If you tell Leo our plans to involve the police, you sign a death warrant for Becca and probably Daddy, too. And you'd still go to jail for the rest of your life—especially with an accessory-to-murder charge around your neck. But if you turn informant, it's likely all charges against you would be dropped."

Sheila frowned but then nodded. She knew a good deal when she heard it. No way would she want to languish in jail for the rest of her life. "What do I have to do?"

A Perilous Plot

"Tell Chief McDonald what you did and what you know."

Sheila looked away, her expression pensive. "I . . . I guess I could."

"Is Leo expecting to hear from you anytime soon?" Tricia asked.

"I told him it was difficult—that you girls were deliberately curtailing my freedom," she added pointedly.

"Can you blame us?" Angelica demanded. It wasn't likely she'd ever be able to forgive her parents for being a part of the initial plot to kidnap her for ransom—hoping to reap at least a part of the payoff.

"I'd better call Ian from home. If Leo is watching, it might look suspicious if I stay here much longer," Tricia said.

"Agreed."

"If we have to, we can all join him on an online call," Tricia added.

"I hope it won't take long. I need my beauty sleep," Sheila complained.

"You can rest all you want once Becca's safe. Whether that's in a hotel or a jail cell is anyone's guess," Tricia said bluntly.

Sheila merely glowered.

Tricia retrieved her jacket and spoke to Angelica. "It's your job to keep Sheila away from a phone so she can't warn Leo of our plans."

"Can do," Angelica said, eyeing her mother. "If I have to, I'll sit on her."

If looks could kill, Sheila might commit murder right there and then.

Tricia held up her hand and crossed her fingers. "Wish me—and Becca—luck."

Angelica nodded.

Tricia wondered if anyone was watching as she walked from the Cookery to Haven't Got a Clue. Once inside, she hurried to her apartment, where she quickly gave her cat a treat so she wouldn't be bothered while she spoke to McDonald. Tricia stabbed her phone's contacts list, found his number, and tapped the call button.

Please answer, please answer, please answer, Tricia silently pleaded, hoping that McDonald wouldn't miss her call—or the mental telepathy behind it. After all, he'd asked her to keep in touch.

"Tricia?"

"Oh, thank goodness you picked up."

"Have you heard from Becca?" he hurriedly asked.

"No, but I have heard from her kidnappers."

"What?"

"We can't risk communicating on official channels, which is why I called your personal cell phone."

"What's going on? Is she okay? What do you know?"

Tricia launched into the story of the entire debacle and how her parents were integral to the plot.

"The gist is they or he—a man I only know as Leo—has kidnapped Becca. I'm sure he was the man she went to meet last evening."

McDonald sighed. "The FBI will have to be notified."

"Yes," Tricia agreed. "But I can't be seen communicating with law enforcement."

"That's what online meetings are for."

"I've been wondering if the man who owned the Rolex and Leo are the same person," Tricia stated.

"It's likely. The owner's name is Leonardo Dixon."

"Aha!"

"Indeed."

"Okay. So I guess I should probably be seen going to the bank first thing tomorrow morning."

"Agreed." Ian sounded remarkably calm for a man whose fiancée was being held for ransom. It was no doubt due to his training.

"Billie Hanson is the Bank of Stoneham manager. We'll have to coordinate with her about the money—or at least a partial amount to show to the kidnapper."

"I need to speak to your mother—to interrogate her."

"We think we convinced her to cooperate with law enforcement. Whether she follows through is anyone's guess. What if she insists on a lawyer being present when questioned?"

"That's her prerogative. However, if she knows something that could prevent a tragedy and doesn't speak to me . . ." He let the threat stand.

A long interval of silence accompanied that. Finally, the chief sighed and spoke again. "I'm going to contact the FBI and get back to you. This could take hours. Are you willing to hold tight?"

Suddenly Tricia felt exhausted. The idea of the planning to come seemed overwhelming. Still, there were potentially two lives on the line—Becca's and Tricia's father's. "I'll do whatever it takes."

"Good. I need to get things moving in the background and I'll give you a call as soon as I know what's what. In the meantime, don't talk to anyone about this. Not your employees, not your boyfriend, not your extended family. Loose lips sink ships," said the former mariner.

"I won't," Tricia promised.

"I'll get back to you as soon as I can. Again, I'll want to talk to your mother and Angelica, as well."

"Right. I'll let them know," Tricia said, and the connection was broken.

Tricia set her phone down and swallowed. What was she supposed to tell Pixie and David? How could she explain furtive absences and terror every time the phone in her shop or cell phone rang?

And what danger would she be exposed to by the criminal she had no memory of? If anything went wrong, she might be the first person he disposed of.

Sudden terror filled Tricia's heart. What if everything went wrong? What if Becca—and her father—were killed because she contacted the authorities?

What if?

It was close to midnight when Tricia answered the online call and Chief McDonald appeared on the laptop's screen. "Have you heard from the kidnappers?" he asked without preamble.

Tricia shook her head. "Nothing."

McDonald nodded, as though expecting the answer. Earlier, Tricia had scanned the note and sent it to the chief. Because of the way Tricia had been contacted, they knew the perps weren't all that tech-savvy.

"The FBI agent in charge will be joining us in just a few moments. She had some problems connecting."

A woman FBI agent? Nothing wrong with that, Tricia surmised. And why was she surprised? Women were certainly capable of holding that kind of responsible position. But her mouth dropped open in shock when the third person logged on to the call.

"Cleo?" Tricia asked. "What are you doing on this call?"

"Hello, Tricia. I know this must be a surprise, but—"

"Shock is more like it." Tricia turned her attention to McDonald. "I thought this problem was going to be held in confidence. Why have you involved the Stonecreek's innkeeper?"

"Until this evening, I was on sabbatical. I wasn't sure I wanted to be an innkeeper. But since I am in the vicinity, I was called back to duty," Cleo explained. "And since the victim has been missing for more than twenty-four hours, and Stoneham is practically on the Massachusetts state line, it's possible Ms. Chandler is no longer in New Hampshire."

A Perilous Plot

"When did you find out Cleo was a member of the FBI?" Tricia asked McDonald, looking at him with suspicion.

"The night of Ms. Murdock's murder."

"And you said nothing?" Tricia asked, irritated at Cleo for misrepresenting herself—and for not being at all honest with her interactions with Tricia and Angelica.

"Ms. Gardener asked for discretion. I gave it to her."

"Now, what's been going on?" Cleo asked crisply.

Tricia sat there, stunned.

The screen changed when Angelica logged in to the call. Her eyes widened in what Tricia saw as anger. "Cleo, what are you doing on this call?" she demanded.

Cleo again briefly explained. "Now, let's get to work."

Angelica did not look pleased.

"I've briefed Ms. Gardener on the situation. Is your mother willing to speak to us about what she knows?" McDonald asked.

"Yes," Tricia answered.

"She's asleep," Angelica said.

"People's lives are at stake," Cleo said firmly.

"I'll wake her," Angelica said, and got up, disappearing from the screen.

"Meanwhile," McDonald said, "it turns out Becca's holdings are based in Boston. She doesn't have enough to cover the ransom from her account in the local bank. They're working with arranging for the money transfer."

Good. At least they weren't expecting Tricia or Angelica to come up with the cash.

Cleo explained how the money was going to be delivered, but Tricia was still in shock at the woman's authoritative status and took in only half of what she said. By the time Cleo finished, Angelica had returned with a very grumpy Sheila in tow. She waived her right to an attorney and spoke more candidly with Cleo and McDonald than she'd been with her children regarding what she knew about the kidnapping scheme. When it came to the part where she spoke about Angelica as the possible victim, Angelica got up and could be seen angrily pacing the living room behind her mother. At one point, she left the room but apparently stayed near enough to listen to her mother confess what she knew about the kidnapping operation and everyone's role in it.

It was then Tricia noticed the call was being recorded. For posterity or as evidence against Sheila?

She didn't ask.

By the time the call terminated, Tricia's head hurt. She glanced at the clock and saw it was nearly two in the morning. Come working hours, it was going to take a lot of concealer to disguise the dark circles under her eyes.

Tricia sighed, hoping she could get some halfway decent sleep. It was a long time until midnight the following day, when she was supposed to drop off the cash, and she was sure the chief would have a lot of instructions for her to follow.

Was she scared? Just a little. *Little?* Talk about an understatement. Tricia was terrified. But she was also ready to drop.

Tricia left a note for Pixie on the cash desk in the store below. She didn't want to leave a text in case it awakened her assistant manager.

Tricia trudged up the stairs to her bedroom and didn't even bother undressing. She just kicked off her shoes, dropped onto the bed, and wrapped herself in the duvet. She was asleep in seconds. And dreamed of faceless villains and nasty outcomes.

TWENTY-SIX

 Tricia woke up late—it was almost ten—and found a text from David on her phone.

Hey, what's happening?

Tricia sighed, knowing she was going to have to tell a whole lot of lies that day, and perhaps beyond. She also found texts from McDonald, telling her when she was supposed to show up at the bank. It was thought the kidnapper would be watching her every move. So she dressed, decided against making coffee, ate half a buttered, toasted bagel, and headed downstairs. Pixie had already opened Haven't Got a Clue for the day.

"Late night?" she asked, wide-eyed.

"Yes, but not what you think."

"Oh?"

"Yeah. For some reason I just couldn't fall asleep," Tricia lied. "Did you get the weekend receipts ready for the bank?"

"Sure. They're down in the office. Are you going to deposit them?"

"Yes. I can do that on my usual morning walk."

Pixie nodded, but this wasn't their usual Monday-morning routine.

"Well, let me know if there's anything I can do . . . you know . . . out of the ordinary."

Tricia tried to tamp down the sudden panic that gripped her. Did Pixie suspect what was going on? How could she?

Pixie squinted at her boss. "Are you okay?"

"Why would you ask?" Tricia said, her voice rising.

"Because you seem kind of freaked out."

"No, I'm not," Tricia insisted, which made it seem like she might be more than freaked out—possibly paranoid.

She tried to calm down.

"I'll just go down to the office and get the deposit."

"You do that," Pixie agreed.

Tricia felt jittery as she traversed the length of the shop and hung on to the banister as she descended the basement stairs. She found the bank pouch, checked the contents, zippered it up again, and went back upstairs. Would she be able to speak candidly to Billie Hanson about what was going to happen? Would having a suitcase full of money be safe at Haven't Got a Clue for the duration of the day? What if a regular everyday robber came into the shop? What if they pistol-whipped both her and Pixie until they gave up the cash? Then what would happen to Becca and Tricia's father?

She was catastrophizing and she knew it, but somehow, she couldn't seem to turn her thoughts away from dark outcomes.

Once back above ground, Tricia grabbed her jacket from a peg on the wall in the back and strode across the shop, hoping she looked cool, calm, and collected—everything she wasn't at all feeling. She shoved the bank pouch into her jacket pocket—a tight squeeze. "I'll be back in about an hour."

A Perilous Plot

"Don't hurry on my account," Pixie said blithely.

Tricia forced a laugh. Pixie wasn't smiling. She knew something was up.

Tricia stepped outside her shop and paused to look around. Was this Leo Dixon character somewhere nearby watching her every move or had he commissioned her father to do his dirty work?

The day was bright and brisk—typical weather for the time of year. Although most of the shops were open, there was a dearth of potential customers roaming Booktown's Main Street. Tricia crossed the street at the light, and headed back north up the road, passing several shops along the way. She paused in front of the Bank of Stoneham, looking up at the granite edifice. It was then Tricia realized she should have taken her walk first and then stopped at the finish to pick up the million dollars in cash. And why had the kidnapper(s) settled on a mere million? Becca was probably worth a lot more than that. Heck, the amount of money she was pouring into her tennis club project at the village's edge had to be at least a million-dollar endeavor. Had the kidnapper taken that into account? Or had the decision been based on the rather modest—for her—accommodations Becca had taken in the village next door? Granted, it was one of the nicer condo complexes in the area, but it certainly wasn't opulent. And did Tricia's assumption that the kidnappers weren't tech-savvy mean they hadn't had the idea to Google the former tennis star's net worth? Random news stories of that sort seemed to pop up on browsers all the time.

Someone brushed against her, trying to get around her to enter the bank, and Tricia realized she must have been standing on the sidewalk for almost a minute. That was sure to bring attention to herself—something the kidnapper wouldn't want. Giving herself a shake, Tricia entered the bank, but instead of heading for one of the tellers, she veered to the right and Billie Hanson's office.

Billie was nowhere in sight, so Tricia sidled into her office and took one of the two chairs in front of her desk, prepared to wait for however long it took before the bank's manager finally appeared. It wasn't long.

Billie, who was rather short and round, always reminded Tricia of a fireplug. She strode into her office, dressed for business in a dark pantsuit. Her hair was cropped short, and her usual manner could be described as brusque. Today, she sounded downright cheerful. "Tricia, I've been expecting you."

Cheerful? The woman sounded positively gleeful. Did she view this whole situation as an escapade—or was she merely a good actress?

"Hi," Tricia practically squeaked. She really needed to take back control of her voice. Billie closed the door to the office before taking the seat behind her desk, and Tricia was glad the bank was located in an older building where there still were real offices and not open landscaping.

"Chief McDonald and I have been coordinating the transfer of funds. We're not quite ready yet," Billie apologized.

"Oh," Tricia said. "How soon will you have the cash?"

Billie seemed to draw inward. "Probably not until the end of our business hours. We've got an armored truck arriving around three this afternoon."

Oh, crap.

"But Chief McDonald told me I should come visit you this morning," Tricia explained.

"Yes. If the kidnappers are watching, it would seem to them that you're here making arrangements to get the cash."

Tricia nodded. "I do have a deposit to make for my store."

"I can take care of that." Billie studied Tricia's face. "Are you all right?"

A Perilous Plot

"I've never been involved in what's essentially a prisoner exchange before."

"This is my second time," Billie remarked. "I was working at a bank in Boston the first time." She turned her gaze to her desktop. "It didn't have a happy outcome."

Why, oh, *why*, had she mentioned that scenario? But Tricia was afraid to ask what had gone wrong with that transaction. Instead, she pulled the bank pouch from her jacket pocket. "I'd appreciate it if you could take care of this."

Billie accepted the zippered bag. "Not a problem," she said. "I'll be back in a jiffy."

Tricia watched her leave, her spirits—already low—drooping even more.

So, she wouldn't have to worry about having a huge amount of cash on her premises until late in the afternoon. And then she'd have to sit on the cash until almost eight hours later. She had better have Angelica and Sheila come to her place for dinner. She cringed. What unkind remarks would Sheila spew upon arriving at Tricia's digs?

It didn't matter. Hopefully, in a matter of days—maybe hours—Sheila would be out of her life forever. The thought cheered her—but only if the woman left Booktown alive and well. The same went for her father.

Billie soon returned with the faux leather pouch and a receipt for the deposit. "Come back this afternoon just before four. I'll personally take care of the transfer of cash and have you sign a receipt."

"It's not my money," Tricia protested.

"No, but it'll be turned over to your care."

Tricia let out a breath. "And I'll have hours and hours before I make the drop. What if I get robbed?"

"Don't," Billie said quite seriously.

It wasn't a helpful response.

Tricia stood. "I guess I'll see you later."

Billie nodded.

Tricia left the bank feeling even more downhearted. How was she going to get through the day? Her anxiety quotient was off the charts. Pixie would know in a heartbeat she was a nervous wreck and want to know why—and, of course, how she could help. She might think there was trouble between Tricia and David, or Angelica. Then again, Pixie had spent time with Sheila the evening before. Yes, Tricia could use that as an excuse.

Tricia decided to try to act as if this was a normal day and took her usual walk around the village, her mind awhirl with every possible thing that could go wrong that evening.

Once back at Haven't Got a Clue, Tricia was happy to find Pixie interacting with a customer. That would give Tricia time to come up with some kind of an explanation about her mood—if asked. If not . . .

Since Angelica was tethered to Sheila for the foreseeable future, Tricia texted her sister with a cryptic message—and also begged off their usual lunch. Instead, Tricia spent the time going to the grocery store in Milford and buying far more food than she needed for the week—and a lot of it pure junk—because it made her feel better. She was pretty sure David would welcome it.

Oh. David. He was another problem. She begged off seeing him that evening, saying it was her turn to entertain Sheila to give Angelica a break from their mother. As anticipated, he wasn't eager to interact with the woman and Tricia again wished her parents could be even a tenth as normal—and kind—as the man and woman who had raised David and his brother.

The day dragged on. While Pixie took care of the shop, Tricia (and Miss Marple) retreated to the upstairs apartment while she assembled the ingredients for dinner for the Miles women. It wouldn't be an elaborate meal, just skinless chicken thighs dipped in egg and seasoned breadcrumbs, a big tossed salad, and baked potatoes. Tricia had a feeling her mother would skip the protein and starch altogether and she didn't care. Once out of their protective custody, Sheila could do—and eat—what she damn well pleased.

At three forty-five, Tricia donned her jacket and headed for the Bank of Stoneham. Apparently, the armored car had arrived earlier than anticipated, and when Tricia entered Billie Hanson's office, she saw a faux leather attaché case sitting on the bank manager's desk.

"It's all here," Bille said. "Would you like to see what a million dollars looks like?"

Tricia frowned. "I guess."

Billie opened the case. The bills were all one-hundred-dollar notes. They were new, which meant they were numbered sequentially. An alert would be sent out should any of them be spent in the US. But as Sheila had said, the money was destined to be sent to Brazil. Who would be looking for those numbered bills in South America?

And how were Leo and John to get those bills to the lower half of the planet without rousing suspicion?

It wasn't Tricia's task to figure that out.

The short walk from the bank to Haven't Got a Clue seemed to expand exponentially. Tricia found herself looking at all the buildings, scanning the rooftops, and feeling terribly vulnerable until she ducked inside her store.

"New purchase?" Pixie asked, eyeing the briefcase Tricia held.

"Uh . . ." Tricia wasn't sure how to answer. "Yeah. I thought I might use it to bring paperwork to the Chamber of Commerce monthly meetings," she stammered.

"Uh-huh," Pixie said. The skepticism in her voice had Tricia convinced that Pixie knew full well what was in the case and what Tricia was up to. Still, Pixie wasn't a gossip. It was unlikely she'd tell anyone—including her husband—what she suspected.

Tricia proffered the case. "I'd better put this away and get some things ready for dinner. Angelica and my mother are coming over."

"That's nice," Pixie said.

The women looked at each other. Pixie seemed to understand that something was going on that Tricia wasn't ready to talk about—yet. It was also understood that as soon as she *could* talk, she would.

Upon reaching her apartment, Tricia retreated to the bedroom, where she stashed the attaché case under the bed. It was as good a place as any to hide it. She returned to the second floor, hung up her jacket, and entered the kitchen to chill the glasses and make a pitcher of martinis. Gin martinis. Sheila could have a glass of wine or a whiskey and soda should she wish, although Tricia also had a bottle of mineral water on hand—just in case.

She sat at the kitchen island and heaved a sigh. She had almost eight hours to wait for the money drop. Was she just supposed to put the case in the gazebo and leave? When was the kidnapper going to release Becca and/or her father?

She sat there for a long time before her phone pinged; a message from Pixie. She'd closed shop for the day and said *See you tomorrow*.

Angelica and Sheila would be arriving any minute.

As if on cue, Tricia heard her sister call and footsteps on the stairs. The door opened and Miss Marple scampered in ahead of Tricia's guests. She plunked down in front of the women, eyeing the stranger with a cold glare.

Sheila looked down at the feline. "I don't like cats," she stated.

"That's all right," Tricia assured her. "I don't like you, either."

Sheila's mouth dropped in umbrage. "Well, that was rude."

"Gee, I wonder where Tricia learned that?" Angelica said thoughtfully with an exaggerated eye roll. The newcomers abandoned their coats to the rack beside the door.

"Come on in and sit down," Tricia encouraged, gesturing toward the living room.

They sat.

Like most cats who sense they are scorned, Miss Marple made it a point to sit beside Sheila on the couch, spreading out until her toes just about touched the older woman, causing her to cringe. Tricia could have sworn the cat was grinning.

"Can I help with anything?" Angelica asked.

"I'm good," Tricia assured her sister. Although after retreating to the kitchen, she banged around for a couple of minutes—stalling for time—before she reappeared with a polished silver tray. *Not* silver plate, David had been happy to tell her when he'd gifted it to her.

"My, going all out," Sheila said, inspecting the small charcuterie board Tricia had prepared earlier. "I don't eat cured meats," she announced.

"Nobody said you had to," Angelica said, accepting the martini Tricia poured for her. "I've been waiting for this *all* day."

"You two are certified alcoholics," Sheila muttered, and grimaced before turning to inspect the label on the bottle of mineral water Tricia had provided before pouring some into a glass.

"We drink to forget," Angelica said.

"Forget what?"

Angelica was about to answer when Tricia interrupted her. "This afternoon, I picked up the you-know-what at the you-know-where," she said.

"No, I don't," Sheila said.

Miss Marple got up and jumped onto the back of the couch, settling within inches of Sheila.

"The money from the bank," Tricia deadpanned. For a woman whose husband might be a hostage, Sheila seemed remarkably calm. Tricia wanted to jump out of her skin and slopped her drink onto the tray.

Sheila scowled.

Miss Marple raised a paw and tapped Sheila on the shoulder, sending the woman into hysterics, her drink flying and scaring the bejeebers out of Tricia and Angelica. Miss Marple went airborne, and Tricia could have sworn she sported a grin.

Sheila slapped a hand onto her chest. "That damn cat attacked me."

"Oh, she did not," Angelica said, and took a hardy slug of her gin. "She was just playing with you."

Tricia gulped from her own glass, knowing it was going to be a long evening.

McDonald contacted Tricia a few times that evening, informing her that several of his officers and members of the Sheriff's Department had been surreptitiously stationed on rooftops around the village, within sight of the gazebo. He seemed worried that she'd received no other instructions from the kidnappers, and Tricia deduced that it wasn't a good thing.

Sheila had fallen asleep on the couch, her mouth open, snoring. Angelica had thrown an afghan over her and retreated to the kitchen, asking permission to clean Tricia's fridge.

"I didn't think it was dirty."

"It isn't, but I've got to do something while you're gone or I'll go crazy."

Tricia glanced at the clock. It was ten to midnight. She swallowed. "I guess I'd better get going."

She'd brought the attaché case down earlier and went to get her jacket and hat. Her phone told her it was cloudy and thirty-seven degrees.

She grabbed the case. "Well, this is it."

"Don't say that," Angelica admonished. It sounded too final. "Hurry home," she said instead, and drew her sister into a bear hug. Pulling back, she adjusted Tricia's hat like she often did for Sofia.

"Thanks. I'll be back in a few," Tricia said, swallowing again before forcing a smile.

"Want me to walk you downstairs?"

"No. Just keep Miss Marple up here. You know, just in case."

Angelica nodded grimly. "Be careful," she instructed.

"I will." And with that, Tricia headed out the door, flicking on the stairwell's light switch.

The security lights were on in the shop. Tricia patted her jacket pocket to make sure she had her keys. Then she walked across the silent store, unlocked the door, closed it behind her, and headed out.

Main Street was eerily quiet, the streetlamps casting long shadows, and with every step, Tricia's hackles rose ever higher.

She crossed the street at the light and headed toward the village green, wondering how many pairs of eyes were trained on her.

Tricia's footfalls echoed between the three-story brick buildings. She kept going—one foot in front of the other—until she entered the small park, taking one of the concrete paths that led to the gazebo. The edifice was always lit at night, but several of the bulbs were dark. Had they burned out or had someone broken or unscrewed them?

As Tricia approached the gazebo, a shot rang out. The globe of the nearest lamppost exploded, sending shards of glass like tiny shooting stars flying everywhere. Instinctively, Tricia ducked, her heart racing.

"Get down!" a male voice shouted, cutting through the darkness. Was that Chief McDonald?

In the midst of the chaos, Tricia remained standing, clutching the attaché case, frozen in shock.

A few feet away, a man stumbled into what little light remained. Catching sight of her, he barreled toward her, knocking Tricia to the ground.

A second shot rang out.

"Daddy!" Tricia hollered.

The once-peaceful area around the gazebo was now filled with a cacophony of voices as uniformed officers poured into the area like bees swarming, guns pointed.

Sirens wailed in the distance, growing louder, echoing the urgency of the moment.

John Miles collapsed onto the concrete walk, his light-colored jacket stained with blood, his hand clutching his side, his eyes wide with what seemed like shock, but instead of groping for Tricia's hand, he reached for the attaché case.

"Daddy, where's Becca?" Tricia implored.

"Leo has her stashed at one of the nudist camp's outbuildings outside the village."

That facility was a seasonal enterprise and no one would have thought of looking for the missing tennis star there.

Chief McDonald was suddenly on the scene. He crouched beside Tricia and John. "We've got an ambulance on the way," he said, noting the growing puddle of blood pooling on the concrete. Whipping off his jacket, he wadded it into a ball and shoved it against John's wound.

"Tell me everything you know about this kidnap plot," he demanded.

"Leo—it was all Leo's idea."

Another shot rang out, but it didn't appear to be aimed at the village green.

"Man down," came a muffled voice over the speaker attached to McDonald's jacket.

A Perilous Plot

Tricia looked to her friend for an explanation.

"Sounds like we're going to need a second ambulance."

"And get a crew to search the outbuildings at the nudist camp on the edge of the village. That's where they'll find Becca," Tricia said.

McDonald was on his feet in a second, barking orders to his officers.

Tricia pushed the attaché case aside and clutched her father's hand. This time, he didn't protest and returned the squeeze. "I'm sorry, princess. I didn't mean to involve you in all this."

"Yes, you did," Tricia told him. "You were originally going to kidnap Angelica for ransom."

"I would have never let that happen," he said, and winced, the pain of his injury catching up with him.

Tricia wasn't so sure.

The flashing lights from the fire rescue ambulance suddenly lit the sky around the village green. Seconds later, two paramedics bounded onto the scene. "Can you move back, ma'am," said the woman clad in firefighter gear.

Tricia disentangled her hand from her father's, struggled to rise from the damp concrete, and stood.

It had already been a terribly long day. She had a feeling it was about to be a terribly long night.

TWENTY-SEVEN

Hospital waiting rooms always seemed to have lights that were way too bright. Two patients had been brought to Nashua's St. Joseph Hospital very early that morning. One John Miles and the other Leo Dixon.

Meanwhile, Tricia had received a text from Chief McDonald that Becca had been rescued, giving her no other information. Becca had previously been pretty glib about threats to her security. Tricia wondered how she'd feel after the ordeal she'd suffered at the hands of Leo Dixon.

It was after three when the surgeon came to talk to the Miles family, reassuring them that Mr. Miles had survived the surgery and—fingers crossed—should make a full recovery.

"I'm afraid only one of you can be with him in the recovery room," the doctor announced.

Sheila glared at her daughters.

"You go," Angelica told their mother.

A Perilous Plot

"I wouldn't have it any other way," Sheila said, and trotted off after the surgeon.

Tricia and Angelica resumed their seats in the nearly empty waiting room. Long minutes passed before Angelica finally spoke. "I'm not willing to do this ever again."

"Do what?" Tricia asked.

"Put up with the crap Mother and Daddy hand us."

Tricia's head dipped. "From what Sheila told us, they're broke. Practically destitute."

"And whose fault is that?" Angelica asked angrily. She shook her head. "I'm willing to bail them out—at least partially. One. Last. Time."

"But?" Tricia inquired.

"But I want them out of our lives," she said with conviction. "And I want it in writing."

Tricia frowned. "What do you mean?"

"That the condition of my offer is that they *never* contact either one of us again."

Even to Tricia that seemed like a harsh request. "Are you sure you want to cut off *all* ties with them? They *are* our parents, after all."

Angelica's resolve seemed to harden. "They haven't acted that way for a long, long time."

She was right about that. But still . . .

"Why don't you think about it for a few days?" Tricia suggested.

"Nope. I've made up my mind." And when that happened, there was no reasoning with Angelica.

Tricia nodded. "We can't just walk away tonight. I mean, Sheila would be stranded here."

Angelica seemed to think about it.

"I have the keys to Bunny's car, which is still parked in Stonecreek

Manor's parking lot. She could drive that until someone figures out what to do about it."

"Bunny had nobody in her life?" Tricia asked.

Angelica shook her head. "Not that she said. As far as I know, the cops haven't located a next of kin."

Tricia felt bad about that. "Sheila's going to need a place to stay tonight and until they release Daddy."

"She can come home with me, and in the morning I'll pack up her stuff, put it in Bunny's car, and put her in a hotel room along the highway until they release Daddy from the hospital. Then they're on their own. I'll have my attorney communicate with them about the arrangements because *I'm done*."

It sounded so cold, so final. But then, Sheila and John Miles had abused the trust their children had given them one too many times.

Angelica turned a jaundiced eye on her sister. "I don't suppose you'd care to take Mother in."

"Not on your life. But you shouldn't have to shoulder the total cost of ridding them from our lives."

"Neither of us have to spend a nickel on those two toxic people ever again. Our problem—if you could call it that—is that we have a moral code. And we sure didn't get it from our parents."

No. They'd learned their best lessons from their paternal grandmother, who had never said a word against their father or mother, but she must have felt embarrassed by the conduct of her only child.

"You can go home," Angelica said. "There's no reason you have to wait for Mother—er, Sheila."

"Well, there is the fact that we drove in together," Tricia said wryly.

Angelica shook her head, blushing. "Oops! I guess I forgot that. I suppose we're stuck here for who knows how long."

"I'm hungry," Tricia said. "What are the odds we could find something to eat here in the hospital?"

A Perilous Plot

"In the middle of the night? None. Vending machine crap and lukewarm machine coffee are probably our only options."

Tricia sighed. "I want French toast with bacon and a big mug of hot chocolate covered in whipped cream."

Angelica offered a wan smile. "It just so happens I have everything to make that in my fridge. If you don't want to just go home and fall into bed, I'm more than willing to make it for you—for us."

"You're on," Tricia said, feeling a burst of sisterly love.

Movement at the room's entrance caught Tricia's attention. Sheila had returned far quicker than she'd anticipated. "I'm ready to go."

"You could at least give us an update on our father," Angelica growled.

"He's asleep. It's been a long day. Let's get out of here."

For a woman who supposedly loved her husband, who had spent the better half of her life bailing the guy out of trouble, Sheila seemed pretty ready to abandon him after suffering a horrific injury. That said a lot about her character. No wonder the sisters had made a pact to divorce themselves from the people responsible for their existence. And yet . . .

Tricia refused to feel guilty.

Angelica grabbed her purse and stood. "Let's go. Tricia's hungry and I'm going to make her a delicious breakfast."

Sheila eyed her second daughter. "She certainly doesn't look like she needs it."

Angelica shoved her index finger close to Sheila's nose, her voice low and menacing. "If you ever make another crack about Tricia's weight, I will personally body-slam you into next week."

Sheila's mouth dropped, appalled. "How dare you speak to me in that tone."

"Get used to it. In fact, perhaps you better not, because come morning . . . We. Are. Done."

Anger blazed in Sheila's eyes for a few long seconds, but it was soon replaced by fear. Had she finally learned that she'd crossed one line too many?

Angelica turned from the older woman, hooked arms with her sister, and they started walking toward the elevators that would take them back to the hospital lobby.

"So," Angelica began, her voice just a little shaky, "what do you think about all the great stuff we found in the Stonecreek's attic?"

Tricia spoke about her wish to help sort the books and place them on the manor's library shelves, well aware that an angry Sheila struggled to keep up as they made their way to the parking garage. Tricia didn't envy the older woman's discussion with Angelica come morning, but she also didn't care. Tricia knew she would always have limited affection for her parents—all based on the past—but like her sister, moving forward she was glad to finally shed those noxious people from her life. It felt deeply disturbing, and yet also freeing.

As they drove back to Stoneham, Tricia couldn't wait until Sunday rolled around once again so she could spend time with Antonio, Ginny, Sofia, Will, David, Grace, and Mr. Everett.

Her real family.

EPILOGUE

 Two days after the failed kidnapping money exchange, John Miles was released from the hospital. He and Sheila spent the next night in the hotel Angelica had booked for them up on the highway before they left to return to Sheila's condo in Connecticut. They hadn't been arrested—yet—but the probability of it happening hung over them. That was their affair. Tricia didn't want to think about the possibility of testifying against them sometime in the future. It was all too much to contemplate just then.

There were no tearful good-byes.

Tricia hadn't heard from Becca, but Chief McDonald had called to say she was doing as well as could be expected. While Becca hadn't been physically hurt during her ordeal, she was deeply shaken and wasn't up to having company. Tricia sent her a card in the mail, apologizing profusely for her parents' participation in the kidnapping plot. Of one thing Tricia was sure; she wasn't likely to be invited to Becca and Ian's wedding.

One less ugly bridesmaid dress to wear, she thought ruefully.

Friday and Saturday came and went. David was attentive and sweet, and Tricia did everything in her power to live a life free from stress and difficult people. Pixie and Mr. Everett also did their best to make Haven't Got a Clue a tranquil sanctuary for its owner.

It wasn't as easy a task as one might think, thanks to the news media, who had taken Becca's kidnapping story and splashed headlines around the world. But never one to miss out on a PR opportunity, Becca gave tearful interviews to several news organizations and online magazines, emphasizing her trauma and promoting the fact that the first of her tennis clubs would be opening soon and she was actively looking to franchise the operation.

Angelica hadn't heard if McDonald had been contacted by her literary agent—and she didn't ask. She was much more interested in studying the results of the surveys from the Brookview Inn employees who'd stayed the night at Stonecreek Manor.

Angelica had also had a long talk with Cleo Gardener, who—it seemed—wasn't at all sure she was ready to retire from the FBI. That saved Angelica the task of firing the woman. Of course, with the inn opening in just over a month, the hunt was on to find a new innkeeper. This time, Angelica would find the perfect person.

Come Sunday, Tricia found herself watching the clock, counting the hours and minutes until it was time for her chosen family to assemble at Antonio and Ginny's place for their weekly dinner.

As usual, she and Mr. Everett arrived together, and the warm welcome they received from the whole gang—and David, who was now a part of that group—made her feel like she'd come home.

Sofia was dressed in one of her princess outfits, dancing and singing to entertain the crowd, who applauded enthusiastically. The wine flowed, laughter and the aroma of lasagna filled the air, and everyone seemed to be in excellent spirits.

And then Grace, with a heart filled with love and compassion,

A Perilous Plot

asked the question Tricia had been dreading. "Have you heard from your parents?" she politely inquired.

"No, and I don't expect we will," Tricia stated, her spirits plummeting.

"Why's that?"

"Because that was part of the deal I made with them," Angelica said, holding a tray filled with bruschetta.

"Deal?" Grace asked, selecting one of the snacks.

"Yes. I paid a bunch of their bills so they don't have to declare bankruptcy. I also arranged to pay their rent for the next five years *and* deposited a chunk of change in our mother's bank account, safe from our father's sticky fingers. I suppose it'll likely be used for their legal defense. Anyway, their end of the bargain is to never contact Tricia and me again."

Grace and Mr. Everett blinked in disbelief. "It must have been a difficult decision for you to make," Mr. Everett said.

"Not at all," Angelica said.

"But . . . they're your family," he protested.

"Blood isn't always thicker than water. We prefer to spend our time with our *chosen* family."

"That's all you guys," Tricia agreed.

David settled on the arm of the couch next to Tricia. "I like the sound of that."

Tricia looked up at him and smiled.

"We're looking toward the future," Angelica said. "Tricia and I have a lot of plans."

Tricia blinked at her sister. This was news to her.

"Such as?" Ginny asked, swirling the wine in her glass.

"We're still in the planning stages," Angelica said confidently.

Antonio raised an eyebrow. "This is news to me."

And me, Tricia thought, feeling flummoxed.

"All will become known in good time," Angelica said cryptically.

And when would that be? Tricia wondered.

She shook herself. She wasn't about to let whatever Angelica was up to spoil her time with the ones she loved best, so she said nothing—for the moment.

Ginny raised her glass in a toast. "To Tricia and Angelica's new business venture."

Tricia raised her glass as well, wondering what plan Angelica had for her future.

She'd just have to wait and see.

RECIPES

Sofia's Favorite Chicken Nuggets

INGREDIENTS
½ cup dry breadcrumbs
¼ cup grated Parmesan cheese
2 teaspoons Italian seasoning
½ teaspoon salt
6 boneless, skinless chicken breast halves cut into 1-inch cubes
½ cup butter, melted
Sweet chili sauce (optional)

Preheat the oven to 400°F (200°C, Gas Mark 6). Combine the breadcrumbs, cheese, Italian seasoning, and salt. Dip the chicken pieces into the butter; roll in the crumb mixture. Place in a single layer on an ungreased 15 × 10 × 1-inch baking pan. Bake for 12 to 15 minutes or until the juices run clear. Serve with toothpick. Optional: use sweet chili sauce as a dip.

Yield: about 4 dozen nuggets

Brie and Raspberry Pastry Cups

INGREDIENTS
1 sheet frozen puff pastry, thawed
⅓ to ½ cup raspberry preserves
4 ounces Brie cheese, cut into ½-inch cubes (36 pieces)
¼ cup chopped pecans or walnuts
2 tablespoons chopped fresh chives

Preheat the oven to 375°F (190°C, Gas Mark 5). Spray 36 miniature muffin cups, 1¾ × 1 inch, with cooking spray. Cut pastry into 36 (1½-inch) squares. Slightly press each square into a muffin cup with your finger. Bake for 10 minutes. Press the center of each cup with the bowl of a spoon. Bake 6 to 8 minutes longer or until golden brown. Remove from the oven and immediately press the center again. Fill each cup with about ½ teaspoon of preserves. Top each with a piece of cheese, nuts, and chives. Bake another 3 to 5 minutes or until the cheese is melted. Serve warm.

Yield: 36 pieces

Recipes

Bruschetta

INGREDIENTS

¼ cup olive oil, plus extra for brushing on the bruschetta
3 tablespoons chopped fresh basil or 1 tablespoon dried basil
3 or 4 garlic cloves (or more if you like a lot of garlic), minced
½ teaspoon salt
¼ teaspoon black pepper
4 medium tomatoes, diced
2 tablespoons grated Parmesan cheese
1 loaf (1 pound) unsliced French bread

In a large bowl, combine oil, basil, garlic, salt, and pepper. Add the tomatoes and toss gently. Sprinkle with the cheese. Refrigerate at least 1 hour. Bring to room temperature before serving. Slice the bread into 24 pieces; brush with olive oil and toast under a broiler until lightly browned. Top with the tomato mixture. Serve immediately.

Yield: 24 slices

Tricia's Easy Peanut Butter Cookies*

INGREDIENTS

1 cup smooth or crunchy peanut butter
½ cup brown sugar, lightly packed

Recipes

½ cup granulated sugar
1 large egg
1 teaspoon of baking soda

Preheat the oven to 350°F (180°C, Gas Mark 4). Line a baking sheet with parchment paper or nonstick foil, or lightly grease a baking sheet with butter, and set aside. In the bowl of a stand mixer or in a medium bowl with electric hand beaters, combine the peanut butter and sugars until well combined. Add the egg and baking soda and mix for another 2 minutes. Roll into small walnut-sized balls and create a crisscross pattern with a fork. Bake for 10 to 12 minutes or until lightly browned. Cool on a baking sheet for 2 minutes, then transfer to a wire rack to cool completely.

Yield: 2 dozen cookies

*This recipe contains no flour.